JAC

The most dangerous killer
is the one you don't see...

When a distraught man calls 911 to report a murder that hasn't even happened, police think it's a hoax or a crackpot until the caller turns out to be a highly respected Doctor. After his warning comes violently true, the killing thrusts Jack Stratton into his first official case as a new detective. Money, sex, and drugs are all motives. Still, these aren't your usual suspects: a tenured professor, a tech CEO, a mathematical genius, and a convicted felon have a million reasons to kill, but who did it? Can Jack follow the trail of victims and catch the mastermind, or will his first case be his last?

Praise for Christopher Greyson's
Jack of Spades

Non-stop action and suspense! Move aside Agatha Christie! Five golden stars...wish I could give It seven!
— Dan Santos — Author of the Insurrection Series

This book grabs your attention from the very first chapter! Don't start this book if you have other things you need to do, because you're not going to want to stop!
— Maree Nickel

Lots of action and a surprise ending! *— Bruce Floyd*

From action to heartwarming reunions - and so much in between - Jack of Spades was hard to put down, and left me wanting more!
— Tasha Stringer

Buckle up and hang on! It starts off in the fast lane and moves at the same pace throughout the book, so don't blink while reading! Jack's investigatory skills, as well as his methodical approach to solving crimes, are on full display. There are also some surprise guest appearances, which add to the fun, realism, and excitement. Jack of Spades will make you think, and there are more twists and turns than a Six Flags roller coaster! You won't want to put this one down! — *Amazon Review*

ALSO BY CHRISTOPHER GREYSON

The Girl Who Lived

One Little Lie

Pure of Heart

The Adventures of Finn and Annie

The Detective Jack Stratton Mystery-Thriller Series:

And Then She Was Gone

Girl Jacked

Jack Knifed

Jacks are Wild

Jack and the Giant Killer

Data Jack

Jack of Hearts

Jack Frost

Jack of Diamonds

Captain Jack

Jack of Spades

Kiku - The Yakuza War Trilogy

A Beautiful Place to Die

Kindle the Fires of War

Dance of Death

This book is dedicated to my friend Robert Tolich. Sometimes, the most important thing a person can do for someone is to listen. Bob has been my sounding board for years as well as a fantastic consultant for all things law enforcement and the hearing impaired. Thanks for listening, Bob.

JACK OF SPADES

WALL STREET JOURNAL BESTSELLING AUTHOR
CHRISTOPHER GREYSON

1

"I want to report a murder that will be committed." Sitting in his unmarked police cruiser, Detective Jack Stratton rewound the recording of the 911 call and played it again.

"911, what is your emergency?"

"I want to report a murder that will be committed." The man's voice was surprisingly calm, considering his words.

"Can you please repeat that?" The operator stuttered. "Did you say this murder hasn't happened yet?"

"You're paraphrasing my statement, but yes."

"And will you be the one committing the murder?"

"Don't be ridiculous. I'm simply reporting it. It is imperative that I speak with a detective. A life hangs in the balance. Will you please connect me?"

"Hold on."

The operator was so frazzled that he disconnected the call.

Jack had parked outside the cliff-side contemporary home to which they traced the calling number. Seeing how someone made the call from a landline, it only took a couple of minutes to get an address. Filled with high hopes for his first official case as a detective, this unusual caller left Jack with mixed emotions. It could be a hoax. Still, the police had a responsibility to vet every reported crime. Jack looked at his detective shield and re-read the words he'd memorized a thousand times. To serve and protect.

How Jack, so fiercely independent, could readily throw himself into the position of a servant was beyond his understanding, but he loved his role. The shield in his hand made him picture a knight of old, protecting the realm. That duty included all threats, even if he doubted the veracity of the call. How could anyone know beforehand if a murder is going to happen?

Jack powered down his window. The sky was a glorious blue, and all the trees had budded. The world around him was a buzz with the newness of spring. Even the breeze seemed charged with excitement. He smiled like a kid on Christmas morning as he gazed once more at the detective badge and remembered what Willy Wonka said; don't forget what happened to the man who suddenly got everything he wanted.

"He lived happily ever after," Jack said aloud.

Down the street, a cherry red Porsche rounded the corner. Jack stared out the windshield as the flashy sports car zipped toward him.

Jack let out a long sigh.

When Jack accepted his new job, he hoped he'd work alone, but Sheriff Morrison paired Jack with Detective Ed Castillo.

Ed skidded to a stop and climbed out of the two-seater. His light-gray suit looked like it would've cost a month of Jack's pay, and his thick, brown hair was gelled and styled. Average height with the body of a boxer, Ed kept in good shape. Jack could tolerate Ed on a personal level, but professionally? Ed tried hard, but Jack always felt he was not so much an actual detective, more like an actor playing a part, wandering around in a costume with a badge. It didn't help that Ed had been harboring a grudge against Jack ever since Jack caught the man known as the Giant Killer. It was Ed's case, and Ed still believed Jack had captured the guy just to show Ed up and make a name for himself.

Ed strutted over to Jack's door, whipped off the dark sunglasses he wore, and stared down at Jack. Ed's long face grew longer. "Here's the deal, Stratton. I'm the lead on this case. You follow what I say and when I say it. I'll listen to your input, but this is my case, and I take point." He thrust out a hand noticeably paler than his spray-tanned face. "Agreed?"

Jack flashed a crooked grin and shook hands. "Sure." He opened the door and got out.

Ed eyed him suspiciously before folding his arms across his chest. "It's nice that your first assignment is going to be an easy one. This guy sounds like a whack job."

"According to the background check, Dr. Samuel Mobley owns the property. He's an orthopedic surgeon at Mercy General."

Ed rolled his eyes. "I doubt the doctor made that call. Look at this pad!" Ed walked up the short driveway as he talked. "This place could be in Malibu. And with that view? It had to run at least a couple million. I'm betting it was probably the doctor's kid playing a prank on social media. You know, posting it for views. We're probably on camera now. Kids do it all the time."

"Dr. Mobley has no children, never married, and lives alone."

Ed's eyebrows knit together. "How do you know that?"

"Background check and social media." Jack tried unsuccessfully not to smile.

Ed pointed at Jack's lapel. "You're wearing a body cam?" He laughed dismissively. "You're a detective now, Stratton. Body cams are for beat cops."

"It helps with taking notes," Jack said, omitting the long list of other benefits cameras provided. From the look on Ed's face, there wasn't a point in defending wearing one, but Jack wasn't about to take it off.

Ed pounded on the door.

"Since I'm learning here," Jack said, "is there a reason you didn't use the doorbell?"

"Good for you asking questions, Stratton." Ed cleared his throat. "You see, an interview begins before you even start talking. That's why I wear a sharp suit. I want to set the tone before the conversation even begins. Give the door a few hard whacks when you get to a house. That way, you show them you're in charge." He pounded again.

Jack kept his mouth shut. This was no way to start things off. His prior military experience had taught him that scaring the person you're about to interview or making them angry because you sound like you're breaking in their door increased the chances they'd grab a firearm if they had one.

The door opened, and a black man in his late sixties, dressed in a stiff blue shirt, tan pants, and brown leather shoes, stared at them from behind thick glasses. His eyebrows rose, and the skin on his bald head furrowed. He leaned forward, supporting his weight on two elbow crutches. "Good morning, gentlemen. I suspect you're from the police department, and this is regarding my earlier phone call?"

"I'm detective Ed Castillo, and this is Detective Jack Stratton. We're with the Sheriff's Department and need to speak with Mr. Mobley."

"It's Dr. Mobley, but please call me Sam. Come in."

The sound of air brakes on the road made Jack turn. A propane truck's warning alarm beeped as the driver reversed, heading for the backyard and a large tank next to the house.

Dr. Mobley waved, and the driver returned the gesture, beeped twice, then pulled the steering wheel hard to the left to avoid running over the bushes at the corner of the lot.

"Propane." Dr. Mobley's crutches clicked on the tile floor as he headed into the foyer. "It was too far for the city to run gas. A small sacrifice for being able to live in an eagle's nest."

As Jack entered the elaborate home, the doctor's words took on new meaning. The entire back wall was made of glass sliders leading out to a deck made entirely out of glass. The view across the valley was breathtaking. With no earth visible, Jack felt like he was standing on the mountain's edge.

"If either of you is afraid of heights," the doctor continued, "I wouldn't recommend going out on the deck. It's perfectly safe. They crafted the deck from the same material as the Skywalk in the Grand Canyon, but it unnerves some."

"We can talk in the living room," Ed said, his voice higher than usual.

"Pardon me for a moment while I turn off the stove." Dr. Mobley inclined his head. "I'll be right back to explain my cryptic phone call."

Jack walked over to the sliders as Ed made a beeline for the couch. The drop-off was sheer. Jack leaned forward until his hair touched the glass. A massive iron support beam was partially visible. The house hung over the cliff by twenty yards.

"Stratton," Ed whispered, pointing beside him. "Sit here, and we'll have him sit in the recliner."

Jack nodded but strolled over to the shelves. Various awards and photographs lined the shelves. Engraved into the plaques were the names of the most prestigious schools — MIT, Stanford, Harvard, and Yale. The object that stood out was a small plastic golden globe with a little plaque emblazoned with the words: *WORLD'S GREATEST SCIENTIST.*

The clicking crutches signaled Dr. Mobley's return. "Mothers are their children's biggest encouragers." He chuckled. "That's her in the photo."

Jack picked up a picture of a young boy and a beaming mother standing on the end of a small dock. The grinning boy held a wet, broken toy plane in his hands.

"We were on vacation in New Hampshire. Lake Winnipesaukee seemed like an ocean to me. I engineered pontoons for my remote control plane so I could launch it off the water. They functioned until a strut failed. My mother thought I was a genius, however."

"That's fascinating," Ed called out from the couch. "But I need to get this report completed. If you don't mind." He held his hand out toward the recliner.

"My apologies for reminiscing. I consider it my greatest award." He gave Jack a wink as he walked over to the chair. "As I said when I phoned the Sheriff's Department, I need to report a murder."

"And this murder hasn't taken place yet?" Ed asked.

"No."

"How did you learn it was going to happen? A dream? A vision?"

Jack sat on the sofa on the opposite end of his partner. If charm schools still existed, he'd buy Ed a gift certificate to one for Christmas. Nothing like starting an interview with condescension and sarcasm.

"Actually"—Dr. Mobley picked up an envelope off the coffee table and handed it to Jack—"the killer notified me by mail."

Ed plucked the envelope from the doctor's hand and turned it over. It was blank. He lifted the flap, and a single playing card slipped out. The backside was a traditional red-and-white pattern. The front of the card was a Jack of Spades, but the jack's face was a skull.

"The death card," Dr. Mobley said.

"It isn't." Ed handed the envelope and card to Jack. "The death card is the Ace of Spades."

"Normally." Dr. Mobley nodded understandingly. "But please allow me to explain. Four years ago, I restarted my idea for a technical project. I hired three people to assist in its creation. Each participating member drew a playing card to represent themselves. I selected the Jack of Diamonds."

"So you think because someone mailed you a Jack of Spades with a skull face, you're the intended target of a murder?" Ed said.

"Considering the current circumstances, yes. Everyone involved in the project had a falling out."

Jack removed an evidence bag from his pocket and placed the envelope and card inside. "What exactly was the project, and who worked on it?"

"It's an aerial delivery system. I know the media overuses the words, but it is revolutionary. It's entirely unmanned."

Ed elbowed Jack in the side. "You're talking about robot flying cars?"

"Nothing that big, and it isn't robots. The system is AI-based and surprisingly non-complex, considering what it accomplishes. There were four of us working on the project. Dr. Navi Patel is a brilliant programmer who teaches at White Rocks Eastern College. She created the AI. Dr. Yan Chen is a mathematical genius who created the algorithms, and Oscar Chambers is the graduate student who assisted with both the coding and the drone."

"And what was your contribution?" Jack said.

"I gave birth to the idea. The design for the aircraft is mine. I hold two different doctorate degrees. My first was in aerodynamics. But, like Icarus, I flew too close to the sun in an experimental craft I designed, and gravity reminded me of my hubris. I broke my back, damaged my spinal cord, and shattered my legs. The doctors who did a poor job of repairing the injuries to my spine inspired me to get into medicine, so I changed careers. But you never forget your first love." He looked over his shoulder and out at the sweeping view. "Four years ago, I restarted the project."

"What was the falling-out over?" Jack said.

Dr. Mobley removed his glasses and cleaned them. "The root of all evil—pride. People falsely believe it's money, but the Devil didn't tempt Adam and Eve with riches. He promised they would be like the Highest. And until this day, we all seek to build our own Tower of Babel and rise to heaven." Dr. Mobley cleared his throat and placed his glasses back on his face. "The time had come to seek investors. Oscar contacted a high-tech company that was seeking a deal for an automated delivery system for pharmaceuticals. Our system was a perfect match. We created a pitch, but each person believed they should receive top billing. Navi felt her AI code was the most important factor, while Yan convinced himself that none of this could be possible without his algorithm. Oscar, filled with youthful megalomania, imagined himself as the real driving force behind the project and insisted all credit belonged to him. I voted for an even split. No one could agree, and our final meeting devolved into profanity and threats. It was all very dramatic."

"Did anyone say they would kill you?" Ed asked.

"Not specifically, but the card—"

"Did anyone specifically threaten to harm you?" Ed continued.

"No, but—"

Ed set his tablet on the couch beside him. "Let me give you some advice, Dr. Mobley. You need a lawyer and not detectives. You're right, pride and money make people do crazy things, but it isn't our job to mediate these disputes."

"What about the other members of the group? I'm concerned for their safety as well," Dr. Mobley said.

Ed stood. "For all you know, the playing card could simply be a message saying the project is dead—not you. Take my advice; talk to a good lawyer."

"In the meantime," Jack said as he moved to stand next to Dr. Mobley's chair and handed him his business card, "if you're concerned for your safety, is there someplace else you could go? Someone you could stay with?"

Dr. Mobley tucked Jack's card in his shirt pocket, picked up his crutches, and, after two tries, rose from the chair. "Unfortunately, my obsession with work was to the detriment of friends and family. In this world, I am alone."

Ed glanced around the house and shrugged. "Maybe it's time for a vacation? But go because you want to. Trust me. I wouldn't give that playing card a second thought."

Dr. Mobley followed them to the door. "Is there any way I can convince you to speak with the other project members?"

"With all due respect"—Ed placed his hands on his hips—"with the Sheriff's Department's limited resources and the fact that no one leveled a direct threat, there's nothing more we can do. Contact us if someone poses a threat, and we'll respond accordingly."

Dr. Mobley nodded and shook both of their hands.

Jack wanted to say more, but with Ed glaring over his shoulder, all he could think of was, "Thank you, Dr. Mobley. You have my card. Call if you need to."

Ed marched down the driveway but headed for Jack's car instead of his own. From the way Ed pulled his shoulders back, he looked locked and loaded for an argument. The last thing Jack wanted on his first day as a detective was to end up in Morrison's office because of a fight with Ed.

Once they reached Jack's car, Ed leveled his gaze at Jack. The serious expression on Ed's face gave way to a chuckle. "What a space cadet! How did that guy ever become a doctor and afford that place? Do you have any idea what he must rake in? Now he thinks that a couple of nutty professors and him created a flying car worth killing over?"

"He's afraid. The reasons for his fear may not pan out to be true, but he's legitimately worried about the playing card." Jack bristled, angling himself between Ed and the house's windows in case Dr. Mobley could see Ed laughing. "You've got to admit, whoever sent that card wanted to send Dr. Mobley a message."

"I agree, but as I said, the message was the project is over, not you're dead! My roommate had Dr. Patel and Dr. Chen as professors when I went to WRE. She's a mouse, and Chen's out-there eccentric, but neither of them would jay-walk, let alone kill someone. You heard Mobley say that no one made a direct threat at the meeting. I'm telling you, Jack, Mobley saying he's worried about getting murdered is blowing this whole thing way out of—"

Time slowed.

Jack's shoulders moved forward as an invisible force pushed him from behind. A deafening roar thundered in his ears as the searing heat of a blast wave slammed into his back and rippled through his chest. Jack smashed into Ed, sending both men flying onto the pavement.

Knocked off his feet, Jack shielded his head with his right arm. His shoulder bashed off the hard road, and he rolled to lessen the effect of the impact.

It sounded like wind chimes in a hurricane as shrapnel hurtled past him, pinging off the cars.

Car alarms blared to life.

Ed groaned and lay on his side.

Jack rose unsteadily to his feet. His ears rang, and his vision blurred, but his Army training overrode his shock. Grabbing Ed by his suit collar, he dragged Ed behind the car in case of a secondary explosion.

A cloud of smoke and debris clung to Dr. Mobley's house. The left corner of the home was gone, and the propane truck had vanished. Puzzled, Jack rubbed his eyes and shook his head. Through the haze, he noticed the rear axle of the propane truck, but it wasn't on the ground. It hung from the branches of a broken maple tree, one wheel spinning freely, black soot rising off the tire, forming giant smoke rings in the air.

Jack fumbled for his phone, his shaking hand pulling something else with it that fell onto the ground. Puzzled, he glanced down. The clear plastic evidence bag lay on the tar. Inside, staring back at Jack, was the grinning skull of the Jack of Spades.

2

Alice Stratton paced across the floor of their apartment, twisting the new wedding ring on her finger. The simple gold band held no diamond yet was more precious to her than the hand it adorned.

"I have to tell Jack, but you know what he's going to do, don't you?" She turned and stared at Lady, her gigantic King Shepherd, lying on the couch.

The dog rested her head on her paws, following Alice with her eyes as she crisscrossed the living room. Lady huffed and rolled onto her side.

"Exactly!" Alice nodded. "If I tell Jack, he'll want to come!"

Lady sniffed the air, bounded off the couch, and charged the front door.

A moment later, someone knocked.

To Alice's surprise, Lady sat and stared expectantly at the door instead of barking.

Alice cautiously peered out the peephole. Mrs. Stevens, her landlord, stood in the hallway holding a large glass baking dish with a plate balanced on top. With her big smile, plump cheeks, and red hair, her rosy disposition was in perfect harmony with her appearance. Alice pulled the chain off the door, unlocked the deadbolt, and grabbed hold of Lady's collar as she opened it.

"Patience! Patience, baby," Mrs. Stevens cooed as she headed into the kitchen.

"That smells delicious." Alice took a deep whiff. Garlic, tomatoes, basil. She'd made some Italian delicacy.

"It's homemade, fresh lasagna. I even made the pasta from scratch! I think I've been binge-watching too many cooking shows."

"Lasagna is Jack's favorite."

"I'm so proud of him. I hope you don't mind, but I wanted to do something special for his first day as a detective."

"He'll love it." Alice inhaled and stopped herself from peeking beneath the aluminum foil. As the scent filled the kitchen, her hunger grew. "I'm so glad you stopped by. I need some advice."

"Really?" Mrs. Stevens set the plates down, and her hands went to her chest. "I'd be honored."

Alice started for the living room, but Lady blocked the way.

"I almost forgot Lady's treat!" Mrs. Stevens uncovered the plate she'd brought, revealing a stack of peanut butter dog cookies.

"Please wait a sec," Alice said, moving into the living room. "Lady, come. Let's show Mrs. Stevens your new trick."

Lady's tail beat the air as she trotted around Alice and stood by her side.

"We've been practicing at the park," Alice explained. "Plug your ears. Okay, Lady. Show them who's the boss."

Lady took two steps forward and looked to the left. Her massive chest expanded as she gulped in air, then let out an enormous bark so loud the picture frames on the wall shook. Lady looked right and barked again. She sat on her haunches, raised her head, and, staring straight forward, barked a third time.

Mrs. Stevens stood there wide-eyed with her fingers plugging her ears. "I can see why they call her a King Shepherd."

"Doesn't she look regal?" Alice smiled.

"She most certainly does." Mr. Stevens handed Lady her treat. "And I am grateful you practiced that trick at the park." She winked, then crossed to the couch and sat.

Lady hopped up on the couch next to her while Alice stood in the middle of the living room.

"As you know, I've been trying to find my grandfather." She had told Mrs. Stevens bits and pieces about the situation, but not everything. She had to be careful what information she shared. Knowing about Alice's grandfather's background could put Mrs. Stevens in danger. "I received word from a friend who may know where my grandfather is."

"That's wonderful news!" Mrs. Stevens slipped Lady another cookie as she scooted forward on the couch. "But I don't understand. Why would you need my advice about that?"

Alice took a deep breath. "The problem is that I need to go with my friend to follow this lead, and Jack just started his new job. He's wanted to be a detective his whole life. I can't mess that up for him by asking him to head off to Timbuktu."

"Why does Jack have to go with you? It's not dangerous, is it?"

"It could be."

"Then you shouldn't go alone!"

"I won't be alone." Alice started pacing again. "My friend will come with me, and she's more than capable of handling herself."

"You're not talking about that woman, Kiku, are you?" Mrs. Stevens's mouth fell open.

The new cookie in her hand tumbled from her fingers and fell to the floor. Lady shot off the couch to gobble up the treat.

"Kiku's really a wonderful person."

Mrs. Stevens's red hair swayed as she stiffly nodded. "I'm sure she is, but whenever she comes over, I end up patching bullet holes in the walls and ceilings. Last time, it was thirty-seven."

Alice ran the palms of her hands down her face. "That's the problem. Kiku can handle herself, but she's a magnet for trouble. If Jack knows I'm going anyplace with her, he'll insist on coming."

Mrs. Stevens's lips pursed. "And he can't go because of the new job."

"Exactly."

"Can you put off speaking to your grandfather?" Mrs. Stevens shook her head before Alice could answer. "No. Of course not. And it's dangerous, so you can't go alone." Mrs. Stevens nodded and sat up straighter. "I know. I'll go with you and Kiku."

Alice's breath caught in her throat. Mrs. Stevens's offer was so dear that the last thing she wanted to do was offend her by laughing, but the image that flashed in her mind of Mrs. Stevens clinging to the back of a motorcycle as Kiku raced down the street almost made Alice stick a dog treat in her mouth to cork the chuckle.

"That is so kind of you, but I need you to stay here and care for Lady. And what if Jack needs something while I'm gone? I couldn't possibly go anywhere without your help."

Mrs. Stevens nodded understandingly. "That's true. You are in a predicament, my sweet. I wish I could be more help. But you know what you have to do." She stood up.

Alice stopped pacing. "No, I don't. What do I have to do?"

Mrs. Stevens smiled and gently touched Alice's arm as she walked past. "Tell Jack the truth. Then it will be his decision to go or not."

"But if I tell Jack, you know he'll go for me. He's self-sacrificing. He always puts me first, but I want to put him first. Isn't that what marriage is all about?"

"Yes. But marriage is also about trust. If you don't have truth, you don't have trust. It's a sticky wicket, as my Henry used to say."

"Henry? I thought your husband's name was Howard."

"Howard was my second husband. Henry was the first. It's hard for me to keep track of them. I should never have had a thing for men whose names start with H. Hank used to say that."

Alice opened and closed her mouth. Mrs. Stevens talked a lot about a husband who passed away a few years ago, but Alice had never known she had been married previously, let alone three times. Apparently, her life was as colorful as her hair.

"And don't worry about Jack." Mrs. Stevens opened the door. "Maybe he can get time off from work?"

Alice nodded, but in her heart, she knew she couldn't do that to him. This was Jack's dream. She owed it to him not to interfere with it.

Mrs. Stevens slipped Lady another cookie before stepping into the hall. "Have you heard from Jack yet? How is his first day going?"

"Nothing yet." Alice shrugged.

"Don't you worry." Mrs. Stevens patted Lady, then waved as she headed down the hall. "If I know Jack, and I do, I'm sure he's having a blast."

3

"Are you okay?" Jack shouted at Ed, who sat on the road, leaning against his car's tire, staring at Jack.

"Did I fall?" Ed held his hands out in front of himself like he was seeing them for the first time. He blinked rapidly and mumbled.

Jack patted Ed down and checked his back for any sign of injury but found none. "You're okay, Ed. Stay here!" Jack yanked out his phone and called dispatch. "This is Officer— Detective Stratton. Request EMS, Fire, and backup at 21 Mountain View Bluff."

The dispatcher replied, but Jack couldn't hear what they said through the ringing in his ears as he stumbled toward the house.

Flames shot up high in the now exposed kitchen. The explosion blew the roof and outer wall off. The steel and stucco construction appeared undamaged outside the blast zone, but the corner of the house nearest the propane tank was in ruin.

"Samuel!" Jack shouted as he walked through the open front door.

Smoke rose from the kitchen, and flames licked above the

broken wall and flickered against the now visible skyline. The force of the blast knocked the cabinets beneath the kitchen window backward into the center island. A pair of brown leather shoes and tan pants stuck out beneath the debris. The enormous pool of blood made it clear that the doctor was dead.

A flash of flame sent a wave of searing heat against Jack's skin. The smell of his burning hair filled his nose. He covered his face and raced outside. Frantically patting down his hair and smoldering suit jacket, he moved away from the fire raging inside the house.

A giant snap behind Jack made him spin around.

The branch holding the axle of the propane truck snapped, and the twisted metal thudded to the ground.

Jack's heart sank.

Where was the truck driver?

As Jack circled the house, burning debris and metal scraps littered the side yard. A line of Japanese maple trees lay at an angle next to a row of fence posts, the fence now missing most of its pickets.

"Hey!" Jack shouted, doubting anyone could have survived if they had been near the truck. But Jack had witnessed miracles in Iraq. Soldiers and civilians he'd been certain were killed somehow lived despite the odds.

Down the embankment on the left side of the yard, he found the remains of the propane truck. It looked like a flatbed now. The metal cylinder that had once been on top sat like a crushed soda can twenty yards away.

Jack headed in that direction, but a noise from the cliffside made him stop. He listened.

Fire crackled. A breeze fanned the flames, and the smoke stained the blue sky.

"Help!" a faint voice called out.

Jack rushed over to the cliff. "Hey! Can you hear me?"

"Help! Help! It's breaking! It's going to break!"

Jack dropped onto his stomach and peered over the ledge. The beefy truck driver hung fifteen yards below, clinging to the rock's surface.

"My feet are slipping." The man peered up at Jack. He was young, and his brown eyes were wide with fear. The man clawed at the rocks above him, sending gravel cascading over his head.

"Don't move!" Jack shouted.

The man was too far down for Jack to reach him. Even if Jack could, there was nothing to hold on to. The nearest object was the maple tree that stood ten feet away.

Jack got to his feet.

"Don't go!" The man cried out, and rocks skidded down the cliff as he moved. "Please! Please don't leave me here!"

"I'm going to get something to lower down to you. STOP MOVING!"

Jack scanned the area. There was nothing in the trunk of his car he could use, and he doubted there would be anything in Ed's sports car. He sprinted toward the burning house.

Ashes rained down as Jack approached the back deck. Coiled on the far end was a water hose. Bounding over the railing, Jack crossed the transparent deck and slid to a stop. As he reached for the water spigot, his stomach flipped. He stared through the glass decking, down the cliff face, at the rocks a hundred yards below.

Glass shattered inside the burning house, and the heat on his arms made steam rise off his skin.

Jack unscrewed the hose from the wall, picked up the coil, and turned.

The glass beneath his feet cracked.

Like standing on a frozen pond too early in the winter, he watched as the cracks radiated out like frozen bolts of lightning. Two feet to his left, a chunk of glass the size of a suitcase slipped free and disappeared from view. Five seconds later, the popping sound as it smashed against the rocks far below snapped Jack into action.

Holding his right hand above the railing, he sprinted across the deck.

Each time his foot touched the smooth surface, the glass cracked and snapped, the broken veins spiderwebbing out in front of him. The safety of the ground drew closer. Now only a dozen yards away.

Behind him, it sounded as if someone had turned on a giant ice machine. The noise grew into a roar.

Five yards.

The deck beneath his feet gave way.

Jack leaped forward. His chest smashed into the railing. The hose coiled on his shoulder dragged his left arm down, but he clung to the metal with his right arm.

He heaved the hose over, then pulled himself up. Once his feet were on solid ground, he glanced back. The deck behind him was gone. Bare metal supports clutched at the sky like skeletal fingers.

Down the road, sirens sounded.

Picking up the hose, Jack sprinted back to the maple tree. He used a clove hitch knot to secure the hose around the trunk, then carefully approached the cliff's edge. Dropping onto his stomach, he fashioned a bowline on the other end of the hose.

"Give me the rope!" The man sobbed, tears streaming down his face. "Please!"

"Stop moving!" Jack started lowering the hose down. "Loop it over your shoulders and cinch it around your waist. I don't know how much weight a hose can hold, so don't climb up! The fire department is almost here."

The man pulled the hose around himself, then grabbed it with both hands. He looked up, then screamed, "The rock's breaking!"

"Don't pull on it!" Jack shouted.

The man panicked. He yanked the hose tight, dragging the slack over the cliff.

Jack seized the hose and set his feet against the ground along the cliff edge. The hose stretched.

The man shrieked.

The hose swayed back and forth along the cliff like a pendulum.

A mix of fire, EMTs, and police sirens blared in the front yard.

Jack wanted to call out but couldn't draw a deep breath as he strained to pull. Hand over hand, inch by inch, he pulled the driver while he feebly climbed.

The man's head appeared, and then his shoulder.

He seized Jack's leg, nearly pulling Jack's foot off the rocks he depended on for leverage.

"Don't grab me!" Jack leaned away from the edge for counterbalance as the wild-eyed man clawed at the ground.

Setting his feet, Jack held onto the hose with his right hand, grabbed the back of the man's collar with his left, and yanked.

The man scrambled onto the top of the cliff, scurrying several feet on his hands and knees before collapsing in the grass.

Jack wearily rose to his feet and started for the front of the house and the emergency personnel gathering there.

The driver raised his head and stared at Jack with red-rimmed eyes. "Thank you. You saved my life."

"Wait here. I'll send the EMTs."

"What happened?"

"Your propane truck exploded."

"How?"

"That's what I need to find out."

4

Sitting in my darkened room, I remotely guide the drone high over the smoldering wreck of the house. The explosion blew off an enormous chunk of the roof directly above the kitchen. Through the smoke, I catch sight of the corpse and smile.

My plan worked—a perfect execution.

I land the drone atop the telephone pole across the street. From this perch, I have a bird's eye view of the beautiful chaos, watching everything happening safely on the computer monitor. Isn't technology incredible?

Despite my success, a sourness in my mouth bothers me. I feel like I've just eaten the sweetest dessert of my life, only to have an odd aftertaste spread across my palate and leave me wondering if some ingredient had gone rancid.

Could I have missed something? Me? No! I saw the corpse with my own eyes.

I stare at the monitor. There's no sound, the view is awkward, and I can't pan the camera, but despite those shortcomings, it's the best TV I've seen in years. The police scanner on the table next to me spewed out a swarm of intense calls. After Detective Stratton called in the emergency, dispatch summoned every available unit and agency to the scene. Police, fire, and EMS were all en route, squawking like crows as they descended on a freshly harvested field.

The show playing before me is both terrifying and spectacular. Awed horror at my hand causing such devastation mixes with the glow of satisfaction from a job well done. Now, this is must-watch TV.

I relax into my chair, but something else is amiss. I glare disapprovingly at my high-backed leather office chair. Usually, I'm fond of it, but the choice is all wrong for today. I should be sitting in a director's chair with my name emblazoned on the back. This is my show, after all. I set the whole affair into motion, and the opening act is going off splendidly.

The other detective is now standing in the street, staring at his battered car. Maybe he's in shock? He doesn't appear injured, but he isn't moving, either. Stratton rushes back over to him. They speak for a moment. Without audio, I can't hear what they're saying. Stratton leads the man over to the grass and helps him lie down.

I reach for the keyboard and zoom in the best I can. The camera angle is crooked, but Stratton's face fills the screen, and the foul taste in my mouth travels down my throat and churns my stomach.

Stratton is what is bothering me. The look on his face is wrong—all wrong. If I asked a dozen psychologists what an average person's reaction would be if they were almost killed in an explosion and then nearly dragged off a cliff to their death, the universal consensus would be fear, shock, terror, and relief they lived.

Jack Stratton shows none of those emotions.

His bright eyes and crooked grin leave no doubt what he's

thinking—he's in his element. Coming to the edge of death didn't leave him weak-kneed and cowering. It fueled him. Here was the rare individual who reacted opposite most men in a life-threatening situation. Fear doesn't pin his feet to the floor; it gives strength to his legs and propels him forward. The more pressure he faces, the greater he pushes back. Jack Stratton is a force to be reckoned with.

There is a flaw in my strategy—an unforeseen risk. I calculated everything regarding my plan down to the smallest detail, including which detective could be appointed to the case. None of the experienced detectives concerned me. They're all mediocre investigators with few problem-solving skills and poor records of solving even simple crimes. The odds had been in my favor that the Sheriff, with his limited resources, would assign the case to the low man on the totem pole. I believed that choice would be most beneficial to my success. Was I mistaken?

I swivel in my chair, click the mouse, and the monitor on my right flicks to life. A few keystrokes later, I'm viewing the file I prepared regarding the newest addition to the detective squad, Jack Stratton. Photos and articles written about him fill the screen.

He's tall, 6'2", fit and handsome. His dark hair and eyes, along with a perfect mouth with the slightest hint of an ever-present grin, give him a bad-boy vibe. But he recently married and just returned from his honeymoon.

His wife is stunning. Petite with shoulder-length dark hair, a bright smile, and gorgeous emerald eyes. But there's a ferocity that emanates from the beautiful bride. In their wedding photo on social media, they stand side by side. From the way they cling to one another, it's clear they have each other's back—two against the world.

The more I read, the more unsettled I become. Stratton is a highly decorated soldier. He's also independently solved several high-profile cases, including catching the infamous Giant Killer.

I settle back in my chair and fold my hands in my lap.

This Detective Jack Stratton is an unexpected glitch I will need to correct.

5

The knock on the apartment door made Alice jump.

Lady leaped off the couch and bounded over to the door.

"Come! Lady, come!" Alice whispered, her heart pounding.

Lady always started barking before someone reached the front door. With the dog's radar-like hearing, no one climbed the stairs without Lady barking.

Why hadn't she detected this person?

Lady whined and trotted in a circle. She still hadn't barked once.

Three rapid knocks reverberated through the apartment. They weren't overly harsh or loud, but each made Alice flinch. Taking a deep breath, Alice marched over to the door and gazed out the peephole.

Standing in the hallway was a gorgeous Asian woman. Her raven hair was so black that the highlights were midnight-blue. She could have been a model with her high cheekbones and exotic beauty.

Alice yanked open the door, and Kiku stepped through.

Kiku wore black jeans, matching sneakers, her signature

red lipstick, and a fuchsia top. She smiled, her pearly but sharp canines added to her wolfish appearance. "Hello, Alice."

"It's so good to see you." Alice hugged Kiku but quickly shifted her hand when her fingers touched the handle of the concealed gun at the small of Kiku's back.

"Did you receive my message?" Kiku's eyes were blacker than usual, and her normal creamy complexion had a dull pallor.

Alice nodded. "I can't believe you found him."

Kiku reached into her purse and removed a nine-inch wooden object. Lady opened her mouth, but Kiku raised a manicured finger, and the enormous dog sat down. "A gift for her Queen. It is all-natural, crafted from the coffee wood root of Tanzania. Do you mind?"

Alice thought the dog treat was so beautiful it could be a centerpiece on her shelf but nodded.

Kiku angled her hand, and Lady gently took the toy and retreated to the couch.

"Please, come in and sit down," Alice said.

Kiku shook her head. "I am afraid that I cannot. There is much to do if we are to leave in two hours."

"Two hours!" Alice sputtered. "Jack won't even be home by then. I can't."

"The man aware of your grandfather's location will not wait, nor will I."

Alice grimaced. Her hands balled into fists. "Hold on a second. There's a minor problem. Jack just started a new job as a detective. It's something he dreamed about his whole life."

"I am very proud of him, but I cannot see how this concerns us."

"If I go, he'll want to come. To help." Alice quickly added.

Kiku smiled knowingly. "The detective worries about what kind of trouble you will get into with me?"

"Let me put it this way. Did you see the news from Hong

Kong a couple of months ago? There were reports of gunfire and explosions at a shopping mall. Hundreds of police swarmed the scene, but the shooter got away. Do you know what Jack said? 'I bet it was Kiku.'"

Kiku's cheeks flushed.

"It wasn't really you, was it?" Alice felt the first sparks of adrenaline kicking in. Just being around Kiku was like watching a storm roll in. You knew something was going to happen. You knew it would be dangerous, but you couldn't run away.

"Your husband will be very successful in his new career, but the solution for your predicament is simple—do not tell him you are going with me."

"I can't lie to Jack."

Kiku laughed. Light, honest, but brief. "I adore your admiration for your new husband. Do you consider an omission a lie?"

"Yeah, it kinda is. What if you went without me?"

"That is not possible. I need your help with this. I can find the man who knows where your grandfather is, but I need you to verify your grandfather's identity before I question him."

"Wait, why do you want to talk to my grandfather?"

"He has information regarding another man that I am searching for. He is the same man who smuggled your grandfather into the U.S."

Alice's nails dug into her palm. Jack would not like this, not one bit. "Sounds like you need my help."

Kiku nodded. "But with or without it, I leave in two hours."

Alice stared at the floor. Kiku had done so much for Jack and her. How could she refuse?

"I will pull out front in two hours. If you are not there, I will be on my way." Kiku stepped forward and gave Alice a quick hug. She smelled like jasmine. "If you refuse, I understand why."

Alice closed her eyes. Kiku's sympathy was like a stab in the gut. It would have been kinder of Kiku to yell at Alice for being ungrateful.

Kiku smiled, then headed down the hall.

Alice paced back and forth, muttering. Why did doing the right thing feel so wrong? There was no way she could tell Jack what she planned to do. If he even suspected that Alice would search for her grandfather or go with Kiku, he'd insist on coming with her. And he'd be right. Going after her grandfather was dangerous. There was such a large bounty on the ex-general's life that even his own brother had tried to collect it.

But Alice had to find her grandfather, and now that Kiku needed her help, she had to go. The smooth metal of her wedding band caressed her finger as she absentmindedly turned it. If she told Jack where, why, and with whom, he'd go ballistic.

It was only one little lie. How much harm could it cause?

6

While an EMT examined Ed for injuries, Jack stood beside the gurney as another EMT took the propane truck driver's blood pressure and bandaged a deep cut on his leg. Jack wrote down all the driver's contact information since he was unsure if his body camera was still functioning.

"Sean, I need you to tell me everything you remember before the explosion," Jack said. "Let's start with how you decided to come here today."

"It was on my schedule." The oxygen mask muffled Sean's voice. "Dr. Mobley fills up his tank three or four times a year."

"Is that typical?"

"Two is normal, but Dr. Mobley runs everything off propane. Is he all right?"

The firefighters had confirmed Dr. Mobley was deceased, but procedure dictated that Jack not disclose that fact yet. "Did Dr. Mobley call for the delivery?"

Sean shrugged. "I don't know. Dispatch gives me the address, time, and amount."

"What happened when you arrived here?"

"There were a couple of cars parked out in the street. I saw

Dr. Mobley talking to you and the other guy. I waved, then backed up the truck. Once I hooked everything up, I ah..." Sean closed his eyes. "I, ah, went and took a leak."

"Where was that?"

"There's a maple tree near the cliff. I saw Dr. Mobley had company, so I didn't want to bother him." Sean turned his head to look at the EMT, who was bandaging his leg.

Jack tapped his notepad with his pen, smudging the page with dirt from the side of his hand. Jack's BS meter sounded its warning. "Your being over at the maple tree explains how you lived, but you're not telling me something." Jack moved closer, bumping the gurney and making Sean look at him. "And since I'm the guy who just pulled you up that cliff, that hurts my feelings. And it makes me angry."

Sean's eyes darted away again. "I'm telling you the truth. I went and took a leak."

Jack tried to guess the reason for Sean's avoidance. "Aren't you supposed to stay next to the truck when filling up the propane tank?"

"Yeah, but you don't have to hold the handle or anything. I was only gone for a minute."

Jack scowled. "Are you really going to make me drag you down to the station for questioning?"

"What?! No!" Sean stared at the EMT, who looked at Jack.

"Give us a minute, would you?" Jack asked the EMT, who nodded and walked away. "I'm giving you two options. Tell me the truth, or you're coming to the station after you get out of the hospital." Jack leaned close and smiled. "And I guarantee you'll tell me the truth then."

Sean's hand shook as he adjusted his oxygen mask. He swallowed. "There's no way I could have caused it. I only had a couple of puffs."

"Were you smoking a joint?"

"No. I was vaping an e-cigarette. But it couldn't have set off an explosion. There's no way."

"You're filling a propane tank, and you start making sparks nearby, but you think there's no way it caused an explosion?"

"I've done it a hundred times. And I already put the e-cig away when the blast happened. I was like, what? Thirty yards away. It was a couple of puffs. I even cupped it."

Jack wrote a note to check with an expert if an e-cigarette could cause the blast, then pointed the back of his pen at Sean. "Let's talk about when you filled the tank. Did you notice anything unusual?"

Sean stared at the sky, his breath fogging the mask on his face. "I got out of the truck and hooked up—" He glanced over to the destroyed house like whatever he thought of could still be there. "The connector on the tank was clean."

"Clean?"

"Connectors sit outdoors, so they get junked up. Mold. Crusted pollen. Crud. But today, it looked brand new. I even checked if some other propane company put their sticker on it. Just in case Dr. Mobley switched companies or something."

"Had they?"

"No. And the tank was almost empty, so I figured I'd ask when I was done and getting Dr. Mobley's signature." Sean rubbed his eyes with the thumb and forefinger of his bandaged hand. "I'm telling you, there's no way I caused it. Is there?" Tears brimmed in his eyes.

"You're telling me the truth about putting the e-cigarette away before the explosion, right?"

"Totally. I took two puffs, took a leak, and when I zipped—" Sean's eyes widened, and he craned his neck to look at the front of his pants. "You don't think my zipper could have sparked or something?"

"That I doubt." Jack closed his notebook. "Let's get you to the hospital, and if I have more questions, I'll be in touch."

Sean nodded.

"All set!" Jack shouted to the EMTs, who loaded Ed into the back of the ambulance. "Are you going to the hospital too?" Jack asked, somewhat puzzled.

"He said he struck his head." The other EMT explained. "We're going to bring him in to get checked out."

"How is Dr. Mobley?" Ed asked.

"He didn't survive the explosion. The M.E. and the fire examiners are on their way."

Ed nodded, then cringed. "Now it's a wait-and-see game. Once the fire examiner determines if it's an accident or not, we can take it from there. That could take a couple of weeks."

Jack drew a deep breath and held it. The thought of waiting hadn't occurred to him. He was about to protest but stayed quiet. Better to ask forgiveness than permission was a mantra from his childhood that drove his parents crazy, but he still lived by it today.

After the EMTs loaded Ed and Sean into the ambulance, Jack started making his to-do list. He needed to contact the other people involved in Dr. Mobley's project. The odds of this being an accident coinciding with Dr. Mobley receiving the Jack of Spades, were off the chart. Jack would still have to check that angle, but his gut told him this was no accident.

Someone murdered Dr. Mobley.

7

Jack stopped outside his apartment to stare at the black-and-yellow Dodge SRT Demon parked out front. The fastest production car on the street possessed an 808 horsepower supercharged 6.2-liter Hemi V8 engine. Something about the car both excited and bothered him. He stared at the dark-tinted windows and wondered if anyone was inside. The longer he stood there, the more confident he felt that someone was peering back.

Running a hand through his dark hair, Jack headed inside. He took the steps two at a time and paused at his apartment front door.

The car parked outside still bugged him. He marched over to the window at the end of the hallway. Standing close to the wall, he peered down at the sports car parked at the curb. As he viewed the passenger side, he recalled the driver's side, and an odd fact emerged. There were gas caps on both sides of the car.

Why?

In answer to his question, Jack realized the Demon could

handle regular gas and 100-plus high-octane racing fuel, cranking the horsepower up to 840.

That must be one serious driver if they installed a separate gas port for racing.

Turning back down the hallway, he strode to his door and unlocked it. A suitcase sat beside the hallway table, and Alice stood at the kitchen island, pen in hand, with a surprised look on her face.

"What are you doing home? What happened to your suit?"

Jack pointed at the suitcase. "Was it something I did?" he joked.

Alice laughed nervously, shook her head, and rushed over to him. Her nose wrinkled, and her eyes widened. "You smell like smoke. Are you okay? Was there a fire? You ruined your detective suit!"

"I am sure glad you got me two backups. I'm all right. After you explain the suitcase to me, I'm hoping I'll be better."

"It's not a big deal. I just realized that I've never taken a day to myself. And after everything that happened with my family, I need a couple of days to unplug from everything. Clear my head."

Alice stared straight into his eyes, and Jack melted. Like kryptonite to Superman, every time he peered into the emerald pools flecked with gold, it made him powerless to deny her anything. Tempted to ask her to stay, his love for her overrode his desires.

"It's just a couple of days? Is everything else good? You know, between you and me?"

Alice wrapped her arms around his waist and hugged him tightly. "I've never been happier. I need to do this. Two days." She gazed up at him. "Please understand?"

Jack nodded. "Can I help with anything? When are you going?"

Alice glanced at the clock. "Shoot! I gotta go now."

"Are you catching a bus?" Jack joked again.

"No, but I, ah, made a schedule. Lady is with Mrs. Stevens. I love you!" She kissed Jack, grabbed her suitcase, and darted out the door.

Jack let his burnt suit jacket fall from his hand and land on the floor. The weeks after returning from the honeymoon had been the happiest he'd ever spent. He woke up every morning, made love to his wife, and went to bed with a smile after making love again. Some days, all they did was stay in bed while Jack waited for the Sheriff to finalize the new job offer.

He never imagined his first day as a detective would end with him alone in an empty apartment.

I need a couple of days to unplug from everything.

Alice's words echoed in his ears.

Does everything mean me too?

He was overthinking this. Alice had been through the wringer. Two months ago, she thought she was alone in the world. Now she knows her family was murdered, and her grandfather, a retired Ukrainian General, suspected of embezzling millions, is still alive but in hiding with a bounty on his head.

That would make anyone need to get away for a few days.

Jack trudged toward the bathroom, stripping off his soiled shirt. Her not wanting him around while she processed everything stung. He understood it, but a part of marriage that he was looking forward to was dealing with things together—the good and the bad.

He removed his holster and set it on the nightstand.

Outside, a car engine roared to life. It was deep, powerful.

The Dodge Demon.

Jack glanced out the window as the car pulled away from the curb. The Demon sped down the street and disappeared around the corner.

Jack's hand froze as he removed his gold detective shield

from his belt. Alice's blue Bug sat further up the street, still parked alongside the curb.

Alice wasn't in it.

He stared in the direction the Demon had gone, and the hairs on the back of his neck rose. Alice had left so quickly that she hadn't said where or if she was going with anyone, and the sudden announcement so confused Jack that he didn't ask.

Wherever Alice was headed, he had a very bad feeling about it.

8

Sitting at his desk in the Sheriff's station, Jack sipped his coffee and read the article on the computer monitor. The black coffee was as bitter as he remembered it but still brought a smile to his face. It felt great to be back.

"I shouldn't be surprised you're here so early," Sheriff Robert Morrison said as he passed through the office. Bob, a tall African-American man in his late fifties, wore the tan uniform of the Sheriff's department without the hat. His curly black hair was short and graying at the temples. "Got a minute to bring me up to speed?"

"Yes, sir." Jack stood and snapped to attention.

Bob sighed. "You don't need to do that, son. It kinda freaks me out when you do."

"Sorry, sir."

"Bob is fine." Bob unlocked his office door and held it open for Jack, who followed him inside.

The Sheriff's office had changed since Bob had taken over for Collins. Sheriff Collins had taken a minimalist approach to decorating and kept no photos or mementos. Bob was the opposite. Pictures of Bob, his wife Meg, and his two sons and daughter sat on the desk and shelves. There were other photos, too—Bob with friends, family, and other law enforcement personnel.

What surprised Jack was that in none of the pictures of Bob and the influential people he was photographed with was Bob wearing his uniform. The people he was with were relaxed, too. From the photo of Bob bowling with the mayor to fishing with the governor, you'd only know who the person was if you recognized their face. Most people displayed photographs in their office as a power play. They wanted to send the message, "Look at all the important people I know." Bob seemed to display the photographs not for others but for himself. He could look across his desk, see a friendly face, and they'd remind him of a happy time.

It was another reason to like Bob.

"So, Jack." Bob sat behind the large desk. "You had a very eventful first day. Thank you for sending the initial report yesterday, but you didn't need to. How are you feeling?"

"Fine, sir. I wasn't injured. Have you heard any news about Ed?"

"They cleared him with the old prescription of taking two aspirin and call us in the morning. He should be in a little later today."

Jack nodded. He was happy Ed wasn't hurt, but he'd been hoping Ed might take some time off just the same. "I've been doing some research regarding propane, sir. I noted in my report that the truck driver used an e-cigarette. From all of my findings, that wouldn't have caused an explosion. Propane tanks are designed with so many built-in safety features that an explosion is almost unheard of. I'll have to wait for the fire examiner's findings, but considering those facts and taking into account the threat Dr. Mobley received, the explosion may have been a deliberate act."

"Sound approach. Could you do me a favor, Jack? Play nice with Ed. He's a good guy."

"I am. I've CC'd him on all communications and let him know how the case is proceeding."

Bob stared down at his desk and picked up a pen. He clicked it twice and set it down. "That's the thing, Jack. Ed is the lead on the case. Technically, he's the one who's supposed to be letting you know how the case should proceed."

Jack opened his mouth and closed it again when he remembered his father's advice—listen twice as much as you talk. Everything you say can and will be used against you.

"The second thing is," Morrison continued, "I need you to talk to someone in the lobby. She filed a missing report the other day, and they're looking for an update."

"I don't know anything about that case."

Bob slid a folder across his desk. "The girl who filed the report is Naomi Wilson. Her grandfather didn't pick her up yesterday, and she came straight here. The grandfather's name is Carl Wilson. He had a past problem with substance abuse."

"And he's only been missing a day?"

Bob nodded. "I sent a uniform to his apartment, and the manager let them in for a welfare check. Everything seemed fine. Can you talk to her now? The front desk said she insists on speaking to a detective."

"Yes, sir." Jack stood up and snapped to attention.

Bob shook his head. "Will you please stop doing that? You're setting an awful example." He pointed out the window.

Jack glanced over his shoulder. Three uniformed officers marched past the office like they were in a parade, saluting as they went. "Sorry, sir. Habit."

"Understood. Hey, did you and Alice do anything to celebrate your first day?"

"We did. Thank you." He picked up the folder from the desk.

"Give her my regards."

"I will." Jack hurried out of the office. Part of the reason he arrived so early was he couldn't stand being alone in the apartment. Lady had slept over at Mrs. Stevens's, so Jack spent the night alone. Nightmares woke him several times, and he finally settled on working instead of staring at the ceiling, wondering where Alice was and how she was doing.

Aunt Haddie had given them the marital advice of holding onto each other, but not so tightly they choke. Alice disappearing without him knowing where violated Safety Rule Number 1. He wouldn't do that to her. Jack stopped in the hallway and glanced at his right shoulder. He half expected to see one of those cartoon angels standing with his arms crossed, laughing at Jack's hypocrisy. Maybe he would do that to Alice, depending on the circumstances, but he'd explain why later.

He'd give Alice until tonight, then ask where she was if she didn't volunteer her location.

Jack opened the door to the waiting-room door.

A young, petite, Black woman marched across the tile floor and stopped in front of him. "I'm here to find out what you are doing to locate Carl Wilson."

"You must be Naomi. I'm Detective Jack Stratton. Why don't we talk in here?" Jack opened the door and pointed to the conference room on the left.

Naomi marched in, crossed her arms, and didn't sit down. "My grandfather didn't come home last night—again. What are you doing to find him?"

Jack pulled out a chair and sat. He set the folder on the table, his notepad next to it, and opened it up. He wrote the date, Naomi's name, and underneath it, Carl Wilson, and underlined it. Hoping he appeared focused and not uncaring, he wanted to dial the tension down, and getting Naomi to take a seat would be the first step. "I'm sorry to ask you to repeat information already in the report, but can you please start at the beginning and tell me a little about your grandfather?"

Naomi's eyes fluttered to the ceiling, but she dragged a chair back and sat down. "He's a hero, a good father, and a fantastic grandfather. Yeah, he messed up a few years back"—her voice rose along with her hands as she gestured wildly—"but he's been clean for a year. An entire year!"

"That's great. Really. But you need to understand that some questions I have to ask will not be easy. They could be uncomfortable, but they're necessary to ask to find your grandfather. Is it a possibility he started using again?"

"No, it isn't! I knew you wouldn't understand. He broke out of that. He wouldn't go back to it. Never."

"Are there other family members he could have gone to see?"

"It's just my dad and me. They don't get along, but my grandfather's been helping me. I'm going into the army. We meet every morning at the Prescott High track so I can work out, and he encourages me. This is the second day he hasn't shown."

Jack flipped the folder open. Carl's contact information was there: name, birth date, and address, but the space for personal data was left blank. "I need to speak to his friends or co-workers."

"Grandpa didn't work anymore."

"What about friends?"

Naomi stared down at the table. "I don't know. My dad and my grandfather had a falling-out. I only recently reconnected with him."

Jack nodded, but the blank sheet in front of him offered next to nothing for information. The only place listed as where he frequented was his apartment. "I'll continue to look. In the meantime," Jack handed her his card, "if he reaches out or you hear anything, let me know."

Naomi snatched the card from his hand and stuffed it into her pocket. "And what am I supposed to do?"

"You said your grandfather hasn't shown up at the high school for two days, right?"

She nodded.

"Go there." Jack stood up and pushed the chair under the table.

"And do what? Sit there?"

"No. Work out. Your grandfather was helping you. He wouldn't want you to stop."

For the first time since he'd met her, Naomi gave a brief glimpse of a smile. "Do you think you'll find him?"

Jack froze. When his foster sister went missing, the detective gave false promises. Jack swore never to do that. "I'm going to do everything I can to find him."

"Thank you."

Jack's gut tightened when Naomi's eyes met his. She hoped Jack would locate her grandfather, but over half a million people go missing in the U.S. every year. Most don't want to be found by whoever is searching for them. If that wasn't the case, and seeing how Carl had an addiction, the odds of this ending well for Naomi weren't good.

9

Jack drove the unmarked police car onto the dirt road while Ed sat on the passenger seat typing another email on his phone.

"How long is your car going to be in the shop?" Jack asked as he parked beside the closed gate.

"Who knows? It's an insurance nightmare. My car insurance wants me to go through work insurance, work insurance wants me to go through Dr. Mobley's home insurance, but they want me to file with the propane company's insurance."

Jack's head hurt just thinking about making that many phone calls. He shut the engine off and got out of the car. The dirt road ended at an open, old, dented red gate hanging on a dead cedar tree and chained to a metal post. A broken-down farmer's wall stretched off to the left and right. Open fields surrounded them in all directions. According to the satellite maps, Dr. Yan Chen's ranch house sat in the woods at the end of the dirt road beyond the gate.

Jack and Ed climbed over the rock wall and started walking. Tall grass stretched off on either side, and trees rose in the distance. At the edge of the tree line stood a six-foot high, chain-link fence that circled the property. The fence was so overgrown and rusty that it blended with the forest.

"What do you know about this guy?" Ed stopped in front of the closed chain-link gate.

"Not much." Jack grabbed the latch. There was no lock, but the bent metal and rust made it challenging to open. "Dr. Chen has no social media accounts, and the only things I could find on the web about him are old articles. He retired from teaching five years ago. Brilliant guy. He holds a PhD in mathematics."

The latch pulled free, and Jack shoved the squeaky gate open.

"I've got a feeling that this is gonna be another nutty professor," Ed said as he followed Jack.

"Don't close it all the way." Jack let the gate swing closer to Ed.

Ed reached out, but instead of grabbing it, he jerked his hand away like Jack had handed him a snake.

The gate slammed shut, and the whole fence shook.

Jack glared at Ed, who shrugged. "It was rusty. I don't want to get that red crap all over my suit."

From the direction of the house, dogs started barking. Jack couldn't tell how many, but it was at least a few. The barking suddenly cut off.

"My good suit is at the cleaners." Ed strutted forward. "Don't worry. We can open the gate again."

Jack fell into step next to Ed as they approached a rundown ranch house. Moss blanketed the asphalt shingles, and several small trees grew out of the gutters. A rock walkway, clogged with weeds, led to a sagging porch propped up by cinder blocks.

The front door swept open, and a man slipped out, slamming the door shut behind him. Inside the house, claws scratched wood, and the door shook.

"Go tell Fincher that my answer is still no."

Jack recognized Dr. Yan Chen from a news photo. The ring of hair circling his bald head was gray and wild. He wore a stained red T-shirt that didn't fully cover his potbelly, plaid pajama bottoms, and sandals.

"Excuse me?" Jack said.

"Tell Fincher to leave me alone."

"We don't know a Fincher," Ed said.

Jack flashed his badge. "I'm Detective Jack Stratton, and this is Detective Ed Castillo. We're with the Sheriff's Department and—"

"Ha!" Yan chuckled. "I know your game. Your boss should know it's illegal to misrepresent yourselves, especially as law enforcement. You tell Seth I'll see him in court."

The name clicked. Jack had seen a hundred commercials featuring the polished lawyer. "We're not with Seth Fincher Law. You can check with the Sheriff's Department. My badge number is 2614."

Yan's bushy eyebrows knit together, and then he burst out laughing. "Did they call the police? Oh, you have to be kidding!"

Ed stepped forward, straightening his tie. "Dr. Chen, this is a serious matter."

Yan laughed harder. "No, it isn't. It has no mass. Get it? Matter? It's a science joke."

"I get it," Ed said, but Jack wondered if he did, from his raised eyebrows. "We need to ask you a few questions about Dr. Samuel Mobley. He died yesterday."

Yan's laugh puttered off like an engine running out of gas. "Wait, you are serious. How?"

Ed placed his hands on his hips. "We're not at liberty to provide details, but Dr. Mobley brought your name up during our investigation."

"Of course he did." Yan ran a hand over the top of his bald head. "I bet he said I was trying to steal his project. Did he claim I wanted all the credit and all the money? Lies. All lies. Sam wanted it all."

"Actually," Jack stepped to Ed's left. "Dr. Mobley said he wanted to share credit equally between you."

"See! That's a lie. He wanted eighty percent and would split the remaining twenty between us. But Sam had no say."

"And why would that be?" Jack asked. "The design was Dr. Mobley's, was it not?"

Yan crossed his arms. "I can't discuss that. There's ongoing litigation."

Jack held up his hand. "Before we get off track, Dr. Mobley was concerned for the safety of the other members of the project—including you. He said threats were made at the last meeting. "

Yan's voice rose along with the red flush in his cheeks. "I may have become agitated, but the entire argument was ridiculous. I provided more to that project than anyone. The formula for the stresses alone was beyond any of them solving. And if I hadn't proposed the honeycomb design for the struts, the drone could never bear any significant load."

The muffled noises of nails scratching on wood echoed from inside the house.

The hair on the back of Jack's neck rose. There were far more than a couple of dogs inside. They weren't lapdogs, considering how the front door shook and how deep the barking had been.

"That may be," Ed continued. "Still, threats were made. Can you please repeat what you said at that meeting?"

"Are you accusing me?" Yan puffed out his chest, but it failed to come close to passing his jiggling belly.

"No, sir," Jack said. "We're simply gathering information, and we're also concerned for your safety. Dr. Mobley said everyone there may be in danger."

"They were all making threats! Navi even said she'd cut Oscar's heart out if he had one."

"That was Navi Patel?" Jack said.

"Yes. And Oscar said that he'd smear our academic records. He threatened to tarnish our names so badly that the only place we could have our next work published would be on toilet paper."

"And what threats did you make?" Ed asked.

Jack winced. He wanted to keep Yan talking, so Ed accusing him of making threats wasn't the way to go.

"I didn't," Yan snapped.

"Did you receive a playing card?" Jack asked. "It may have been delivered in a plain white envelope."

"No. Now, if you will excuse me, I'm done talking."

Ed winked at Jack and stepped onto the stairs. The porch groaned. "Dr. Chen, you could be in danger. For your safety, it's best if you speak to us. Am I making myself clear?"

"I appreciate your concern for my safety." Yan's puffy face softened, but his mischievous grin set Jack on edge. "I can watch out for myself."

"But we strolled right through your front gate," Ed said. "I don't think your security system is that secure."

"Oh," Yan chuckled. "I wasn't talking about the fence. I have my own security system."

"And what is this security system of yours?" Ed asked.

Chen reached back and yanked the door open. A large pack of pit bulls jumped, writhed, and bit the air like alligators in the zoo at feeding time. And the only thing keeping the dogs from crossing the threshold was Chen blocking the way.

"Let's get going, Ed." Jack walked backward. "We're leaving, Dr. Chen. Thank you for your time."

Ed leaped off the porch and hurried after Jack.

Jack was halfway to the gate when Ed stopped and turned

back to the house. Ed cupped his hand to his mouth and yelled, "We'll be back!"

"What was that?" Dr. Chen held his hand to his ear and stepped to the side, clearing the way for the dogs.

"Run, Ed!" Jack shouted, as half a dozen pit bulls poured through the open front door.

Jack sprinted for the gate, with Ed racing behind him.

Claws scratched the ground, sounding like rakes digging through the gravel.

The front dog, larger than the rest, howled.

Back on the porch, Yan cackled and sarcastically called out, "Stop, doggies. Sit. Come back."

Jack reached the gate first. He jerked at the rusted latch, but it didn't budge. He kicked the latch, and it still didn't move.

"Open it!" Ed shrieked.

The pit bulls rapidly closed the distance. Their yellow teeth glistened with saliva, and they flattened their ears against their thick skulls.

The pack was on Ed's heels. He'd never reach the gate before they took him down.

Jack's first instinct was to reach for his gun. He didn't want to put the animals down. It wasn't the dogs' fault their owner was psychotic. He seized an old, metal driveway reflector off the ground. The thin rod flexed like a pool noodle as he swung it, the reflective red circle at the end bouncing around.

The wimpy weapon made the dogs skid to a stop. They barked and snapped their jaws, darting forward and quickly shifting back while Jack swung the reflector at one, then another.

"Climb the gate!" Jack shouted and swept the rod in a wide arc.

Ed clambered over the gate and dropped to the other side.

Jack shouted, stamped the ground, and swung the rod hard.

The dogs skittered backward.

The plastic reflector dislodged from its circle, flying off across the lawn. The metal rod snapped in two like broken pasta.

Jack turned and jumped for the fence. Metal scraped his hand as he grabbed the top rail and pulled himself over.

The huge lead dog sprang after him. Teeth chomped the air next to Jack's face, coming so close that spittle splashed his cheek.

The metal prongs at the top of the fence impaled Jack's jacket sleeve. For a moment, he hung suspended against the fence.

The dogs were on one side and Jack on the other, but the snagged fabric of his coat kept him pressed against the metal.

Another dog lunged forward and slammed against the chain link, followed by two more.

Like a scuba diver in a shark cage, Jack bounced against the metal.

Planting his feet against the chain link, Jack pushed off. The seam on the arm of his jacket ripped, and Jack pitched to the ground, landing hard on his side.

Ed had run ten feet away and stood with his hands on his knees, trying to catch his breath. "If those dogs had gotten hold of me, they could have killed me."

Jack stared up at the sleeve of his new jacket, hanging off the fence and flapping in the wind like a windsock. "It's a good thing Alice is out of town. This is the second suit I've ruined in two days."

"I'll tell you one thing." Ed stomped to the gate but kept a safe distance from the barking dogs. "That nutcase just jumped to the front of my suspect list."

Yan whistled, and the pack came running back to the house.

Jack's eyes narrowed. "Dr. Chen has full control of those dogs. He could have stopped them from chasing us."

"How are we going to talk to him now?" Ed said.

"I'm coming back later, and I'm bringing backup."

10

Ed parked the car in a visitor space outside the new technology center at White Rocks Eastern College. Jack stared at the building, but his focus wasn't on the glimmering glass and steel structure. Memories of Michelle, his foster sister, floated through his mind like falling snow. As the photographs drifted downward, they twisted and turned, allowing Jack to catch a glimpse. Then they were gone—Michelle riding her bike, opening a Christmas present with a massive smile on her face, and seeing her and Aunt Haddie making cookies.

Ed banged on the car hood. "Are you coming or what?"

Jack wiped his eyes and shoved open the car door. The two of them made their way past a steady stream of students into a vast, open foyer. They checked the directory and headed upstairs to the door labeled ROBOTICS LAB.

A dozen workbenches filled the brightly lit room. Each was topped with a computer and a robotic arm sitting next to it. Ten of the tables had students standing around them. Some worked alone while others were in pairs and a few trios.

In the back of the lab, a middle-aged woman with light-brown skin, darker hair, and thin glasses sat working at a ten-foot square table. A thick cable connected the computer she was typing on to what looked like a giant silver ball sliced in half with a dozen metallic arms sticking out of it. She kept her eyes focused on the monitor when she called out, "I'm sending ADA around with next week's assignment. Let her scan your badges and make sure you double-check that she gives you the correct package."

Double doors in the far wall bumped open, and something that resembled a wheeled lunar rover drove out. The white machine was slightly bigger than a storage trunk, with three wheels on each side and a robotic arm on top. It rolled over to the first table. The students held their badges in front of the scanner on the arm. A moment later, a package appeared out of a slot on top. Once the student picked up the container, the machine moved to the following table.

Jack read the initials painted on its side as the robot passed by, A.D.A. Automated Delivery Assistant.

Jack and Ed continued to the back of the room.

The woman sitting at the computer lifted her chin, pushed her glasses higher up the bridge of her nose, and tilted her head. "May I help you?"

"I'm detective Ed Castillo, and this is detective Stratton. We're with the Sheriff's Department. Are you Dr. Navi Patel?"

"I am. Pardon my surprise. I didn't think you'd come so quickly."

Ed did a double take. "Why did you think we'd come?"

"I called this morning. About the threat?" Navi reached into the pocket of her navy pants and removed an envelope. "I received this in the interoffice mail this morning. There's no note, only a playing card."

Jack pulled out a pair of gloves, put them on, and took the envelope. The outside had been sliced open. Inside sat a playing card — a Queen of Hearts with a skull face. The only writing on the envelope was DR. NAVI PATEL. COMPUTER DEPARTMENT.

"Is there a more private place we could talk?" Ed asked.

Navi stood up and addressed the class. "I need to speak with these gentlemen." She glanced at her watch. "I will be back in eighteen minutes. Make sure you upload your code to the Gordon 2042 by the time I return." She smiled at Jack. "Please follow me."

"What's the Gordon 2042?" Jack asked.

Navi pointed to the multi-armed robot. "The future of cooking! It slices, dices, and makes your order in a quarter of the time." She laughed and walked over to a door in the room's corner. They followed her into a small workroom, with shelves lined with robotic parts and benches littered with tools and circuit boards.

Navi held onto her right elbow with her left hand. "I hope I'm not wasting your time, but the card was unnerving. I recently participated in a project that ended with bruised egos and hot tempers."

"The aerial delivery system with Dr. Mobley?" Jack asked. "Dr. Mobley received a similar card."

"A Jack of Spades with a skull face," Ed said.

Navi sagged against the table like she might fall over, and her complexion paled. "Is Sam aware of what it means?"

"What do you believe is the meaning?" Jack asked.

"It's a threat. A direct warning." Navi shivered. "The meeting got so heated, but I never thought the project would end like this."

"When we spoke with Dr. Mobley, he stated that at your last meeting, threats were made," Ed said. "Did you hear any of these statements?"

"Positively. Everyone was saying them. Male pride is a dangerous thing when wounded. Oscar, Sam, and Yan were all flinging around promises of lawsuits, restraining orders, and personal vows of revenge."

Ed took out his notepad and pen. "Do you recall anything specific that anyone said?"

Navi bit her lower lip and gazed at the floor for a moment before slowly continuing, "It was so confusing. There was so much testosterone and screaming. You should have seen it. Their veins bulged, and spit flew from their mouths as they ranted. They were all trying to shout over one another. Perhaps Oscar was the loudest, but I remember him specifically saying —you're all dead. All of you!"

"This was Oscar Chambers?" Ed asked.

Navi nodded.

"What about you, Dr. Patel?" Jack said. "While everyone else was shouting and clambering for credit, you said nothing?"

"What was the point? It would have fallen on deaf ears."

"So you're officially stating that you didn't want to receive any credit for this project?" Jack asked.

Navi stiffened, thrust out her chin, and said, "Never! If anyone deserved the most credit for the delivery system, it was me." She jammed her finger against her chest.

"Yet you never expressed those feelings?" Jack said.

The angular features in Navi's face sharpened. "I stated my beliefs at the start of the meeting. I did so courteously and professionally."

Ed glanced up from his notepad. "Dr. Mobley told a different version of that story. He stated you made threats as well."

"Sam is lying. It's as simple as that. But I will say that if there was something Yan, Oscar, and I agreed about, it was that Sam wouldn't be mentioned."

Jack crossed his arms. "How could that be? Wasn't the aircraft based on his design? And didn't he have a patent?"

Navi frowned at Jack the way a teacher scolds a student for

giving an incorrect answer. "As the saying goes, Sam was a day late and a dollar short. His patent had expired."

"But he worked on the new project, correct?" Jack said.

"That's not the correct question. You should ask if Sam brought any new ideas to the table, and the answer is no. All of his contributions were historical data now."

"What about fair attribution?" Jack said.

"This is business. Business is not fair. Did any of the other members receive cards?"

"Not that we're aware, but we're still checking with everyone." Ed cast a sideways glance at Jack before continuing. "Considering this threat, I must make you aware that Dr. Mobley was killed yesterday."

Navi's face pinched. "No!"

Ed nodded. "Is there—"

Someone knocked on the door, followed by three loud bangs and several giggles. "Dr. Patel?" A boy called out in a sing-song tone. "The Gordon 2042 waits for no human!"

Navi folded her hands in front of her chest and exhaled. "I need to think. Please excuse me while I process this information." She crossed to the door and opened it.

A crowd of students rushed away and surrounded the table with the massive robot with a dozen arms. Six students stood to the side of the table, and one, a thin kid with thick, round glasses, waved his hands dramatically.

"The Gordon 2042 will now create the ultimate BLT sandwich!" He pointed at a young woman sitting at the computer, who reached high into the air and slowly lowered her finger toward the keyboard like she was launching a missile.

The robotic arms sprang to life. While Jack and Ed had been speaking with Navi, students set up unique food items in different sections around the robot. A stack of bread, a pile of bacon, a tomato, lettuce, a cup of mayo—there was even a toaster. The robot moved in a blur of motion. It sliced, diced, and stacked food items with the utmost precision until it reached for the lettuce.

Metal scraped against metal when two of the robot's arms clipped each other. A third arm, carrying a mechanical hand full of bacon, slammed into them. With a loud bang, the entire table shifted an inch.

A fourth arm shot forward. Whatever it gripped in its hand snapped free and flew directly at Navi.

Jack instinctively reached out. Something squishy slapped against his palm, and his tightening fingers turned the tomato to mush. His smile faded as he looked at Dr. Patel.

Some of the tomato juice splattered her face and ran down her cheek. Navi brushed it with her hand and then stared at her stained fingers. "That is a bad omen. I think I am in real danger, Detective."

11

Alice awoke sitting in the passenger seat of Kiku's car, her chin resting on her chest. Blinking, she sat up and stared out the windshield at the sun rising over the palm tree-lined street.

"Good morning, Alice." Kiku slowed down and turned right. "I need to stop and get supplies and connect with my contact. We are almost there."

"Where is there?" Alice rubbed her stiff neck and yawned.

"My house."

Alice sat bolt upright. She'd never been to Kiku's house and hadn't been sure until now that her mysterious friend had one. She gazed around the quiet suburban neighborhood with surprise. The tree-lined street with little ranch homes was far from the ultra-modern city penthouse she'd imagined.

Kiku reached up to the visor and clicked a button on a remote. The garage door to the house on the right opened. The simple white stucco ranch had a reddish clay tile roof. A fence ringed the well-maintained property. Kiku parked the car inside the garage as the roll-down door shuddered to a stop behind them.

Alice groaned and stretched as she stepped out. "Thank you for driving. I thought you were going to wake me up for my shift?"

Kiku popped the trunk and hefted out a large duffel bag. "You needed the rest, and I do not mind. Driving helps me think."

Alice reached out to open the house door for Kiku.

Kiku's arm shot forward, and she seized Alice's arm. "Wait!"

Alice jerked her hand back from the doorknob as if it were a hot stove.

Kiku pushed in an electrical socket on the wall. Something clicked, followed by a buzz, and the red light above the plug changed to green. "My apologies. I needed to turn off my security precautions."

Alice exhaled. "No problem. For a moment, I thought I would get my head blown off if I opened the door." She laughed.

Kiku smiled, "No. But it would not have been pleasant."

Alice swallowed as Kiku entered the house.

Her home was an open Floridian design. The tiled floor led to a bright kitchen with a screened-in lanai. On the right were a bathroom and a living room with a bedroom beyond.

Kiku eyed the counter. "Please excuse the dust."

"You should see my apartment." Alice lied. She tried to keep her home as clean as time permitted. "Besides, you've been so busy. When was the last time you were home?"

"I have never been here." Kiku set the bag on the counter and walked to the kitchen table.

Alice's eyebrow rose.

"This is not my home. It is a Yakuza safe house. We have many in Florida. Tourist destinations are an ideal cover. Here, one raises less suspicion, leaving a house unoccupied for long periods and then, with different people arriving. The Airbnb trend makes it even less conspicuous."

"Where is your home?"

"I rent a condo but do not truly have a home. I consider myself a wanderer."

A wave of sadness and compassion washed over Alice as she looked at Kiku. How alone and adrift she must feel.

"Your beautiful green eyes give your heart away, Alice. I am fine. My lifestyle demands that I remain flexible and unencumbered. Through my lens, it is freedom."

"You're amazing! I wish I could read people the way you and Jack can."

Kiku shoved the kitchen table aside. The legs squeaked on the tile. "We will not be here long. I only need to pick up a few things." Kiku placed her hand on the corner of the baseboard, then pushed. A muffled metal click sounded, and the baseboard slid forward like a drawer. Different guns, weapons, and ammunition covered a four-foot-long, three-foot-wide tray.

Alice stared at the rows of weapons, many she had never seen before. The gravity of the situation once again weighed heavy on her shoulders. This was no game she was playing. There was a price on her grandfather's head, and the men on the hunt for him were greedy, unscrupulous, and ruthless. They would go to any length to find her grandfather. And if they found Alice first, they would use her to get to him.

Kiku removed a cell phone from the drawer and closed it. "Please, make yourself at home." She pointed to the fridge. "There will be drinks in there and frozen food. Anything here is yours. I need to make a brief call."

"Sure." Alice smiled and set her bag down. She did not know what exactly was going on. She couldn't make this place home, not even for a second. Not without Jack. Her home was wherever he was.

The refrigerator held only water, energy drinks, beer, and wine. Alice removed two water bottles. She could hear Kiku's voice from down the hall as she shut the refrigerator door. "I request you waive his immunity." There was a long pause, and then Kiku said, "I understand. Goodbye."

Kiku's heels rang off the tile floor as she marched down the hallway and back into the kitchen with a stern look on her face.

"Is everything all right?" Alice handed Kiku a bottle of water.

"There has been a complication. Vidal Navarro, the man who knows the location of your grandfather, is not staying at the Gulf Hotel as my contact believed he would be. He is in the wind."

Alice pinched the bridge of her nose with her forefinger and thumb. "That's more than a complication—that's a disaster. How are we supposed to find my grandfather without Vidal?"

Kiku sipped her water, then crossed over to the drawer. "I have other means." Setting the bottle down, she opened the secret panel again. "Fausto Rossi knows everything that goes on in Miami. We will contact him." Kiku picked up a large pistol, aimed down the sight, then set the gun down with a look of displeasure. She repeated the process twice more until she reached a Glock. Racking the slide several times, she smiled. "This will do." She placed the gun on the counter and stacked boxes of ammo next to it.

"Can you trust this guy?" Alice asked.

Kiku placed another handgun beside the Glock. "Fausto is a player who has no loyalties and deals with anyone with money. He is not to be trusted, and this will be dangerous. Are you still sure you want to see this through?"

Alice nodded. "I didn't mean to, but because of the acoustics with the tile, I overheard you when you were coming down the hall. You asked if someone would waive immunity. Who is this Fausto guy, a diplomat?"

"Alice, you are aware the more you know, the greater your danger?"

"Yeah. The booby trap entry door got my attention. Then I

saw the James Bond drawer of death and destruction. I figure I'm up to my eyeballs in this, so I may as well ask questions to get a heads up as to what we are in for. So, is Fausto some kinda diplomat?"

"Similar." Kiku closed the drawer. "To the Yakuza, Fausto and Vidal are considered neutral, like Switzerland. They both have a certain level of protection that I requested Takeo rescind. Takeo does not want me to harm them to get them to speak."

"I don't want anyone to get hurt, either. I just want to find my grandfather. Can we pay them to tell us?"

"The reward for your grandfather is so exorbitant; you could not afford it."

Alice crossed her arms. "But if Takeo is the head of the Yakuza, and your boss, even if he is your boyfriend, don't you have to obey his rules?"

"I am supposed to. Takeo has ordered me not to kill them."

"And you're okay with that?"

Kiku smiled. "Of course."

Alice exhaled. She wanted to find her grandfather, but realizing that Kiku wouldn't harm the men made her breathe easier. "That's a relief."

"Good." Kiku finished the water. "Get your bag. We are leaving to find Fausto."

"And when we find him, you're not going to kill him, right?"

Kiku's eyes turned even darker. "I will not kill him, but I will make him talk."

12

Jack and Ed stood waiting in the lobby of the Patricia E. Reynolds Business Center at White Rocks. The modern campus building was four stories of steel and glass filled with classrooms, lecture halls, and offices.

Ed rechecked his phone. "Oscar said he'd meet us here fifteen minutes ago."

Jack glanced at his phone and the social media accounts of Oscar Chambers and shrugged. The smug, handsome graduate student had plastered his academic accomplishments on every social platform and networking site Jack found.

"I'm giving him five more minutes, and then I'm going to knock on doors." Ed stuffed his phone back inside his suit jacket.

"Here he comes." Jack pointed to the staircase leading to the second floor.

Oscar Chambers was even more pretentious in person. He nodded, smiled, and winked at several people while he strode down the stairs and across the foyer. He oozed a certain smarm, typically reserved for politicians and playboys. His wavy, dark hair was styled to appear somewhat wild, but Jack was sure that

Oscar sculpted each out-of-place curl. Oscar wore blue jeans, tan boat shoes, and a dark turtleneck with a blue sports coat. He flashed a perfect veneer smile as he shook Ed's hand and Jack's. "My deepest apologies for keeping you waiting. I was dealing with a critical call."

"We appreciate you taking the time to speak with us," Ed said.

"I assume this is about Dr. Mobley? If he filed some sort of complaint before he died, you'd have to go through my attorney."

"It's not regarding a complaint," Jack said, then pointed to a high table with four stools circling it next to the windows. "Can we talk over there?"

Oscar nodded and fell into step beside them. "He is dead, right?" His lips mashed together, and he ran a hand through his hair. "The rumor mill on campus is going wild. I can't believe it."

"Were you two close?" Ed asked.

"Not really." Oscar pulled over a stool and sat at the round table. "I was closer to his work than I was to him. Dr. Mobley was a very innovative designer. His work was dated, of course, but for his time, it was excellent."

"Could you please explain your relationship with Dr. Mobley?" Ed flopped his notebook on the table and clicked his pen. "How did you two meet?"

Oscar pressed his left forefinger and thumb to his eyes and held up his right hand. "I'm sorry. I can't."

"Take a minute," Ed said. "We understand that this is very distressing."

"It's not that." Oscar sniffed. "My allergies are killing me, and I can't discuss the project with anyone. My counsel has advised me not to."

"You've already spoken with an attorney about this?" Jack asked.

"Sam threatened to sue me. Of course, I went to an attorney. I'd like to help, but my hands are tied."

Ed dropped his pen onto the pad. "Are you refusing to assist in a murder investigation?"

Oscar's eyes widened, and he shook his head. "No! I want to help, but I'm stuck in the middle." He stared at Jack. "You're Jack Stratton, right? Michelle Carter's foster brother?"

The mention of his murdered sister cut him like a knife. He longed for the day when he could picture Michelle's smiling face without a flood of pain.

"I am."

"Michelle was my friend. We were in classes together. I'm the one who set up the memorial study room in her honor. I'm a good guy. Please understand that I want to help, but what can I do?"

The words knocked Jack for a mental loop. He'd been at the opening ceremony for the memorial room, but he couldn't bring himself to go in. Jack didn't know that Oscar had not only been a friend of Michelle's but helped to preserve her memory.

Jack cleared his throat. "You don't have to get into details of the project, but someone made a threat against Dr. Mobley before his death. One was also made against Dr. Patel. We're here to check on your safety and let you know that you may also be in grave danger."

"You mean the playing card?"

"Did you get one, too?" Ed asked.

Oscar nodded. "King of Clubs with a skull for a face."

"Do you still have it?" Jack said.

"No. Someone put a blank envelope on my car. The card was inside. I pitched it." Oscar looked down at his hands. "If I say something, can it stay off the record?"

"It doesn't work that way. We're not reporters." Ed clicked his pen. "Also, we already know a great deal. We just need you to corroborate the facts."

Oscar rolled his eyes. "That's assuming that what you've been told are the facts. If you've only spoken with Navi and Sam, I doubt you've gotten the truth."

"Then tell us the truth, Oscar," Jack said. "What happened at the meeting?"

"Sam's involvement with the project was more of a courtesy. Years ago, he designed a precursor of today's drones. But Sam glamorized the past. His ideas were dated."

"Why did you keep him around?" Ed asked. "If he wasn't contributing to the project?"

"Kindness," Oscar said. "In reality, this was my project. As part of my graduate work, I developed a modern automated aerial delivery system. I interviewed many old designers, and Sam was one of them. I didn't know it would inspire him to revive his old work. He poured money into his old design but, excuse the pun, it wouldn't have gotten off the ground. He was putting lipstick on a pig. When his project failed, I invited him to some of our tests. Sam believed it was a collaboration, but it wasn't. Then he demanded credit—and money."

"And that's when things went south?" Ed asked.

"Sam threatened to sue us all and stormed out. He was relentless after that. Calls. Threats. Texts." Oscar's brow furrowed. "Can I ask how he died? Are you certain it was related to the threats?"

"He was killed in a propane explosion at his home," Ed said. "We're exploring all possibilities. Hopefully, it was just an accident."

Oscar nodded. "I hope so, too, especially after receiving that card. You didn't say anything about Yan. Have you warned him?"

"We tried." Ed frowned. "He's not the most approachable guy."

"The dogs?" Oscar chuckled. "You should email him and have him meet you. That's what I do. I'll give you his email.

Ed wrote down the address Oscar gave him

"Dr. Mobley said that you approached a tech company to invest. What company was that?" Jack asked.

Oscar shrugged. "There were no talks with any companies. We hadn't yet reached that point."

"Until we conclude the investigation," Jack said, "we're asking all of you to take extra safety precautions. Is there any chance of you getting out of town for a few weeks?"

"None. This is the busiest time of my life." Oscar glanced at his phone. "Speaking of which, I have to teach a robotics class." He shook Ed's hand, then turned to Jack. "I'm sorry about Michelle. She was brilliant. I mean that."

Jack nodded. He pictured the little girl who overcame so much to go to college, and his chest swelled with pride. He handed Oscar his card. "Call me if you think of anything or see anyone that makes you uneasy."

Ed stepped forward and thrust his card into Oscar's still outstretched hand. "Be certain to notify me first, okay?"

Oscar nodded. "Sure. Sorry. I have to go."

As Oscar hurried back up the staircase, Ed turned to Jack.

"We need to get some things straight, Stratton. Nothing big. Nothing bad. Just some operating procedures." He picked up his notebook.

Jack glanced at the page before Ed closed the book. There were only a few notes concerning the investigation. The rest of the page, Ed had filled with a bulleted list entitled JACK.

"First off, I'm the point of contact for everyone involved in this case. I know you got new business cards that you're dying to use, but hold on to them for now. Second, I lead all interviews, so let me do the talking. It would be better if you take the approach of watch and learn. See how I do things, and later we can talk about how you can put that into practice when I think you're ready. Third, this case is your primary focus. I know Morrison threw you a bone with that missing person case, but odds are, the guy started using again. It's only been a few days, so you should take a wait-and-see attitude with that one. Give it a week, and I'm sure he'll show up at some clinic or homeless shelter. We need to prioritize."

While Ed prattled on, Jack glanced down at his badge. He got his first detective shield when he was six. Aunt Haddie brought it home for him, but it came with a catch. She asked him to help find Michelle's friend's missing doll.

But Jack refused.

"Uh-uh." Young Jack shook his head. "She's always mean to me, Aunt Haddie. I'm not helping her."

Aunt Haddie crouched in front of him and pointed at the plastic gold badge on his chest. "Have you ever heard of the Golden Rule?" she asked.

Jack shrugged. Being raised by a prostitute addicted to drugs and alcohol, he hadn't heard many rules at all.

"Jesus said, in everything, do to others what you would have them do to you. That's the Golden Rule."

Jack's little face scrunched up. "What about the bad others?"

"Everyone." Aunt Haddie smiled.

"But you're nice, Aunt Haddie. I like you. I'd look for your doll."

"You'd help me even if we're different?"

Jack nodded.

"Everyone's different, but we're all one race—human. That means we're all in this together, even if we're different." She pointed at her dark skin and Jack's white arm. "Take us. We're just different shades of brown. And some people are tall, and others are short. Some are nice, and some are not so nice."

"She's really, really not so nice."

Aunt Haddie touched the star on his chest. "You want to be a policeman when you grow up, right?"

"I'm going to be a detective!"

"Do you know that when you put that badge on, you promise to help everyone? Rich, poor, black, white, nice, and not so nice."

"Even the mean ones?"

"Even the mean ones."

"What's that rule called again?"

"If you forget, look at your golden badge. You'll remember."

Ed snapped his fingers. "Stratton, are you listening? I said you need to focus on this investigation."

"Yeah." Jack glanced down at his gold detective badge again, and Aunt Haddie's words rang clear and loud in his ears. In everything, do to others what you would have them do to you.

"Those are your marching orders, Jack. I expect you to follow them." Ed said.

"You're absolutely right, Ed. You're the lead on this case, and I'll follow how you want me to operate."

Ed smiled smugly and nodded in agreement.

Jack continued, "Regarding my other cases, I expect you to show that same courtesy to me. Carl Wilson's case is my case. I'll handle it how I see fit."

Ed's smile vanished. He raised his arm and pointed at Jack. "I knew bringing you back was a bad idea. I told Morrison not to rehire you, let alone promote you."

Jack shrugged.

"I'm going to go talk to him. I'll let him know what you just said."

Jack shrugged again.

Ed squeezed the notepad in his hand so hard it buckled. "If I were you, I'd be worried. Morrison's going to listen to me."

"Why do you think the Sheriff will listen to you now? He didn't listen to your opinion when he hired me."

Ed swore and stormed out of the building.

Jack pushed the stools back under the tall table and strolled toward the exit. Ed stomped down the sidewalk like a battering ram, sending students scrambling to get out of his way. Ed reached the car first. He glanced back, flipped Jack off, grabbed the door handle, and vainly tried to open it.

Jack held up the keys. The car ride home was already going to be uncomfortable enough, but he couldn't help flashing a crooked grin.

Ed hung his head. He muttered something to himself. It was clear he was seething, but Jack didn't care. He had to stand up for his principles and if that made Ed upset, so be it.

And there was much more at stake than Ed's bruised ego. Carl Wilson was missing, and Jack needed to find him.

13

Jack stared at the sign for the Willamina Inn, a faded, poorly screen-printed bed sheet tacked to the side of the building to cover the original sign and name—Hearthside Lodge. The L-shaped ranch building was split into a dozen rooms rented long-term, daily, or by the hour.

The five men and two women milling out front scurried away like rats as Jack made his way to the front office. They disappeared into different apartments, closing the doors and drawing the curtains.

Opening the main entrance door, the mixed aromas of marijuana, stale cigarette smoke, and body odor made Jack hold his breath. A bell chimed, announcing his arrival, but the front desk remained deserted.

The small waiting area held a soda machine and a bench against the wall covered with dusty stacks of free flyers offering everything from real estate listings, apartment rentals, and tourist attractions. From the yellowed paper, Jack doubted any were current.

"No rooms!" A man shouted through the partially open doorway behind the desk.

"I need to speak with the manager," Jack shouted back. "Police business."

Something fell over. Heavy footsteps thudded across the floor, and the door slammed shut.

"Give me a minute," the same man called out.

More banging sounded inside the room along with muttered cursing. A greasy-haired man slipped out the door, pulling it closed behind him a moment later. His eyes were yellowish and bloodshot, set deep into blackened sockets. His hands shook, but he glared at Jack with simmering defiance. "I've got rights. Do you have a warrant?"

"I'm not searching the place, and I don't care about you smoking dope." Jack held up his badge. He kept it lifted until the man finished inspecting it. Jack never understood why some detectives flashed their badges quickly. It always made him think of the movies where the person wasn't a cop, and the badge was really a Burger King gift card. He wondered if whoever they flashed it to remained suspicious for the entire interview. "This is a wellness check."

"A wellness check? What's that?"

"We've received a report of a missing person, Carl Wilson. I want to make sure he's okay."

The man's eyes darted to the floor. "Can't help you with that."

"Are you the manager? What's your name?"

"I don't have to answer that."

"Yeah, you do." Jack set both hands on the countertop.

The man's yellow eyes blinked, and he wiped his nose with the back of his hand. "Bernie Strickland. I'm the owner."

"I want to see Carl Wilson's unit."

Bernie shook his head.

"If you make me get a warrant—"

"It ain't that." Bernie raised his hands in protest. "Carl don't got a place no more."

"When was the last time you saw him?"

"Three days ago." Bernie shrugged. "Rent's due Monday. He's a week-to-week. No exceptions."

"Where are his belongings?"

"I tossed them this morning."

The muscles in Jack's arms tightened. "That's illegal."

Bernie shook his head. "No, it ain't. He didn't pay."

"You are required to hold on to his possessions for a minimum of fourteen days."

Beneath his greasy hair, Bernie's forehead wrinkled. "What are you, a lawyer?"

"Where'd you pitch them?"

Bernie jerked his head to the side. "Out back."

Jack held open the little swinging gate to the counter. "Show me. Get moving."

Muttering, Bernie grabbed a set of keys from under the counter and started down the narrow hallway. Making their way past a soda machine with an Out of Order sign hanging off it, Bernie stopped at the metal door at the end and unlocked it.

Trash and garbage littered the patio behind the hotel. Rusted window air conditioners, three old toilets that looked and smelled like they were still being used, and a large green dumpster closed with a chain and padlock crowded the concrete pad.

"Gotta keep it locked to keep people from digging through it and dumping their crap." Bernie removed the chain, the lid landing with a loud clang as he shoved it open. "Have at it." A snide grin formed on his thin lips as he held his hand out.

Jack shook his head. "You're going in."

Bernie crossed his arms. "Ain't gonna happen. You can take me to jail before I do that, but since I haven't broken any laws, you can't do that either."

"You're right." Jack grinned. "But if you don't go in there and get everything you removed from Carl's apartment, I'm coming back with a warrant to take this hotel apart to look for evidence. And, for my safety concerns, I'll bring the health inspector, the fire inspector, and drug-sniffing dogs. Or you can get in there and get Carl's belongings. Your choice."

Bernie's eyes bulged like jaundiced balloons ready to pop. He glared at the dumpster, shook his head from side to side, and ran both hands through his greasy hair. "This is harassment." He grumbled before leaning halfway into the dumpster. He pulled out a green bag and a cardboard box and set them on the ground. "That's it." He wiped his hands on his pants. "Everything."

Jack peered inside the dumpster. In the back was a cardboard box that matched the one Bernie had just removed. "Get that one, too."

"I can't reach it."

"Climb in."

Bernie stomped forward until he was right in Jack's face. He was four inches shorter than Jack, so he had to settle with lifting his chin high and glaring up at him. "I'm not climbing into a dumpster for nobody. Arrest me. Search the place. I don't care."

Jack softened his tone like he was speaking to a child. "Did I forget to mention that I'll also have to seize your billing records? I have to check when Carl paid and then double-check those results with the IRS, and then there are the state's room occupancy excise taxes to check."

Bernie swallowed, and his bulging eyes deflated. Swearing under his breath, he climbed into the dumpster. Light-blue bags crunched and broke as he waded through the trash to the back. "I could get a disease in here!" he shouted, his voice echoing off the steel. He grabbed the box, hefted it onto his shoulder, and started back.

"Before you get out," Jack said, taking the box, "look around to make sure you missed nothing of Carl's."

"I'm telling you, that's everything." Bernie grabbed the side.

Jack blocked his exit. "You lied once. Check again."

"Look!" Bernie flailed his arms around at the garbage. "I put his stuff in two boxes and a green bag because I ran out of the blue ones. I'm positive that's it." He pointed to the pile at Jack's feet. "I'm a hundred and ten percent certain." Bernie tilted over the edge of the dumpster and slid out. "Two boxes, one bag. That's it."

Jack opened the boxes. Inside were some shoes, toiletries, and books. On the top was a photo frame. It was a picture of Carl Wilson when he was young. He stood in his Army dress uniform beside a grinning woman, who smiled proudly. The trash bag held only clothes.

"Are we done here?" Bernie rubbed at a fresh stain on his shirt. "I need to take a shower."

Jack wanted to let him know he was long overdue for one but held his tongue. He might need to come back and didn't need to alienate this guy further. "Don't have this bin emptied until Friday. Lock it up, and don't put any other trash in."

"Where am I supposed to put the garbage?"

Jack glanced around the filthy patio. "I'm sure you'll come up with a place." He picked up the boxes and got a hold of the bag too. He started around the building without wanting to navigate the narrow hallway with them. "Thank you for your help," Jack called over his shoulder.

"We're good, right? You're not gonna send nobody else here?"

"We're good." Jack kept walking.

Trash and litter cluttered the path behind the building, but Jack couldn't stop glancing at the windows. As he passed the rear windows of the apartments, eyes peered out of the darkness. Fear filled some, and others narrowed with contempt. An old man waved. A child darted out of sight.

Guilt washed over Jack. He drove by the Willamina Inn

daily and never thought of the lives inside. They were all someone's sons or daughters—people living in the shadows, fighting demons on their own.

Seeing the photograph of Carl Wilson inside the box hit home. Jack had one just like it on his mantle. Would his demons have dragged him here if he hadn't met Alice?

Jack marched around the corner and headed to his car. Aunt Haddie's words rang in his ears. There, but by the grace of God, go I...

14

Sitting in my car, I stare at the large screen on the dashboard. The mapping program displays my vehicle as a blue dot and highlights Jack Stratton's car in green. The detective is a busy man.

He's on the move again. I watch as the green dot heads north on Court Street. Technology is incredible, but a part of me yearns for the days when I'd have to follow closely behind Jack's car or risk losing him.

There's no chance of that now. The tracker I placed on his car enables me to wait until the risk of him seeing me is nil. It takes some of the fun out of the game, but I can't be too careful with him. I overheard him telling his neighbor that his lovely bride has gone away for a few days. Now Jack's undivided attention is laser-focused on solving the case. Should I be worried?

I start the engine of my car and follow him. He's out of sight now and heading straight down Jefferson Ave. I wonder where?

I'm becoming a little too obsessed with Jack. Last night, I binge-read his life story. At least what I could find online. How does the child of a prostitute and a murdered father rise out of that life unscathed? The question haunted me until I awoke.

He doesn't.

Jack may look like he has it together, but he's defective. He has to be. I'm no psychologist, but Jack's scars have to run deep.

I tick off Jack's potential issues as I wait at a red light. Abandonment. Trust. Hatred of authority. Defiance disorders. Risky behavior. Lack of impulse control.

Why did he ever choose law enforcement as a career? It's like a child getting hit by a truck who goes for a job as a bus driver.

Yet Stratton is capable. He's thorough. And he's become a problem.

I may have to put a stop to his meddling soon. On the one hand, it would be easy to kill him. A well-placed explosive or bullet would be simple yet effective. But if Jack dies, that would kick the hornet's nest of law enforcement. They'd come down on the town in a swarm to avenge one of their own.

No. I still have too many on my list. I'll have to delay killing Stratton.

Delay?

Hmm.

If I can't kill him, perhaps forcing him to pause or knocking him off the case would suffice. There's always poison. Only enough to result in a trip to the hospital. Not enough to cause death. Would that work?

Probably not. There would be tests, and if the doctors detected the poison, that would rile the hornets into attack mode.

An accident could work too. Cut his brake lines or set his apartment on fire while he's sleeping? I do love a good fire.

No. I need to keep a low profile until my work is complete.

What if one of those things didn't happen to Jack but someone close to him? I don't know where Alice went, so she is not an option. But he has that dog. Would he stop working if that beast died or got sick? Maybe.

Or his landlady. They seem close. Would he take time to care for her if she fell down the stairs? She probably has kids of her own to do it.

His birth mother is in a psychiatric hospital near here. A facility like that would be well guarded.

His parents live in Florida. They'd be an easy target, and I have their address courtesy of the internet. If I take a plane that will leave a trail quickly discovered. No. Not an option.

The green dot is slowing down and pulling into a parking lot. The building is only two blocks ahead, so I don't bother zooming in on the map.

The County Morgue.

Yes. Jack is a busy man. I watch him get out of his car and head inside. He's looking around as he marches toward the building. Always the soldier, he moves like a warrior on the battlefield.

My resolve fades. He is a force to be reckoned with. It isn't wise to let this detective go unchecked. Perhaps I should put an end to Stratton sooner than I thought.

I circle the building. I want to continue trailing the detective, but I notice the clock on my dashboard.

There's not enough time. I can't wait for him to come out. I have things to do and people to kill.

15

Jack loathed going to the morgue. The stench of death permeated the building and clung to Jack even after he left. Entering the morgue felt like descending into a crypt. Always cold, the air inside was dense, seeming to press in from all sides. Jack waited for the Medical Examiner in the lobby outside the examination room.

He couldn't sit. Not in here. Pacing, he ran down his to-do list and tried not to think about where Alice was or what she was doing.

A large door swung open, and Mei Lai, the M.E.'s assistant, stood on the threshold, her white hospital coat nearly touching the shiny linoleum floor. The petite woman gave a friendly wave and held the door open for Jack.

"Hi, Mei."

"It's nice to see you again. Congratulations on rejoining the force."

"Thank you." There was something different about her that Jack struggled to put his finger on. Her shoulder-length dark hair was the same. She still wore her rectangular blue-and-pink glasses, but something had changed.

Then it hit him. Mei was painfully shy, but now she confidently met his gaze. Her badge provided a reason for the confidence boost. Dr. Mei Lai — Medical Examiner.

"You got promoted!" Jack held up his palm, and she returned the high five. "I didn't know you were a doctor. I apologize, Dr. Lai."

"Oh, please call me Mei." Mei blushed and beamed all at once. "Neil retired. Over twenty people applied from all over the country. I never thought I'd get it."

"But you did. Congratulations."

"Thanks. I'm glad things are working out—for both of us. The wedding was wonderful. Did you have a nice honeymoon?"

Jack inhaled as he thought about how to respond. He and Alice barely survived their honeymoon, but they spent the last three days in the Bahamas locked in the bridal suit. That made it all worth it and still brought a smile to his face. "It was fantastic. If you get a chance, we loved the Bahamas. It was a trip we'll never forget. It was a blast."

"Speaking of blast." Mei glanced over her shoulder into the examination room. "This one is pretty rough. Would you rather review the report?"

"I can handle it." Jack squared his shoulders. He was a soldier and had seen things no one should witness.

Mei walked over to the gurney, where a body lay covered with a sheet.

Jack stared, confused. Dr. Mobley had stood almost six feet tall. The body on the table was under four and a half feet long.

Mei pulled back the sheet, and Jack's stomach clenched. The corpse looked like a shark attack victim that had been bitten almost in half. His legs and six inches of his stomach were there, but the upper torso was gone.

"Dr. Mobley had been standing in front of the kitchen window before the blast," Mei explained, her voice so quiet

Jack moved closer to hear her. "The steel and stucco construction of the house, the stone countertop, and the lower cabinets protected his legs. There was virtually no new damage to his lower extremities."

Mei cleared her throat and continued. "Dr. Mobley was injured in his twenties." Mei sniffed. "He crashed his airplane and extensively shattered his legs. No one believed he'd walk again, but Sam showed them."

A familiarity with how she said his name caught Jack's attention. "Did you know him?"

"He taught several classes at the college. I loved him as a teacher. He was a patient man. He even wrote a letter of recommendation for me." She pushed her glasses up the bridge of her slender nose. "I pulled his medical records from the hospital and cross-checked them with current x-rays to verify his identity. Because of the severity of the injuries, it's impossible for me to say the exact cause of death besides the explosion. Typically, in a blast event, secondary injuries lead to death. Flying debris, shrapnel, even blunt force trauma. Here, metal from either the propane tank or another source severed his torso."

"Was there anything out of the ordinary in your findings?"

"I'm still waiting on toxicology and several other lab reports, but no. All of his injuries are consistent with an accidental explosion. We recovered multiple fragments from the site that I still need to process, but they're heavily damaged and burned."

Jack lifted his chin. He liked Mei and didn't want to say anything to dampen her newfound confidence, but she needed to be careful with every word. "You said accidental explosion. I never used the term accidental, and you shouldn't include it in any report."

Mei flushed a bright red, and her eyes darted to the floor. "Yes. An explosion. It would be presumptuous of me and beyond my expertise to say the cause. Thank you for pointing that out."

"How many times have you gotten my back? I needed to clarify in the event this ever goes to trial. Lawyers have a field day over a misstated word."

"I didn't think it could have been anything different. He was in the process of getting a propane delivery when it happened. And Sam was such a nice man. He set my ankle after I broke it hiking in Dogwood Park last year. The emergency room at Mercy General was packed. I sat there for hours, but when Sam started his shift—he took care of me." Her expression hardened. "Can I ask you a favor, Jack?"

She'd never asked for anything in the years he'd known Mei. "Sure."

"If this wasn't an accident, find who was responsible. You don't meet many people like Sam. He was kind."

Jack nodded. As Mei pulled the sheet back over what was left of the good doctor, he remembered the photograph of Sam as a child, smiling with his mother at Lake Winnipesaukee.

Sam's death wasn't an accident. The skull playing cards were too coincidental for Jack to believe otherwise. They were calling cards of death, and it was time for Jack to find their dealer.

16

Alice peered at the street, crowded with throngs of partygoers dancing to the beat of the music, spilling out the open doors of the Parthenon nightclub and cascading down from the balconies above. Inside her mind, her list of doubts swirled like dust in the wind. Was the man Kiku looking for even inside the club tonight? Even if he were, would he help them?

Kiku smiled confidently. “Relax, Alice. Fausto is here. And he will tell me how to find your grandfather.” Kiku pulled the car to the curb and handed the keys to the valet, who ogled Kiku. Dressed in a red dress that hugged her curves, Kiku drew the men's attention from her car to her.

Alice straightened her simple tan summer dress but held her chin high. Woefully modest compared to the woman dancing on the sidewalk waiting to get into the club, her outfit drew snickers from a group of giggling women, but to Alice’s surprise, many men also stared at her.

“Stay close to me,” Kiku said as she marched toward the hulking security guards stationed at the front of the club.

"Where's your pass?" A towering man with arms as thick as Alice's waist blocked Kiku's path.

Alice expected Kiku to slip him a bribe, but Kiku leaned closer to the man and said something that was drowned out by the music. Whatever she said made the security guard swallow and let her pass.

The crowd parted out of Kiku's way as she strolled inside. Kiku moved like a panther, each step filled with such grace and power that it commanded respect—and fear.

The beat of the music assaulted Alice as they made their way through the club. She could feel the bass vibrating up her legs and through her chest. Alice hovered at Kiku's heels as she marched to the stairs, somehow knowing exactly where she was going.

Men shouted offers to buy Alice drinks. She politely shook her head, but every few steps, someone new asked until Alice held up her wedding ring and pointed to it. Men still offered.

Feeling like a swimmer breaking out of the water, they reached the stairs, and the crowd thinned. Two more security men immediately moved aside as if they were expecting them. One unhooked a velvet rope that blocked the way. Halfway up the staircase, Alice looked back at the sea of people and marveled they had made it through such a mob.

The second floor had more dancing, but the crowd was a fraction of the size of the one on the first floor. A woman on a mission, Kiku headed straight to the back right corner of the room. Rounding the end of the long bar in the center of the room, she aimed toward an open lounge section. A couch and chairs circled a low table cluttered with drinks. Several women and three men sat laughing and talking.

A thin man in a black suit with an earpiece stood off to one side. He held his hand over his ear, nodded, then crossed to one of the men sitting down. The man's laughter snapped off, and he sat bolt upright, scanning the club. He noticed Kiku and stood, almost knocking the women seated on either side of him to the floor.

The man, dressed in black slacks with a yellow shirt unbuttoned to his belly button, waved his arms and shouted in Italian to the group. The two men with him cleared the women out of the lounge area, so only the thin man and the man in yellow remained.

"Buona sera, Kiku." He bowed low, then strode over with his arms outstretched. Like he'd hit some invisible wall, he stopped outside Kiku's personal space and gave a polite bow of his head. "Buona sera," he repeated to Alice but took her by the shoulders and kissed her cheeks. "Welcome. Please sit. What can Fausto Rossi do for you?"

Two waitresses hurried over and started cleaning off the table.

"I wish to speak to you somewhere more private," Kiku said.

"Of course. Certainly." Fausto stepped out of the lounge area. "My office is over here."

Fausto led the way to a closed door, with Kiku and Alice following and the thin man coming behind.

Alice didn't care for the thin man at all. Something about his lack of expression and the stare of his brown eyes made her uncomfortable.

Fausto held open the door, and all four went inside. The room was a large and traditionally furnished office. A desk sat in the back with four chairs in front of it. In the corner were a wide leather couch and a coffee table.

While Kiku and Alice took the chairs in front of the desk, Fausto and the thin man crossed behind it. Fausto sat, and the thin man stood behind him on his left.

The thin man cupped his hand to his ear, and his expressionless face turned grim. He leaned forward and whispered something to Fausto, whose only reaction was a slight flaring of his nostrils.

"They did not search me," Kiku said. "I am armed, of course."

"Of course." Fausto motioned the thin man to step back. "Can I offer you a drink?" He reached for a crystal decanter on the corner of the desk.

"No, thank you," Kiku said.

Alice politely shook her head and gave a tight smile.

"How is Takeo? Does he wish to discuss a business matter?"

"Takeo is well. And no, this does not concern the Yakuza's interests. This is personal."

Fausto spilled some of the liquid he was pouring onto the desk. Ignoring it, he corked the decanter and held up his glass. "Cin-cin."

"Alla nostra salute." Kiku said. "I acquired a vehicle I wish to test. Word is, you have a new Corvette?"

Fausto blinked twice and exhaled. He looked back and forth between Alice and Kiku, laughed, and gulped half his drink. "Are you talking about a race? You can't be serious. Your Demon versus my Vette? Is that really why you came? Wonderful!"

"Only if you and I drive."

Fausto polished off the drink and poured another. "I didn't think you'd give me a chance to redeem my name. You know you only won because of my mechanic's failure."

"You do love to cast blame." Kiku smiled. "You pushed the car past its abilities—and yours. That is why the engine blew. The fault, mio amico, was your own.."

Fausto's eyes flashed with anger, but he covered it with a laugh. "Tomorrow night? Circle the City?"

Kiku shook her head. "Scramble for the Coast."

Fausto thought about it for a moment before replying, "Agreed."

"Do try to show some restraint this time. I want to drive away in your Vette, not have it towed."

"You don't have a chance, Kiku. I am speed. Why do you think my mamma named me Fausto?"

"Because she was a superstitious woman. Your name has nothing to do with speed. It means lucky."

Fausto grinned. "Then either way—I win!" He laughed and polished off the rest of the drink.

Alice followed Kiku out of the room, angry and confused. All they discussed was a stupid race. Had Kiku forgotten why they'd come?

The two made their way back through the throngs of dancing people. This time, no one dared offer to buy Alice a drink. The men looked at her scowling face and headed in a different direction.

Once the valet had returned their car, and they were safely down the road, Alice shifted in her seat to face Kiku. "What was that?"

Kiku held her finger up to Alice's lips to signal her to stop talking. "Please hand me a tissue. There are some in the glove box."

Alice nodded in understanding and opened the drawer. Kiku pointed to the black bag in the compartment's corner, which Alice handed to her.

Kiku removed a device that opened to the size of a curling iron and began scanning the car. As she swept it over the dash, the detector emitted a green flashing light. When she reached the cigarette lighter, it glowed a steady green. Kiku removed the lighter, then inspected it.

Alice pointed at her ear.

Kiku nodded, powered down her window, and tossed the lighter out. "Thank you for following my lead," Kiku said. "Now we may talk."

Alice exhaled, then sat bolt upright. "What was the deal back in the club? You didn't even ask Fausto about Vidal."

"My apologies, but that was never my plan."

"What are you talking about? You said you would help me find my grandfather; the only way to find him is through this guy, Vidal. And the only one who knows where to find Vidal is Fausto."

"That is all correct. But Fausto will never willingly tell me where Vidal is. I will have to use other means of making him talk, and since you prefer I refrain from killing people, it complicates things."

Alice sat back in her seat. "I don't want you to kill anyone, but why would that complicate things?"

"If I were alone, I would have put a bullet in the thin man's head, and Fausto would have told me anything. Problem solved."

Alice's stomach flipped. Kiku's casualness in speaking of killing a human being made her look away.

"Before you judge me," Kiku continued, "know this. The thin man is evil. He has the blood of many innocent people on his hands."

"Couldn't you just have him arrested?"

"We come from two different worlds, Alice. I adore your heart. If you knew mine, it would repulse you. Please do not take this as an insult, but in some ways, you are so sweetly naïve. There is only one way to stop evil like the thin man—death. I spared him tonight because you were there. I will get Fausto to talk tomorrow. That is the best I can do without killing anyone. Would you rather I go back to the club and execute my original plan?"

"No. Tomorrow is fine." Alice turned and stared out the window.

How she missed Jack. He'd know what to do. Doubt swept over her. She thought this might take a day, maybe two. And now, the reality of her situation slapped her in the face. Kiku was correct. Alice was naïve. But Alice had followed Kiku down the rabbit hole, and she couldn't turn back now.

17

Sitting in his empty apartment in front of his computer, Jack missed Alice's company and her computer skills. He felt like a hack as he plodded along, digging up any information he could regarding the people involved in Dr. Mobley's delivery system. This was his first official death investigation as a detective, and the pressure he placed on himself was already mounting.

Jack took a USB stick out of his pocket and stuck it into the computer slot. He believed in having a backup of his body cam footage. With incidents between police and civilians being uploaded to the internet, Jack wanted to make sure he could always show his side of the story.

Like Aunt Haddie said, "Any story sounds true until someone tells the other side and sets the record straight."

The phone beside him rang, and the caller ID made him smile — FINNIAN CHURCH.

"What's up, buddy?" Jack answered the phone. "Thanks for the wedding present. Please tell Annie that Alice and I love that..." Jack closed his eyes as he struggled to remember the gift.

Then, like a contestant on a game show, he blurted out, "Crockpot!"

"You're such a terrible liar, Stratton. Do you think I'd believe you're all excited about a kitchen gadget?" Finn laughed, and so did Jack. "And you can tell Annie yourself. We're heading to Darrington for a job."

Finn and Annie were not only friends but also insurance investigators.

"Can I ask what you're looking into?" Jack asked.

"That's the reason I'm calling. We caught the insurance claim regarding Dr. Samuel Mobley's house. Because of the value, the insurance company wants us right on it. I called the station, and they told me you're working the case."

"I am. It's an active investigation." Jack said. "There are certain things I can't discuss."

"I understand. But I have some information that you may find useful. For starters, everyone and their brother tell me it's a million to one that the explosion was an accident."

"A million to one still leaves one."

"It does," Finn said. "But I've been on the phone for hours with a dozen propane safety experts. They all say the same thing—an explosion under those conditions is impossible."

Jack checked his notes. "What about the propane driver smoking an e-cigarette? Could that have caused the explosion?"

"Not unless all the fail-safes failed, and the driver was holding the hose next to his face while he was lighting the e-cig."

Jack flipped back his notes and stared at a sentence he'd circled. "The propane driver said the fuel connector was clean. He said they're usually junked up, but this one looked brand new."

"I know the fire investigator. I'll pass that information on and have her look for it."

Jack felt guilty not telling his friend about the threat to Dr. Mobley, but he couldn't. "How much was the insurance on the house?"

"Dr. Mobley had a minimal policy. He had downgraded it earlier this year. If he lived, he would've regretted the decision."

"Thanks, Finn. Do you guys need a place to stay? You can crash here. Alice's old bedroom is now a guest room."

"Hanging with the newlyweds? No thanks. I need my beauty sleep."

"Alice is, uh, visiting friends. It's no problem."

"In that case, that'd be great. Let me check with Annie. See you, Bud. Stay safe."

"You too." Jack hung up the phone and wrote the fact that Dr. Mobley had downgraded his insurance policy. Finn had just saved him time by checking the accidental explosion angle. When they served together, Jack had never known a more thorough soldier. If Finn looked into something, his word was gold. He'd still have to contact the companies officially, but he could do that later.

Jack wiggled the mouse, and the computer monitor came back to life. Various articles about Yan, Navi, Sam, and Oscar filled the screen. Yan was the only one who had not received a playing card.

Connecting his phone to his computer, Jack uploaded the photograph of the skull-faced Jack of Spades that Dr. Mobley had received. He performed a reverse image search. Not only were the cards available online, they were currently on sale in three different stores in Darrington. He wrote the store's contact information down and yawned.

He rubbed his eyes and checked the clock—ten past midnight. Before bed, he decided to switch gears and review his missing person case. Standing up, Jack stretched and walked over to the two boxes and the bag next to the door. His shoulders slumped as he stared down at the pile.

In this world where most people raced to grab the most possessions before they died, Carl Wilson was atypical or doing a very poor job of accumulating stuff. As far as Jack knew, all Carl owned sat at his feet.

The bag and first box contained clothes, a pair of shoes, and toiletries. The second box held several books, a thick Bible, two photographs, several gospel tracks, a stack of business cards, and what looked like a plastic poker chip. Turning the chip over, Jack realized it wasn't for gambling. It was a year sobriety marker from Alcoholics Anonymous. The business cards weren't traditional either. They were invitations to an AA meeting:

Downtown AA. Meets in The River CC Basement. 6:00 AM

No phone number. No name.

Jack closed his eyes. He could picture Chandler standing beside him saying, "There's a reason for the anonymous in the title, buddy."

"I'm wondering why Carl has a dozen of them, genius," Jack shot back.

His friend was long gone, but there wasn't a day when Jack didn't think about Chandler and Michelle. Maybe it was going to the college or even this missing person case, but Jack felt the guilt over their deaths rising within him.

For the first time in a long time, he wanted a drink. Alice wasn't here. She'd never know. For one night, he could drown all the memories and forget everything. The memory of the old man in the Willamina Inn peering out the window made Jack shudder.

I could buy a bottle, but it would cost me more than I want to pay.

Pushing the thought aside, he took the photographs out of the box. One was of Carl in his uniform on his wedding day, posing beside his bride. The woman was beautiful, and they both looked so happy. The following photograph was of Carl, his wife, and a small boy. They were standing in a field and holding hands.

Jack knew from the background report that Carl's wife had died three years ago while he was in prison. They never divorced. The other closest relative was Naomi's father, but she'd said he and Carl had a falling-out.

"Not much to go on," Jack said.

Lady lifted her head, looked directly at Jack, and scratched the carpet where she was lying.

"I swear you understand me. Are you telling me to keep digging?"

Lady huffed, set her head on her paws, and closed her eyes.

"And that's your way of saying, Yes, stupid, keep looking."

Jack turned to the first box. The books inside were all written by Christian authors. C. S. Lewis, R. C. Sproul, and a trilogy by William Gurnall entitled A Christian in Complete Armor. The Bible was worn and dog-eared. Jack fanned it open, and a rainbow of colors flashed on the pages. Carl had highlighted large swaths of verses and made notes in different colored pens.

Jack held the Bible with a cover flap in each hand, then turned it over. He shook it back and forth, and a single piece of paper fell out. Lifting it off the table, Jack scanned the church bulletin. The date was three weeks ago. On the back was a list of fill-in-the-blank questions and Bible verses. On the front was a picture of a man leaping between two peaks. His jacket billowed out behind him like a cape. The image left you with the impression that the man was trying to act like a superhero, but his successfully making the jump wasn't a guaranteed thing. On top of the illustration was printed: Today's Sermon—Do what is right, not what is easy.

None of the blanks were filled in on the back, and neither was the section for the notes. There were several creases in the pamphlet like it had been crumpled, then smoothed out. Turning the paper back over, he checked the address. The River Community Church. 43 Martin Luther King Ave, Darrington.

Jack glanced at Lady. "Looks like we're going to church."

18

Alice sat on the edge of the tub in the hotel's bathroom, pressing her phone against her ear, waiting for Jack to pick up.

"Alice?"

"Hi, babe. How was your day?"

"Good." Jack sounded tired. "I caught my second case. A missing person. He's a veteran."

"You have to work them both? At the same time?"

"Sometimes detectives have to juggle dozens of cases."

"But you always give it a thousand and ten percent. How can you do that for two?"

"Where there's a will, you find a way. I'm fine." Jack cleared his throat. "Are you, ah, having a good time?"

"I'm missing you." Alice clicked her fingernails. She wanted to spill it all and let Jack know where she was and what she was doing. But from the tension in his voice, now was not the right time to let him know she was with Kiku. "Hopefully, I'll be home soon."

There was a long pause. She could picture him in the living

room, staring at the phone with a hundred questions but not asking out of respect for her.

"I love you, Jack Stratton."

"I love you, angel. Be careful, okay?"

Alice inhaled. She wasn't any good at hiding secrets. She could tell Jack knew she was up to something. "You too. Night."

The phone disconnected, and Alice stared at the blank screen. They were a team, but she was keeping him in the dark. On the one hand, she felt like she was protecting him, but on the other, she felt dirty.

Wiping her eyes, she washed her hands and strode out of the bathroom. Kiku had changed into a black summer dress and strappy leather shoes. Alice yearned to exude sex appeal like Kiku, even though her intended audience was one. She made a mental note to start by gradually updating her wardrobe.

"I need to go out and get supplies." Kiku picked up her purse and headed for the door. "I will be back in a few hours."

Alice glanced at the clock. It was almost one in the morning. "Hold on a minute. We need to talk."

Kiku raised a perfectly manicured eyebrow.

"No offense, Kiku, but I'm not just along for the ride. We're trying to find my grandfather. I want in on your plan."

Kiku's crooked smile reminded Alice of Jack. "To be honest, my plan is always a work in process. To reach our goal is like traveling on a stream. The water flows and moves, and I adapt as I go."

"Well, I'm in the boat rowing with you, so start clueing me in." Alice crossed her arms.

"May I remind you that you are the one who asked for my assistance?"

"You don't need to." Alice laid her cards on the table. "I'm completely in your debt and beyond grateful. But I don't sit on the bench for anyone, so I need to work this job with you. And I seem to remember that you need to ask my grandfather a question, too. So what's the plan, and how can I help?"

Kiku crossed the room to the desk, flipped open her laptop, and pulled another chair next to hers. "Marriage has done wonders for your self-confidence. It is a good thing I care for you. If not..." Kiku clicked her tongue and smiled.

Alice hesitated before sitting down. She didn't know if she should thank Kiku or be nervous about what Kiku didn't say.

Kiku logged into her laptop and then explained. "Fausto will never willingly reveal Vidal's location. I need to talk to Fausto alone. The best way to isolate him is with the race. He always drives solo. I will get to Fausto before the finish line and sell him a life insurance plan of sorts."

"Oh, I get it! You're going to convince him to tell you where Vidal is, and he gets to live!" Alice beamed, pleased with herself. Her smile disappeared like the sun behind a cloud. "I'm kinda afraid to ask how you will convince him."

"That is a question best left unanswered."

Alice fired off her next question without taking a breath. "What is the Scramble for the Coast?"

"Street racing is an underground passion here. There are several courses they use." Kiku pulled up a map of the city on her computer. "The Scramble for the Coast starts at Fausto's Parthenon nightclub and ends here." She pointed at a spot far up the coastline.

Alice stared at the map of the city and the spiderwebs of roads. "It's called a scramble because you can pick any route?"

"Yes, but there are only a few viable choices. From the Parthenon, the drivers head down the major boulevard to North Street. Here, they face three choices. They can take First Avenue, a straight shot up the coast but the longest to travel. Or they can head to Franklin, which meanders, but the track isn't that difficult. Or you can make for Orange Blossom and try to navigate the Rattlesnake. Those roads wind like a serpent along the coast. Most take the easier paths depending on the car and driver's style."

"Will there be other drivers?"

"Possibly dozens. It matters how greedy Fausto is. All the drivers must pay an entrance fee. He will also hire one or two to act as his wingmen."

"How will you isolate Fausto with so many other drivers?"

Kiku shrugged. "That part of the plan I am still working on. I am certain Fausto will take the Rattlesnake; he is known for taking risks. But we will still need to stop the other racers. I will take a drive and check for pinch points on the roads. Then all we need to do is create roadblocks."

Alice stared at the monitor. Kiku's plan made sense. If they got rid of the other drivers, Kiku could grab Fausto when he was alone. "How are you going to make these roadblocks?"

"That is what I need to figure out."

Alice bit her lower lip. Once again, she missed Jack. As a policeman, he would be livid at the mention of a race through the city, but he'd also come up with a solution. Alice's eyes lit up. "What if we call the police?"

Kiku smiled politely. "They would shut down the race."

Alice shook her head. "We tell them the race is going down at First Avenue. They'll set up a roadblock and stop any drivers that go that way."

"Very good," Kiku nodded approvingly. "That's one route down. To block off the other road, we can create a traffic jam. We'll schedule deliveries."

"You'd have to order a lot of pizzas to create a traffic jam."

Kiku laughed. "I was thinking on a larger scale. Furniture. Appliances. Huge delivery trucks sent to the same location."

"It's not as foolproof as a roadblock, but that works."

"A competent driver can bypass a roadblock." Kiku grinned impishly. "Trust me; I have personal experience. Because of that, we will need to have eyes on the roads to see if any drivers make it. If this was a Yakuza-sanctioned operation, I could pull in men to watch the streets, but I cannot do that now."

"I can get you as many eyes as you need." Alice switched from the map program to an internet browser. Her finger flew across the keyboard and the monitor filled with various cellular trail cameras for sale. "Looks like we need to do some shopping."

"I believe we have a plan." Kiku patted Alice on the back.

Alice sighed. "You still need to beat Fausto. How did you do it before?"

"I sabotaged his car."

"You cheated?" Alice's voice rose along with her eyebrows.

"I won."

"That's still cheating. Can't you do that again?"

Kiku shook her head. "Fausto will have his car watched closely, and this time, winning does not matter. We want him to reach the finish line."

"How are we going to stop the drivers protecting him?"

Kiku's eyes grew cold. "Leave that to me."

19

Jack strode through the basement doors of The River Community Church, and no one even glanced his way. That was a good thing. The group of twenty bleary-eyed people sitting in the 6:00 a.m. meeting were alcoholics. While on their way to rock bottom, most had had multiple run-ins with the police and could usually pick a cop out of a crowd faster than finding an orange in a bushel of apples. But here, Jack blended in. Maybe it was his rough childhood. His mother had dragged him through so many crack dens and drug houses, Jack had probably spent more time with addicts than anyone here.

Taking a seat in the back row, Jack scanned the room, trying to figure out who was running the meeting. Getting information about a particular person was challenging in a place where anonymity reigns. And the minute he opened his mouth to ask questions, everyone would know he was a cop and scatter towards the nearest exit.

They arranged the chairs in a ten-by-ten grid with a column created down the middle for people to walk. No two people sat next to each other. A podium stood in the front, where one person stood at a time to share their story of how they used the program to quit drinking and maintain sobriety.

The tales were heartbreaking. The first speaker was a woman whose drinking spiraled out of control to the point she had an affair, then lost her husband, kids, and the house. After being fired from her job, her new boyfriend set off for greener pastures. Now she was trying to rebuild a life at fifty-seven.

Two more people shared their journeys, but Jack noticed when a one-legged man hobbled up to the podium. In his forties, he wore jeans and a collared shirt. His dark hair was short and peppered gray. He said he'd been a teacher until a car struck him while riding his bicycle. He lost his leg in the accident and gained an addiction to painkillers. When his prescription ran out, he turned to alcohol, but it didn't satiate the pain. He switched to opioids he bought on the street.

His wife knew he was playing a dangerous game of Russian roulette with drugs, most likely manufactured in someone's garage. Desperate to save her husband, she tracked him down, called the police, and had him arrested for possession. Since it was his first offense, the judge allowed him to go to a halfway house and get clean.

He still hurts but does other things to manage the chronic pain. He committed to his sobriety and his wife, working his program, which includes daily meetings to help ensure he doesn't fall again. Now he's loving life, clean and sober.

Jack was so wrapped up in the story he didn't see the clock. It was now five past seven, and everyone headed for the exit except two men and the man with one leg. His crutches clicked off the cement as he walked over to Jack.

"Welcome. I'm Tom."

"Jack Stratton."

"Nice to meet you. First time at a meeting?"

"Actually, no, but today I'm looking for someone. Carl Wilson. I'm a detective with the Sheriff's Department."

Tom rested his weight on one crutch and covered his mouth with his other hand. His eyes rounded with concern. "I've been worried about Carl. He comes daily to help set up and take down the meeting room. He hasn't been here for several days now. I knew..." His voice trailed off. He hopped to the left, held onto a chair back, and sat down, his crutches clattering on the floor.

"You knew what?" Jack took the chair next to Tom.

"I told Carl to speak to someone. They have people he could talk to. People who could help."

"Did he relapse?"

"No. No." Tom vigorously shook his head and let out a small chuckle. "I know we say an addict is always an addict, but rock bottom was different for Carl. AA isn't a religious organization, but Carl had a Damascus Road experience. When he gave his testimony, you could tell the scales fell off his eyes. That man had an encounter with God. He was a changed man."

"Then why were you telling him to speak with someone?"

"I really shouldn't say anything. This group is a safe place to share; if I tell you about Carl, I'm violating his trust."

"I get it, I do. My birth mother was an addict, but if she'd gone missing, I'd sing like a canary to help find her. Please, help me find Carl."

The man drew in a ragged breath and slowly nodded. "Carl had a problem with drugs. Not with getting them—stopping them. Let me back up and explain. Carl and my addiction stories are very similar. When Carl was in the army, his helicopter crashed, which shattered his body. The older he got, the more surgery he needed, and the pain worsened. He got hooked on prescription drugs. Listening to the news, you wouldn't know it, but it's an epidemic. Crazy bad. When Carl got out of prison, he felt led to stop it."

"What do you mean by *felt led*?"

Tom sighed and stared down at the floor. "Carl believed

God wanted him to stop the drugs on the street. He didn't hear God's voice out loud but in here." He touched his chest. "That's what Carl meant by being led. Like God told him."

"That sounds dangerous."

"That's what I told him." Tom crossed his arms. "If you tell someone in here, God doesn't want you to do drugs, that's one thing. When you go out in the street and tell a dealer to stop peddling that poison to kids because Jesus loves you? That can get you killed."

"Is that what Carl was doing?"

Tom shrugged. "I don't know. There was a kid that had been coming in here. Young boy. Teenager. He relapsed, OD'd, and died. Carl found out the kid OD'd on prescription pills. He kept saying the kid could have been his grandkid." Tom stuck his tongue in his cheek. "It didn't matter to Carl that he was black and the kid was a redheaded white boy. It didn't matter to him at all."

"Do you know this kid's name?"

Tom shook his head. "No. He always sat in the back with Carl. Everybody referred to him as Kid."

"Do you know who Carl was going to speak to?"

"No. I wish I could be more help, but he didn't say. I tried to tell him to go to the police, but he wanted to give the person a chance, you know? He thought he could talk to them."

"Do you think he confided in anyone else here?"

Tom's lips pressed together. "I don't think so. Like I said, Carl was on fire for God, but his zeal came off like he was a holy roller. Besides the kid and me, people gave Carl a wide berth."

Jack removed his card and handed it to Tom. "If you think of anything, or anyone that may know something, please call me."

"I will."

Jack left the church and headed for his car. He had more reason to be concerned for Carl's safety but no names to go on.

Taking out his phone, he texted an old friend on the force. If anyone had a lead about drugs, it would be Mark Reynolds. He worked undercover for years and knew the ins and outs of Darrington's drug trade.

A man pushing a shopping cart loaded with green bags crossed the street ahead of Jack and steered his cart closer to Jack's car. Jack had left the windows halfway down but wasn't worried, even with this area being a rough neighborhood.

The man reached the rear passenger side window, stopped, and peered in.

The entire car rocked back and forth.

The man's mouth fell open. Cans rained off the grocery cart as he shoved it forward and hurried away and down the street.

Jack chuckled.

He didn't need to lock the car. Not with Lady inside. The 125-pound King Shepherd was the best alarm he'd ever had. But that wasn't why he brought her to work with him today.

Jack needed Lady for a special assignment.

20

Jack stood outside Dr. Chen's chain-link fence and checked his phone. Still no reply from Ed. Jack suspected Ed was at the body shop trying to convince them to begin work on his battered and beloved car.

Jack texted: @ DR CHENS FOLLOWING UP ON CARD

Ed texted back: GD LUCK W THAT

At the dilapidated house, Jack stared across the front yard, its uncut grass swaying in the breeze. The curtains were drawn. No lights were on. On the right side of the yard, the dog pen sat empty.

A familiar glow ignited in his core. The same feeling that arose when a person neared the first crest of a rollercoaster sent a warmth racing through his veins. Cupping his hand to his mouth, Jack shouted, "Dr. Chen? It's Detective Stratton. I want to speak with you."

The entire pack of pit bulls barreled around the corner of the house. Two crashed into each other, rolling across the gravel, scrambling to their feet, and continuing their charge.

The alpha dog threw himself into the gate, the mental clanging and flexing outward.

Jack took an instinctive step back.

His retreat emboldened the animals. Their white teeth clacked, and spit flew from their jaws as they snapped wildly at the fence and clawed at the metal.

Jack stuck his fingers in his mouth and whistled. He had no idea if this plan would work. The closest he came to dog psychology was watching a couple of episodes of The Dog Whisperer. But dogs were pack animals, and they always followed the leader.

A deep, full roar rose above the barks and snarls of the pit bills. The grass parted in the field behind Jack as a massive, still unseen form raced through the overgrown vegetation.

The pit bulls fell silent as they waited to see what threat rushed at them through the grass.

Bounding into view, Lady pounced from the brush and landed with her front legs shoulder width apart, and she held her head high. She marched to Jack's side.

The pit bulls snarled.

"Okay, Lady. Show them who's the boss." Jack repeated Alice's new training instruction.

Lady took two steps forward and looked to the left. Her huge chest expanded as she gulped in air, then let out an enormous bark so loud Jack wanted to stick his fingers in his ears. Lady looked right and barked again. She sat on her haunches, raised her head, and barked a third time, staring straight at the pit bulls.

To Jack's delight, the sat down. Marching forward, he stopped with his hand on the latch. All hesitation regarding his plan vanished when Lady trotted beside him, and the alpha pit bull lay down and rolled over on his back, its paws in the air and his belly exposed.

"Smart dog," Jack said as he opened the gate.

Lady entered, sniffed the alpha dog, and growled.

"Easy, girl," Jack said, patting Lady's head. "You won. They surrendered."

Lady's body was stiff, and she remained on guard. The alpha pit bull whined, scrambled onto its belly, and crawled backward.

Jack noticed the dark brown stain on its muzzle and side.

Dried blood.

But the dog didn't appear injured.

Jack drew his service pistol. He thought about putting the pit bulls outside the fence, but he couldn't just let them go free. A pack like that could wander off and kill someone.

With his gun drawn, Jack marched to the side yard's kennel. He opened the gate, pointed, and ordered, "Inside."

One by one, the pit bulls filed past Jack, with Lady bringing up the guard at the back of the herd.

The alpha paused. He stared at Jack with big brown eyes, hung his head, and trotted into the kennel.

Jack closed the door, the metal clasp ringing loudly in the silence.

Turning his attention back to the house, Jack eyed the closed front door. Nothing moved. The shades in the windows on this side were all drawn too. The gravel driveway turned into a path that circled the home. If Dr. Chen were inside, he'd hear Jack approaching by the crunch of his shoes on the gravel.

Jack cupped his hand to his mouth, but his tightening throat prevented him from calling out.

Something wasn't right. The situation felt off. And if there was anything the war taught him, it was to listen to his gut.

Jack circled the kennel and flanked the house by crossing the grassy backyard. He scanned the windows as he went, keeping Lady behind and to the right. A mid-sized garden shed with moss on its shingles sat in the left corner.

The rear door of the home was open. Shadows covered the entrance, preventing Jack from seeing anything inside. Using a tree for cover, Jack pressed his side against the bark and stared at the open back door. In some ways, he was grateful Ed wasn't here. Other cops thought Jack was too paranoid. Too careful. And Jack knew nothing he could say would convince them otherwise.

It was another reason that Jack preferred to partner with ex-servicemen or veteran law enforcement with live fire experience. Getting shot at convinced someone to take every situation seriously far better than a lecture about it.

The house was silent. Small tires had matted the long grass leading up to the rear walkway. The path was about as wide as a riding lawnmower, but the grass hadn't been cut, just bent over.

Lady's damp nose touched his hand, and Jack flinched. Having her at his side took some getting used to, but he was grateful she had his back.

Jack sprinted across the open distance. Lady bounded behind him. When he reached the cover provided by the side of the house, he paused and caught his breath. Insects hummed, the electric meter behind him whirled, and his heart thumped in his ears. A bead of sweat rolled down his temple.

Jack started forward.

Lady followed slightly behind. So far, all her training was paying off, and she exceeded his expectations. She wanted to charge right in, but she begrudgingly kept her place.

Jack peered in the first window. The home was dark and crowded with boxes, books, and stacks of paper. With all the clutter, Yan fit the profile of a hoarder. The tall piles prevented Jack from seeing if anyone was inside.

Ducking low, Jack crossed beneath the window. He was only a few feet away from the open door when Lady cut him off, pressing her shoulder against his leg.

He gently tried to prod her back, but she pushed against his thigh and growled. She used her muzzle to shove him back, away from the door.

Jack's sweaty fingers tightened on the grip of his gun. He had to go forward. Not only was it his job, but the need to confront the darkness was part of his DNA. With his left shoulder pressed against the house siding, he stopped at the open doorway and listened. The hum of insects grew louder. Or was it his imagination?

Giving himself a silent countdown of five, Jack breached the doorway. His gun swept the kitchen, taking everything in at once—the overturned chair, the half-eaten food on the table covered in flies, the pool of dried blood on the floor, and the body of Dr. Yan Chen lying on his back, his gray, lifeless eyes open and staring at the ceiling.

From the kennel in the side yard, the alpha pit bull let out a mournful howl. The dog knew his master was dead.

21

Alice hung up the phone and smiled proudly as she crossed another company off her list. So far, she'd scheduled a dozen deliveries, and it wasn't yet lunchtime. The sound of the garage door rising made her spring from her chair.

"Kiku!" Alice shouted as she headed toward the bedroom.

Kiku was already strolling down the hall, a pistol at her side and her phone in her hand. She smiled, tucking the gun behind her back. "Two of my friends have arrived."

Alice followed her through the kitchen and out front. An old pickup truck and a purple sports car were parked in the driveway. Two men, similar in height but opposite in build, waited next to the purple car. One was Japanese, thin and wiry, with shiny, medium-length black hair and a weak chin. The other man was a portly Korean whose enormous smile lit up his round face.

"This is Jimmy." Kiku pointed at the thin man. "And Hwan." Who waved and smiled even more.

"This is my friend Alice." Kiku raised an eyebrow at Jimmy.

"What?" Jimmy held his arms out from his sides. "Why do you always give me a look like you're telling me to behave?"

“Because she has to,” Hwan said as he shook Alice’s hand. “Nice to meet you. Congratulations on your nuptials.”

“Oh, you’re married?” Jimmy frowned.

Kiku scowled.

Hwan elbowed him in the side. “Dial it back, Captain Obvious.”

At the mention of her wedding, the aching spot in Alice’s chest hurt a little more. She missed Jack so much, but the faster she could find her grandfather, the quicker she could get home.

“Come into the kitchen,” Kiku said. “We need to talk.”

While Hwan and Jimmy headed to separate bathrooms, Alice got four water bottles from the refrigerator.

“I asked them to come to help with the race,” Kiku said.

“I figured that out.” Alice opened her water and leaned against the sink. “Anything else in this plan that you’re not telling me?”

Kiku nodded but said nothing.

“Don’t take it personally,” Jimmy said as he entered the room, wiping his hands on his shirt. “Kiku never tells anyone everything about her plans.”

“She tells me,” Hwan said as he walked in.

“No, I do not.” Kiku pointed to the chairs.

“Ouch,” Hwan said.

Kiku smiled and handed Hwan a chocolate bar.

“And she knows a man’s weakness.” Hwan peeled off the end of the wrapper and took a bite. “But I’m not complaining,” he mumbled.

A knock on the inside garage door made Alice jump.

Kiku drew her gun, sprang beside the door, and held her finger to her lips.

“Don’t shoot!” A young boy called out from inside the garage. “It’s only me.”

Kiku glared at Jimmy and Hwan as she holstered her gun.

“I didn’t bring him!” Jimmy said.

"I have no idea how he got here," Hwan added.

"Don't give them a hard time," the boy yelled, still on the other side of the door. "I hid—"

Kiku yanked the door open and dragged the boy inside.

Alex stumbled through the doorway and straightened when he saw Alice. "Hi, Alice." He ran a hand through his dark hair. "Nice to see you again."

"Have you lost your mind?" Kiku dragged Alex toward the living room.

"Hey! I came to help!" Alex protested.

"You were supposed to stay in Universal Studios," Kiku snapped. "You would think a fifteen-year-old boy left with his own hotel room and a credit card at an amusement park would stay put."

"I'm not a dog or a baby. I can help! You know I can hold my own when it hits the fan." Alex held up his hand and smiled.

Alice's green eyes widened as she noticed Alex was missing a finger.

Kiku glared at Hwan and Jimmy. "I hold you two responsible. How did you not know he was in the back of the truck?"

Alice stood up. "What's done is done. Alex is here. Maybe there's something you can find for him to do to help." She winked at Kiku.

"I can see you winking." Alex made a goofy face and winked back. "Don't patronize—Ow! Ow!" Alex winced as Kiku pinched his ear.

"We do not have time for this—all of you, sit." Kiku ordered as she moved to the head of the kitchen table, dragging Alex into the chair next to her." The clock is ticking. Hwan, Jimmy, and Alex will see that the cars are ready for tonight. Jimmy, have you contacted your friend?"

"It cost ten grand, but I've got his spot in the race."

"Excellent. Alice and I will head out to set up the cameras."

"Do you need another driver?" Alex asked.

"You do not have your driver's license," Kiku said.

"This whole thing isn't legal," Alex shrugged. "So I don't see my not having a license as that big a deal."

"It is." Kiku stared at Hwan. "Did you bring the equipment I requested?"

"I've got everything, but getting it installed in your car is going to be cutting it close."

"Alex will assist you," Kiku said. "Alice and I will return shortly."

While the guys headed to the garage, Alice went to get her purse.

Kiku stood waiting in the kitchen when Alice returned.

"Kiku, I ah," Alice cleared her throat. "I don't know how I can thank you for all this."

"No thanks are necessary between friends." Kiku nodded. "And I am not doing this just for you."

"I'm sure Jack appreciates it too."

Kiku's eyes met Alice's. There was a darkness in Kiku's stare that chilled Alice. "Nor am I doing it for him. I seek something for myself as well."

"What?"

"That I cannot tell you until the time is right. In the end, if we succeed, I will be the one thanking you."

"I doubt that." Alice smiled.

Kiku didn't. "We will take the truck. I need to speak to Hwan for a moment first. I will meet you outside." She inclined her head and walked out to the garage.

Standing in the kitchen alone, Alice felt a sense of dread wash over her. She knew so little of Kiku, but the things she knew scared her. Kiku had helped Alice many times, but what could Kiku possibly want from finding Alice's grandfather?

22

While Jack waited for Ed, the crime scene techs, and animal control to arrive, he carefully examined the kitchen. The back door rested open against Yan's bare foot, which flopped on the tile at an old angle. The doctor lay on his back, his arms spread wide at his side. When Jack interviewed him the day before, he wore the same outfit, a stained red T-shirt, plaid pajama bottoms, and sandals.

Bullet holes peppered his shirt. Judging by the size of the wounds, they were large caliber. Jack didn't want to touch the body or even enter the kitchen before they photographed it. The tiles were covered with bloody paw prints but no shoe prints.

Inside the kitchen, a shadow flickered past the far wall.

Jack drew his pistol, pressed his shoulder against the door frame, and shouted, "Darrington Sheriff's Department! Come out now!"

No one answered.

Jack calmed his breathing, his finger covering the trigger, ready to pull.

A cool breeze blew from behind him and brushed his

cheek. Using his foot, Jack opened the kitchen door a little wider. Light filtered across the floor, but the house was empty and still.

A faint tap drew his attention to the ceiling. A mylar balloon with gold stars gently floated in the breeze, bumping along the ceiling as it went.

Backing away from the doorway, Jack stared at the gravel path leading to the door. There was little chance of finding shoe prints.

Lady whined as she paced back and forth in the backyard. She didn't want to leave Jack, but the poor King Shephard hated the stench of death.

Retracing his steps, Jack decided to put Lady back into the car and wait for Ed to arrive. They walked on the edge of the gravel road until they reached the gate, Jack vainly scanning the ground for any trace of shoe prints. Jack let Lady into the car, and she flopped onto the back seat with her head down. A serial killer had murdered her original owner, leaving Jack to wonder how much the poor dog had gone through.

"I think we've both seen too much, girl." Jack opened the glove compartment and put one of Mrs. Steven's dog treats on the seat. Usually, the gigantic dog would scarf it down, but what they'd just found had made her lose her appetite.

Sirens sounded in the distance. Jack watched as four vehicles, all with emergency lights on, raced down the road. A Sheriff's cruiser led the pack with Ed in the passenger seat.

As a half dozen law enforcement personnel parked and got out, Ed cupped both hands to his mouth and shouted, "Listen up, everyone! Come on! Gather round right here. Give Detective Stratton and me a minute before you do anything. Comprendo?"

Ed marched over to Jack and motioned him to follow.

They walked over to the gate, and Ed stopped. His neck was

flushed red, and his lip twitched. "What gives, Jack? Are you gunning for my job? Because let me tell you something—"

"Hold on, Ed."

"No, you hold on, Stratton. This is my case. Mine! You promised Morrison everything would go through me, and the first thing you do is try to show me up?"

"What are you talking about?" Jack held up his phone with Ed's text message on the screen. "You said I could go talk to Dr. Chen."

"But I never thought you'd get past his dogs. I submitted a request to have Animal Control accompany us. Do you know how stupid I look that you just come here with your Dogzilla and get in?"

Jack suspected Ed wanted him to be offended by referring to Lady as Dogzilla, but he liked the nickname.

"I asked you, and you said to go in. And for the record, I don't care who gets the credit. Do you want it? Take it. I seriously don't care. I'll tell Morrison it was all your idea."

Ed eyed him suspiciously.

Jack held up his hand. "I'll write it all up on the report that way."

Seemingly satisfied, Ed nodded. "What do we have?"

Jack explained about getting past the dogs and finding Dr. Chen shot in the kitchen.

"Where are the dogs now?" Ed asked.

"In the kennel. They won't be a problem."

Ed stuck his fingers in his mouth and whistled. "All right, everybody. Gather around for your marching orders."

Jack looked away so Ed wouldn't see him roll his eyes.

Ed instructed everyone as to their roles. He had a uniformed officer stand at the gate with orders to allow only law enforcement personnel through. Everyone else followed him. Leaving Lady in the car, Jack led them down and through the gate to the main house. He followed the same path he took earlier around the house's perimeter.

Everything was as Jack left it, including the balloon floating in the kitchen. While crime scene photographed the scene, Jack and Ed began searching around the back door.

"I've got casings," Ed said, pointing to the tall grass next to a flowerpot. "I see two."

"We'll have to bring out a metal detector. Dr. Chen took three shots to the chest," Jack said, looking between the door and where the casings were. "The killer would have fired from the doorway."

Ed nodded. "He probably walked right up and knocked. Chen opened the door, and Bang! Bang! Bang! Chen dies where he falls, knocking over the chair."

Jack frowned.

"You got a problem with that theory, Stratton?"

Jack wanted to say that he had a problem with the giant chip on Ed's shoulder but held his tongue. "No, Ed. I'm just wondering how the shooter got past the dogs."

Ed's eyes widened. "That is weird. Maybe the dogs were in the kennel?"

Jack shook his head. "They were out when I came."

"Maybe the shooter was a dog guy?" Ed shrugged.

"Or he knew Dr. Chen," Jack said as he searched the backyard.

An hour later, crime scene gave them the green light to go in. Jack and Ed slipped on medical booties and entered the house.

The kitchen was cluttered and cramped, but the only thing that appeared out of place was the tipped-over chair. Shining his flashlight around the dimly lit room, Jack stopped the beam on a white envelope sticking out from under the cabinet. Next to the envelope was a red card splattered in blood.

Jack and Ed moved closer.

It was a birthday card with a photograph of a cake. The envelope itself was blank. Reaching into his pocket, Jack took out a pen and opened the card.

Inside was a blood-stained Seven of Spades with a large red X written in marker over it.

"Ed, we need to go warn the others."

23

Watching the scene unfold beneath the camera lens of my drone, I'm seething. I slam the side of my left fist against the car's door panel.

"It's too soon!" I scream at the ceiling of the car. "They weren't supposed to return to Yan's until I killed the others!"

I'm parked far enough away that I don't have to worry about anyone hearing me. I need to be concerned they don't catch sight of the drone. Especially Stratton.

I fly the drone a little lower. It's tricky resting my elbows against the steering wheel and watching the monitor clipped to the dash. The drone hovers above the top of the trees behind Yan's house. Any lower, I'd risk one of the propellors catching a leaf and crashing.

Visibility is the biggest drawback of my eyes in the sky. They're so easy to spot, especially against the day sky. To counter being detected, I launched it here, then flew inches above the treetops until I reached Yan's backyard.

At least I have a method of checking on their progress. I wanted them to find the body, but I didn't think it would be so soon. Stratton cheated. He brought that hellhound. It's a shame and a dent in my plan. Not only are the murders being discovered out of order, but I also wanted Yan's death scene to be terrifying.

If Stratton hadn't come along when he had, those mutts would have gotten hungry with no Yan to feed them. Well, not exactly! Yan would have been their dinner. What a gory sight. Bits and pieces of whatever was left of Yan's carcass strewn about, drenching the kitchen in blood. That would've been priceless.

Stratton and his dog ruined it.

I should return the favor. He's getting too close, too fast. I need to slow him down without dragging the entire Sheriff's Department down on my head.

No. Stick to the plan. This is a hiccup. A minor annoyance that doesn't even need to be addressed. So what if Yan doesn't get the ultimate indignity of being consumed only to fertilize his own lawn? He's dead. That's what counts.

The drone shifts in the wind.

Down at the house, Stratton, crouching near the back door while he places another shell casing into an evidence bag, stands and turns around.

I zoom in on his face, and my heart stops.

Stratton is staring at the trees. He's squinting, shielding his eyes from the sun.

Can he see the drone?

No. It's too small, too far away, and the sun is in his eyes.

But there's no doubt where he's looking.

My fingers freeze on the remote. What should I do? Without thinking, I pull down the joystick as I shut off the engines. The camera lens shakes violently as the drone plummets into the tree. It only drops a few feet before it stops, caught in a branch and staring at the sky and some leaves.

I exhale loudly and start breathing again. The machine was expensive, but I'd rather let it rust and rot in a tree than expose my plans. That can't happen. Not yet.

Others still need to die.

24

Jack's new priority was locating the remaining members of Dr. Mobley's project and warning them of the danger they faced. While Ed searched for Oscar, Jack headed to the technology center at White Rocks Eastern College. After checking in at the front desk and finding Dr. Patel's office empty, he started back to the robotics lab.

Halfway down the hallway, he stopped beside a simple bronze plaque fastened to the wall outside a glass-walled room.

The Michelle Carter Memorial Study Lounge
The task of the modern educator is not to cut down jungles but to irrigate deserts. — C. S. Lewis

Michelle had selected that quote for her high school yearbook. Inside the room, several students sat hunched over desks, studying. One girl leaned back in her chair, stretched her arms out wide, and smiled at the ceiling. Whatever she was trying to understand, it appeared she'd found her answer.

Jack swallowed, and his eyes burned. Michelle would have made a fabulous teacher. If only... He clamped his eyes closed, his hands balling into fists. All her life, Michelle had struggled to overcome. Michelle's parents had died in an apartment fire, leaving Chandler and her to enter the foster care system. But with Aunt Haddie's love and guidance, Michelle had blossomed. She'd been a fighter and wrung the best education she could get out of the system, believing it was her ticket to improving her life and the lives of the people around her.

A madman cut her dreams short.

Jack marched down the hallway, trying to drive the guilt out of his mind. Michelle's death wasn't his fault, but that didn't stop Jack from mentally flogging himself into a spiral of depression. That was a pit he couldn't fall into. With Alice gone, he didn't even want to go near the edge, but as the pressure of the case built, he wanted that drink more and more.

Dr. Patel wasn't in the robotics lab either. Some students had seen her earlier in the day, but no one had in the last hour. Jack handed out one of his last business cards and made a mental note to grab more from his desk.

Heading down the staircase, Jack glanced through the massive glass windows and noticed Navi pacing outside. She spoke into her phone, her left hand dramatically raising then slashing the air like a hatchet.

Jack hurried down the steps, out the front door, and around the corner.

Navi's back was to him, and he heard every word of her conversation.

"I don't know what I have to do to get your attention. You tell Sabrina Hall that without me, there is no deal. You call me as soon as you get this message or so help me—" Navi stopped speaking when she turned and noticed Jack approaching. Without saying another word, she hung up.

"I didn't mean to interrupt your phone call, Dr. Patel, but

there's been a development. In light of the threat against you, I would appreciate it if you would accompany me to the Sheriff's Department."

"A development?" Navi glanced nervously around. "Did something happen?"

"Yes, but it would be best if we discussed this privately. My car is over there in the visitor spaces. I can give you a ride back afterward."

"How long will this take?" She checked her phone. "I have a lecture in three hours."

Jack didn't want to panic her, but he doubted she'd be holding the class after he broke the news of Yan's death. "It shouldn't be too long."

"I must say, you have me worried, Detective."

"As my aunt always says, better safe than sorry."

Jack led Dr. Patel to the parking lot, but she insisted on following him in her car. Fifteen minutes later, he was holding the door open to interrogation room 3. The room was painted a light yellow and had a gray carpet. A metal table sat in the middle, with two chairs on either side.

"Thank you for coming with me, Dr. Patel. I appreciate you taking this time. I have to make you aware that as a matter of policy, everyone I bring in here, I need to inform them of their rights. You're not under arrest and free to go, but under law, I need to make sure you know your rights."

This was part of the job Jack didn't care for but was necessary. Navi could be a potential victim, or she could be the perpetrator. It was Jack's job to find out which. To accomplish that, he needed to question her.

"I understand." Dr. Patel sat opposite Jack while he read her rights and took down her personal information in a notebook. A camera in the upper left corner of the ceiling recorded the interview, too. "Did you find out who sent me that playing card?"

"Before we move on to that, we're trying to establish the whereabouts of a few individuals, including yourself. Were you at the college this morning?"

"No. Well, yes. I stopped by my office to pick up a few things. "

Jack rocked back in his chair, trying to appear as casual as possible and create a rapport. "I don't want you to be nervous, Dr. Patel. It helps if we know where everyone was, that's all. So walk me through what you did this morning. What time did you leave your house?"

Navi exhaled and folded her hands onto her lap. She pulled at her ear, and her face pinched like she'd taken a bite of a lemon. "I think it was about seven thirty in the morning. All things considered, I didn't sleep well last night. I drove to the college, arriving around eight to pick up some papers. Then I went to the range and then out to lunch with a friend."

The feet of Jack's chair thumped off the floor. "Wait a second. Did you say you went to a gun range?"

"Yes." Navi crossed her arms. "I'm licensed to carry. And with someone threatening me, I felt it best if I practiced."

"So you handled and fired a gun this morning?"

"Yes. Why?"

"I don't know many academics who carry. I'm impressed." Jack folded his hands behind his head, stalling while he scrambled not to raise suspicion just yet. "As a police officer, we encourage people to take steps to defend themselves. What kind of gun do you have?"

"A 9mm SIG Sauer. It's locked in my car."

"That's a nice gun."

"I'm never without it. And the longer you go without telling me why you've brought me here, the more nervous I'm getting."

"There's no easy way of saying this, Dr. Patel. We think your safety may be in jeopardy. Dr. Yan Chen was murdered."

All the color rushed from Navi's cheeks. She clutched her

bag to her stomach and started slowly rocking back and forth. "No. That can't be. Yan? Are you certain?"

Jack nodded.

"When? How?" She gasped, her eyes flying wide and her mouth falling open. "Wait! Is that why you were asking where I was this morning?"

"We're trying to establish a timeline and—" Jack said.

"How was Yan killed? Was he shot? This is ridiculous. I had nothing to do with Yan's death. No one was—"Navi clamped her mouth shut. "I'm done talking."

Jack leaned back in his chair. She hadn't asked for a lawyer, but she was close to doing so. "I would have to caution you against that. Your life could be in danger. I want to help."

A myriad of emotions played across her face. Her shoulders rounded as she cradled her bag. "I think I need to speak with a lawyer."

Jack set the pen down on the notepad. "That's your right. But let me tell you something. If you had anything to do with this, you need to come clean. And if you had nothing to do with it but know what's going on, you need to be careful. I don't want you to be a third victim."

As Dr. Patel stared at Jack, he felt like he was watching her floating down a river, heading for the falls. He'd thrown her the rope. Would she take it?

"I'm sorry, Detective." She stood up. "We're done."

Jack nodded and led her out of the station.

Dr. Patel took out her phone and pressed a few buttons.

"Who's Sabrina Hall?" Jack asked.

Dr. Patel's hand shook as she stuffed the phone into her pocket. "I don't have to answer that."

"I was just wondering." Jack shrugged. "You mentioned her name when you were on the phone."

"No. I didn't. You're mistaken."

When they reached the steps, Jack's eyebrows rose as he

watched Dr. Patel's car pulling up to the curb. Dr. Patel hurried down the stairs and opened the door.

A deputy coming into the station stopped next to Jack, her jaw dropping open as she pointed to the empty driver's seat as Dr. Patel got in.

"No way!" The deputy exclaimed as she yanked out her phone and started recording. "It's one of those self-driving cars! How lucky is she?"

Dr. Patel got behind the wheel and gunned it out of the parking lot. A sense of dread washed over Jack. His gut was telling him she wasn't lucky at all. She was involved in a bad jackpot, and it could get her killed.

25

Jack reached his car when his phone rang with a call from Ed.

"Hey, buddy," Ed said, "Any chance of you doing me a favor? If you can't, no problem. I already left a message for Oscar."

"You didn't speak to Oscar in person?"

"I had to stop by the shop and try to get them to finish my car. They only want to touch up the paint job, but it needs a full redo. You can't paint only one side because it won't match. I haven't made it over to the campus yet. Are you still there?"

Jack wanted to smack Ed upside his head. He was supposed to head straight to Oscar, notify him about Yan's murder, and convey the fact Oscar could be in danger himself. Not to mention Oscar was now one of two living suspects Jack needed to interview.

"You just worry about your car," Jack said sarcastically. "I'll tell Oscar there could be an immediate threat to his life."

"I knew you'd understand. Thanks." Ed hung up.

"Moron." Jack glared at his phone. He switched to his map app and pulled directions to Oscar's off-campus apartment.

Stopping every twenty yards for jaywalking students, he finally made it down the campus's crowded primary thoroughfare. Apartment buildings and homes dotted both sides of the street. Most houses had been converted to student housing, but some posted fraternity signs or belonged to other college organizations. After two blocks, the stores began—coffee, pizza, tacos, and boba tea seemed in vogue.

Parking in front of a brick duplex, Jack rechecked the address. With a BMW, a Tesla, and a new Audi parked in front; they didn't fit the mold of cars students drove when Jack went to college. But the address was correct.

Jack tried Oscar's phone number again as he marched to the door. The call went straight to voicemail. After leaving another message, Jack rang the bell.

A lanky young man with thick, brown hair sticking out like he'd just woken up answered the door. He stood there, blinking at Jack, clearly confused.

Jack held up his shield. "I'm Detective Jack Stratton with the Darrington Sheriff's Department. Is Oscar Chambers here?"

The man did a double take. "Are you serious? I totally didn't believe him."

"Believe who about what?" Jack asked.

"Oscar said he was helping you guys out with an investigation. I thought it was total bull. But here you are."

Jack was tempted to correct Oscar's lie immediately but didn't. "What else did Oscar say?"

"He said Dr. Mo got murdered, and whoever killed him was after him, too."

Jack checked his body cam. The red light was steady, meaning it was recording. "And you are?"

"Jim Parson. I'm Oscar's roommate. He's not here."

"Do you know where he is?"

Jim shrugged. "Could be with his new girlfriend. They were going at it like bunnies and were super loud. I told him it was like listening to a porno while I was trying to study, so I figured he split to get more privacy."

"What's the girlfriend's name?"

"Bree. I don't know her last name."

"What does she look like?"

Jim ran both hands through his hair and exhaled. "I think she was brunette. Maybe blonde. I only saw her once, but I was in the middle of a game. She never hung out. She'd drop in, they'd go at it, and she was gone again. I'd hear her, mostly."

"And Oscar could be with her now?"

Jim held his palms up and out.

"Did Oscar say anything about why someone wanted to kill him?"

"Oscar was working on this big project. He insisted he couldn't say anything about it—unless he was drinking, and then he told me everything." Jim laughed. "He got like three professors to work on it, too. Dr. Mo was one of them. I liked that guy. Did he really get blown up?"

"He's deceased."

The man ran his hand through his wild hair, making it stick out even more. "No way. I thought Oscar was lying about that, too. That's messed up."

"Did Oscar mention who he believed could be behind the killings?"

"Yeah." Jim nodded rapidly, his hair waving like a troll doll on the dashboard of a convertible. "He was sure it was Dr. Patel. He said she was a cold-hearted narcissist."

"Oscar said to you that Dr. Navi Patel was responsible for the killing?" Jack repeated.

"Yeah. She wanted all the credit for the project. Oh, and so did Che."

"Who is Che?"

"Dr. Yan Chen. I know he's Asian, but doesn't he look like Che Guevara?"

Jack shook his head. This stoner wasn't making much sense, but seeing how he was doing so much talking, he wasn't about to cut him off. "What did Oscar say specifically about Dr. Chen?"

"He knew Che killed Mo. Oscar was positive. I was chillin' and smoking a, ah, a cigarette, and Oscar was burning it up. Mad. I was like relax and offered him some, ah"—he ran his hand through his hair and self-edited out whatever it was—"but Oscar was like no way! Are you listening to me? Che killed Mo! He was yelling and waving his arms. It was messing with my Feng Shui."

"You said earlier that Oscar thought Dr. Patel killed Dr. Mobley."

Jim's face pinched. He stretched out his arms, holding onto the door frame, and rocked up on his toes. "I guess Oscar thought that both of them were the killer. First, he said it was Patel, and then he was like, it's Che, man. Che is the one."

"Did Oscar say why he suspected either of them?"

"They wanted credit for the invention, but their arguing was all for nothing. It was Oscar's project. While they were working on it, he did all the legal stuff."

"What kind of legal stuff?"

"Patents and rights and all that junk. It was his, so he had to cover his ass. He's a smart guy. When he sells it, he's gonna be the next Bill Gates. You're talking billions."

"Did he mention where he planned to sell it?"

"Oh, yeah. Wait here." Jim hurried inside the apartment and returned a moment later with a canvas tote bag. "They gave Oscar this when he made his pitch." Opening the bag, Jim started removing items. "A USB stick, a mouse pad, and a cool laser pointer." He pressed the button, shining the red light on the door.

One thing all the items had in common was the name

printed on the merchandise and the bag—Eagle 247 Technology.

"You said that Oscar already made a pitch to this company?"

Jim nodded.

"When was that?"

Jim rocked his head from side to side, closing one eye each time. "It had to be a little over a month ago?"

Jack took down Jim's information and gave him a card. "If you talk to Oscar, please tell him I need to speak to him as soon as possible. It's urgent."

"Will do!" Jim winked and shut the door.

Jack hurried back to his car. He wanted to speak to Oscar more than ever now. He would still warn him, but Oscar just moved to the top of his suspect list.

26

Jack typed away at the keyboard in his apartment as Lady lay under the desk, resting on his bare feet. "You're going to make me fall asleep, girl." He yawned and glanced at the clock. It was almost nine, but he needed to go out and meet a friend soon.

The computer screen filled with information regarding Eagle 247 Technology. The high-tech firm was local, boasting a partnership with the college and its graduates. Their focus was on automated machines, and, from the posted videos, they were very good at it.

Like watching an episode of *Star Trek*, Jack sat back in his chair and stared wide-eyed as robots danced, automated cars drove around a garage and parked, and a swarm of drones put on a laser light show. The videos were slick, coming off like a Hollywood film rather than a simple demo reel.

Flipping over to the staff page, the photograph of the CEO filled the screen—Sabrina Hall. The fifty-four-year-old had an impressive résumé that scrolled over two screens. From humble beginnings to the Ivy League, she started and sold several businesses before founding Eagle 247 five years ago. In addition to her business and academic achievements, Sabrina was an intelligent, articulate, and attractive speaker who'd been featured in dozens of magazines and shows.

Dr. Patel mentioned a Sabrina Hall when speaking on the phone. Jack loaded the video from his body cam. After watching the clip, he leaned back in the chair, crossing his hands behind his head. Dr. Patel lied when she said she hadn't been talking about Sabrina Hall. Why? And what was the deal they were discussing?

Lady scrambled to her feet.

Jack winced as the gigantic dog stepped on his foot.

Lady bashed into the desk as she raced to the door.

Jack grabbed the swaying computer monitor to keep it from falling over. "Easy, Lady."

Lady trotted to the front door.

Jack strolled over and took hold of her thick collar. His hope of Alice appearing disappeared when someone knocked. A quick check of the peephole brought a smile back to his face, and he yanked open the door.

Finnian Church and his girlfriend, Annie Summers, stood in the hallway. The tall ex-soldier grinned broadly as he clasped Jack's hand. "Good to see you, buddy."

"I didn't expect you so soon. Are you keeping this guy in line, Annie?" Jack was careful to face Annie when he spoke so she could read his lips.

"It's more of the other way around!" A huge smile broke across Annie's heart-shaped face, and she shook Jack's hand.

"Come in. You know Lady."

"I think she's growing, buddy," Finn said. Dressed in gray slacks and a neatly ironed white shirt, he straightened a silvery-blue tie as he walked into the apartment.

"I hope not."

Annie crouched in front of the dog and rubbed her ears. "Is Alice in?"

The question made the dull ache inside Jack hurt a little more. “She took a few days off to recharge. Can I get you guys a drink?”

“Actually, we stopped by to see if you wanted to grab a late dinner. Processing Dr. Mobley’s home took longer than expected, so we decided to spend the night.”

Annie held up her phone. Because of her deafness, she also used text-to-speech apps to understand conversations.

“Where are you staying? Have you checked in yet?” Jack asked.

“No, but there’s a motel—“

“Not on your life.” Jack shook his head. “You guys can stay here. I especially need the company with Alice out of town.” Jack checked his watch and frowned. “But I have to meet a guy in half an hour. Why don’t you guys get something to eat? I’ll fix up the guest room and meet you back here after.”

Annie stared down at her phone, and her blue eyes widened. She glanced at Finn and nudged his side with her elbow.

“That’s okay,” Finn said. “We were going to get a double at the hotel.”

“Don’t be ridiculous. You’ll take my room and Annie can have the guest room. I’ve got a case I’m working on, so I’ll be up late researching on the computer and crash on the couch.”

Finn protested, and Jack flashed his badge.

“Shut up, Finn. I’m a detective now, so I can arrest you both.”

Annie laughed, light and happy.

It made Finn smile. “Congratulations again, Jack.”

The tightness around his eyes when he said the words made Jack remember Finn had also dreamed of a career in law enforcement. An RPG had not only cost Finn his left leg but his goal as well.

“I heard on the grapevine that you are killing it in the investigation business," Jack said.

Annie stepped forward. "Finn is absolutely brilliant. He's so successful that he's now the lead investigator for the company."

Finn's neck reddened. "It's all Annie. She's the one who's solved everything."

Annie shook her head. "He's being modest."

"I need to be honest. Both of you are so humble and cute, it's upsetting my stomach," Jack said.

Finn gave him a playful but hard shot in the arm.

"Ow. Speaking of cases," Jack continued, "did you find anything out at Dr. Mobley's?"

"We didn't find any additional evidence, but the information you gave me about the propane connector was spot-on. I passed it along to the fire examiner's office, and you were right. The connector was brand new, and it had been modified."

"Modified to do what?"

"She couldn't say. They found the remnants of a circuit board inside and sent it up to the state lab to see if they can come up with anything."

"Did they get any information from the board? Maybe we can track the manufacturer," Jack said.

"There wasn't much left of it, but everyone I spoke to in the propane industry said they'd never seen anything like it. It's foreign, and there is no reason for anything to be in there, especially something electronic."

"I took photographs of the board. I'll send you the pictures," Annie offered.

"I appreciate that."

"You don't look shocked," Finn said.

"I'm not," Jack explained Dr. Chen's murder and the connection between him and Dr. Mobley.

Finn sighed. "I may join you burning the midnight oil. My report to the insurance company will be much more complicated."

Jack's alarm beeped. "I'm sorry, but I've got to meet this guy about another case I'm working on. So is it a deal? You'll stay?"

Finn looked at Annie, who nodded. "Thank you, Jack," she said. "Alice said you'd give someone the shirt off your back, and it's true."

At the mention of his wife, Jack wondered what she was doing right now. Knowing her and the time, she might be curled up and asleep.

Lady trotted over, carrying what was left of an enormous bone. She opened her mouth, and it dropped to the floor with a clatter.

"What is that?" Finn chuckled. "The remains of a dinosaur?"

Jack laughed. "Lady's been working on that ever since Alice left."

"Where do you even get a bone that big?" Annie asked.

Jack's laughter trailed off. The bone had been a wedding gift from Kiku. "A friend of ours gave it to Lady. I think you met her at the wedding. Her name is Kiku."

Annie nodded. "She was very nice."

Finn nodded, too, but said nothing. Jack didn't take it as a slight on his friend. Kiku gave off a vibe that set some people on edge. Sometimes, being around her, the hair on Jack's arms would rise the same way it did if he got too close to an electrical transformer. Kiku was like a high-voltage wire. Unleashed, she'd kill you. Maybe it was the soldier in him, but Finn also picked up on that danger.

"Does Kiku live nearby?" Annie asked.

Jack shrugged. He didn't know where Kiku's real home was, but right now, he was more concerned with who Kiku was with. He stared back down at the large bone.

You're just being paranoid. There's no way Alice went someplace with Kiku. Is there?

27

Alice strode through the crowd outside the Parthenon nightclub. She felt alive in a very visceral way, with the music pulsing through her chest and excitement racing up her spine. She strutted beside Kiku, and the crowd parted out of their way to let them pass, staring at them like they were superstars.

Kiku wore a red-and-white leather racing jacket with a black top and skin-tight white jeans. Because of the Florida heat, the choice of the coat surprised Alice until she realized Kiku used the outfit to conceal three different pistols.

They had settled on Alice wearing a steampunk biker outfit. Round sunglasses, leather top hat, black leather fringe vest, white tank top, blue jeans, and black combat boots. Alice somehow stood out among the wild display of clubbing attire yet still blended in. But there was another reason for her costume—Hwan had hidden a camera in the hat.

"You shoulda let me come." Alex's voice in her earpiece caught her off guard. "Oh, man, look at that."

Alice angled her head, turning toward the row of shiny racing cars.

"Not the cars," Alex said. "Look right. There's a girl in a pink—"

Kiku interrupted. "Hwan, keep Alex off the channel until he has something pertinent to say."

"Will do. Sorry. Over." Hwan said, then whispered. "Shut up, you idiot."

"Did you see her?" Alex's voice rose.

"I did. Maybe Alice will—"

"You are not muted." Kiku snapped.

"Oh, crud. Sorry again. Over." Hwan said.

Alice hid her grin. Kiku was a professional, but despite her hardness, she had a habit of bringing outsiders in and protecting them. Alex had been in the foster care system until Kiku rescued him. She saved Hwan off the streets in Hong Kong. Even Jimmy owed Kiku for taking him in. Three lost puppies, all under her care.

Kiku stopped at her car and scanned the long row of vehicles. Her face was a confident mask, but a storm raged in her black eyes.

Alice counted thirty cars, including theirs. There were only supposed to be ten. Jimmy's purple sports car sat almost at the end on the right. She couldn't see him, but his bright purple car stood out even among the flashy automobiles.

"Kiku!" Fausto emerged from the crowd. "My apologies, but there's been a minor change in the number of racers. People begged me to let them participate when word got out that I was driving in the race. How could I refuse?"

"Oh, how could you? But seeing how you are now tripling your money on this race, I want an extra fifty grand when I win," Kiku said.

"You wanna bet extra?"

"It is not a bet. You changed the rules. You sweeten the winner's purse."

Fausto stared at Alice. His eyes traveled slowly up and down her body in a way that made her want to slap him, then take a shower.

"Tell you what." Fausto gave a lecherous grin. "I'll up my bet a hundred grand. You throw in your assistant?"

"Deal," Kiku said. She stepped so close to Fausto that they were cheek to cheek. She whispered something in his ear as she placed her hands on his sides and kissed his left cheek, then the other.

Fausto clapped and licked his lips like he was eyeing a steak as he grinned at Alice. "What a wonderful night! Let's get started."

As Fausto danced back to his white-and-red Corvette, the thin man slipped out of the crowd and followed him.

"Did you just bet me?" Alice found her voice.

"I do not bet." Kiku walked over to the driver's side.

"No, you did!" Alex squawked over the microphone. "You totally bet Alice to that sleazebag."

"Hwan! Control him now." Kiku opened her door and slipped inside.

The communications channel went silent again.

"Before you get upset"—Kiku held up her hand as Alice entered the passenger seat—"remember, this is not a race. We are here to isolate Fausto and gather information. That is all. So, no, I did not use you as a wager. I simply wanted him to keep his guard down and went along with what he was saying."

"He doesn't know any of that. He thinks I come along with the winner's trophy!" Alice shot back.

"Then we had better not lose. Take this and put your seat belt on." Kiku handed Alice a cell phone.

Alice glanced at the gaudy gold and pearl case. "Is this yours?"

"It belonged to Fausto until a moment ago. We cannot have him calling for backup, so I relieved him of his phone once he lowered his guard."

Alice smiled as she buckled her seat belt. "You are good."

"Jimmy, are you ready?" Kiku asked.

"Waiting like Hwan watching a bao bun steam."

Kiku's laugh sounded like a glass wind chime on a warm spring day—the kind of laugh Alice liked most, because it made her smile. Alice couldn't remember ever hearing her friend laugh before. Not like that. But the glimmer in Kiku's dark eyes dimmed as she watched the woman holding a flag at her side strut into the middle of the street.

Engines roared to life.

Kiku gave the car some gas. The machine vibrated and hummed. Alice's hand moved instinctively to the door handle. She didn't know if it felt more like she was on a rocket ship or a massive beast, but she realized they were about to take off either way.

"Dear God, please keep Kiku, Jimmy, and me safe. Please help us find my grandfather. In Jesus' name, amen."

Outside, the crowd cheered and scrambled to the sidewalks.

Kiku revved the engine.

The woman raised her arms. The green flag fluttered in the breeze.

Alice took a deep breath.

The woman's arms dropped, the flag slashing downward.

Tires squealed. The smell of rubber and gas filled the air.

Alice jerked forward into her seat belt, her hands hitting the dashboard as Kiku rammed the car into reverse and shot back into the near-empty parking lot. Kiku jerked the handbrake up. The vehicle spun 45 degrees, and she released the handbrake and mashed the gas pedal to the floor.

Alice thought she might throw up as the force slammed her back against the seat.

Stragglers in the parking lot scrambled to get out of the way and hid behind cars and telephone poles as the red Demon screamed across the parking lot.

"I thought we wanted to catch Fausto," Alice said. "Not lose him!"

"Fausto padded the race with his own drivers. They would have blocked us in to prevent us from ever catching him," Kiku yelled over the roar of the engine.

"We've got one, two, three... at least a dozen racers heading to First Avenue. The state police are there, ready and waiting. Over." Hwan said.

"Let me know if any make it past the roadblock." Kiku cut the wheel and steered for the main road. "Is Fausto headed for Orange Blossom?"

"He is," Jimmy said. "I'm right behind him."

"Kiku, you should be coming out on North Street, but you're at least six cars behind Fausto. Over," Hwan said.

"You don't have to say 'Over' every time," Alex said before quickly adding, "Just checked the cameras at the end of Franklin. No one is getting by there. The whole thing is a parking lot. A fight even broke out between two delivery drivers."

"How many cars are headed to Franklin?" Kiku asked.

"Only seven."

Alice frowned. "That leaves eleven racers, including Fausto, us, and Jimmy."

Kiku flashed a grin that reminded Alice of Jack. "Hold onto your hat, Alice. You are in for a ride."

28

Sitting in his idling car, Jack worked down his list of questions. He'd parked at the far end of the closed shopping center. There were still a few cars left, employees finishing closing up, or perhaps some commuters who preferred to save a couple of bucks and opt for the longer walk to the train.

A silver Taurus pulled into the lot and headed his way. It stopped, then backed up next to Jack on the passenger side. Detective Mark Reynolds, mid-thirties with black, wavy hair, stepped out and slid into Jack's passenger seat. Mark was five foot five, and his handshake was firm, like an ironworker's.

"Jack."

"Mark. I appreciate you coming."

"I can't stay long. Are you psychic or something? I was going to call you when I got your text. But you tell me what you want to know first," Mark said.

"I'm working on a missing person case. The man's name is Carl Wilson. You made the collar six years ago, and I was hoping you could tell me who Carl ran with then."

Mark took out a pack of cigarettes. "Do you mind? I really need one now."

"Go ahead." Jack powered down the windows. He didn't care for smoking, but he was the one asking for the favor. "Is there something about Carl Wilson I should know?"

Mark flicked his lighter, and the cigarette puffed to life. He held the pack out to Jack, who shook his head. "You might need one too after I tell you this." He took a long drag and blew the smoke out the window. "I busted Carl Wilson along with eighty-seven other people. It was one of the largest busts in county history. But it wasn't unique just because of the size."

Jack wasn't on the force then. He remembered the case itself but not the specifics.

"It got national news because of the prescription drug angle. We took down everyone from the junkie on the corner to two pharmacists, a surgeon, and Sweet Sally."

"The lady who made those homemade pies?"

"Don't laugh, but that's how they were delivering half the stuff. My wife loved those pies. To this day, she still gives me a hard time."

"And the drugs were prescriptions?"

"Yeah, but you're talking about some real rocket fuel stuff. The painkillers were powerful enough to send someone over the moon or six feet under."

"How does that setup work on a large scale? I thought people sold their own prescriptions or got fake ones. How does that scale up?"

"Fast when you have corrupt doctors involved. There were enough prescriptions written to medicate California."

"What part did Carl play in the scheme?"

"User and low-level dealer. He was mostly dealing to support his habit. He had no priors, so the judge went easy on him. From what I heard, it didn't matter. Carl lost his job, and then his son stopped showing up to court." Mark's voice wasn't too deep but had calmness and patience, like a teacher's.

"I heard Carl got sober. He became a Christian in prison."

Mark stared at Jack for a second, the end of his cigarette glowing an angry red. "Not to sound like the pessimist I am, but that's why they say there aren't any sinners in foxholes. Everyone claims they found religion in prison. Is it real? God only knows, but as for me, I'm from Missouri. Show me."

"A friend of Carl's said that Carl befriended a young kid who OD'd. He said Carl took it hard and thought of talking to the dealers. Do you know who Carl got the drugs from when he was using?"

"That would've been a guy named Donnie B. He ran the scene before Carl went into the joint. Died of hepatitis a year ago."

"Has anyone stepped in to fill Donnie's place?"

"A few people are moving up, but you can always find prescription drugs on the street." Mark took another drag on his cigarette, then threw the butt out the window. "Now, I'm not saying I think this, but did you ever consider that Carl was playing this friend?"

"How do you mean?"

"Carl was a hustler in his day. Prison and rehabilitation don't go hand in hand. If anything, when a guy gets out, he's worse than when he went in. For all you know, Carl wanted this friend to tell him who the dealers were so he could score. Hell, Carl could have been the one feeding the kid the drugs he OD'd on."

"I didn't get that read off the friend. He believed Carl turned around."

"Again, you're going off hearsay. The Carl Wilson I knew would stab his mother for a score. And that brings me to why I was going to reach out to you. You're working a new homicide?"

"Two now. Dr. Samuel Mobley and Dr. Yan Chen."

The muscles in Mark's jaw flexed. "I don't know about Chen, but Dr. Mobley was part of the Sweet Sally bust."

"Dr. Mobley was dealing prescription drugs?" Jack said in surprise.

"No. Sam was a good man who helped us. He went undercover and wore a wire for a year. Without Sam, we never would have busted the others."

Jack ran his hand over his mouth. Maybe he'd been looking at this whole thing from the wrong angle. "But Dr. Mobley was involved in another project. All four of the members received a threatening playing card, and one of the others was murdered."

"How?"

"Shot, close range in his kitchen."

"And Carl Wilson is in the wind? Who reported him missing?"

"His granddaughter."

"I'm no homicide detective, but I know people. I want you to imagine something and then ask yourself a question. Okay?"

Jack nodded.

"Pretend you're a junkie. You need drugs to live. Without them, you itch, your insides burn, and your brain feels like it's melting. Now imagine you're Carl Wilson, and you get yanked off the street and stuck in a box. For years you sit there itching and can't scratch it. It drives you mad thinking about it, but you can't stop. All you focus on day in and day out is the guy who put you there. You spend your nights dreaming of what you'll do to him when you get your chance. Then you get out. You've got nothing, and the guy who put you in the box wants for nothing. Dr. Mobley is all happy in that big house, and you're living in a crappy little apartment smaller than the cell you got out of. You're gonna kill that man, but there's no way you're going back in the box. So you come up with a plan. You'll kill Mobley and another guy to throw suspicion off of you. Not saying that's what happened, but is it possible?"

Jack stared out through the windshield into the darkness.

Doubt slammed down on him like a sledgehammer. Maybe Mark was right. There was logic to his theory.

"I don't envy you, kid." Mark opened the door and got out. "You caught a helluva jackpot for your first case. But if you want my opinion, you're looking for a missing person who doesn't want to be found. You know why? Because he's your killer."

29

Alice sat pinned back in her seat as Kiku cut the wheel and the Demon slid into the curve. Pumping the brake, Kiku cut back to the left and jammed the gas pedal to the floor. The engine roared, and the car shot forward. They raced past telephone poles so quickly, they appeared as an endless picket fence.

"Alex, what is the status of the police roadblock? Did any vehicles make it through?"

"Negative. Three cars tried to double back. Two are out of commission, and the third has four cruisers chasing him down."

"Good. Hwan, what is the status of the cars in the traffic jam?"

The light ahead turned red. A truck started to pull forward.

Alice grabbed the roof handle as Kiku laid on the horn but kept the wheel straight ahead.

The truck slammed on its brakes.

Alice stared at the driver, who held up both middle fingers.

Hwan clicked his microphone. "No one made it around the traffic jam, either. Five of the seven cars doubled back. Over."

"Why did the other two drivers not continue?" Kiku asked.

"They're fighting with the delivery drivers. The police are there now. Over."

"Keep an eye on the other five cars. Hopefully, they will make for First Avenue and get caught in the roadblock."

"Kiku, here's who is in front of you," Hwan said. "Fausto is in the lead with the thin man right behind him. The thin man is driving the bright-green car. There are five other racers in front of you, including Jimmy."

"I can see you, Kiku!" Jimmy shouted into the radio. "You're right behind me."

"I know. Are you ready? It is time to implement your plan."

"Woo hoo!" Jimmy yelled. "Almost to the straightaway."

"What's Jimmy's plan?" Alice asked.

Kiku rolled her eyes. "I do not care for the name, but his idea is solid, and, with Hwan's expertise, it should work."

"I love the name!" Alex said.

"Thanks, kid." A touch of pride rang in Jimmy's voice.

Kiku pulled alongside Jimmy's car. She reached out to the dash, her finger hovering over a normal-looking button. "Hitting the nitro in three, two, now."

Alice felt like someone had punched her in the chest as gravity crushed her against the seat.

Kiku passed the three cars on the left like they were standing still.

Alice glanced in the side mirror. The purple glow of Jimmy's headlights showed he was right behind them.

"Hwan, you are a master of speed!" Jimmy's voice shook. "But I need a little more to get in front."

"Don't hit the second boost yet!" Hwan warned. "You need—"

"Warp speed, baby!" Jimmy shouted.

"Jimmy, do NOT press that button!" Kiku glared in the rearview mirror.

Alice's eyes widened.

Behind them was a flash of flame, and the purple headlights shot forward even faster. Jimmy's car passed them on the right and pulled alongside the thin man's car.

"Initiate your plan, Jimmy!" Kiku ordered.

A bright flash gleamed from the thin man's car.

"The creepy dude is shooting at me!" Jimmy shouted as his car rocketed past the thin man.

"Do not pass Fausto." Kiku's eyes blazed. "Hit the switch, Jimmy, or our deal is off."

"No, way. I want the Demon." Jimmy said. "Initiating Losing Bowel Control... NOW!"

Alex laughed.

Underneath Jimmy's car, a metal plate fell off and liquid poured out. Jimmy swerved back and forth, spewing the liquid across the width of the road.

Kiku steered the car onto the sidewalk.

"Is that oil?" Alice asked, her voice rising.

Beneath Jimmy's purple race car, a little red flash erupted into a blast of flames.

"Your car's on fire!" Alice screamed. "Jimmy! You're on fire!"

Jimmy swore.

"I told you not to hit the second button so soon!" Hwan admonished.

Jimmy's car slid to the left, straightened out for a moment, then swerved to the right. The car spun completely around.

"Houston, we have a negative on this launch trajectory!" Jimmy shouted into the microphone. He was trying to sound brave, but there was terror in his voice.

Alice watched in horror as the burning car spun toward the side of the road.

"Cut to the left, Jimmy!" Alice said.

"I've got no steering. I'm along for the ride."

"Can you jump?" Alex asked.

"I'm going ninety miles an hour," Jimmy said. "I can't jump."

The purple car hit the grass and slid across the forecourt of a tall building.

Kiku sped up.

"Kiku, stop! Stop!" Alice grabbed her arm.

"We cannot." Kiku stared into the rearview mirror. "Fausto is still ahead of us, and we need to reach the interception point."

"What about Jimmy?" Alice asked.

Kiku said nothing.

Alice stared in horror behind them. Jimmy's car was in flames when he left the road. Finding her grandfather wasn't worth his life.

"Go back, Kiku. Please?" Alice pleaded.

Kiku focused on the road, her knuckles turning white on the steering wheel.

"He needs our help!" Alice shouted.

"It's Jimmy." Alex pleaded. "You can't leave Jimmy behind."

Kiku glanced at Alice, and all hope of her stopping vanished. Kiku's eyes were stone cold.

Alice swallowed. Kiku might have been capable of leaving Jimmy, but that wasn't Alice. She eyed the keys dangling from the ignition. This had to stop.

"I'm okay! I'm okay!" Jimmy's voice crackled over the microphone. "The car is toast and sinking in a pond, but I can get out, and judging from the sirens, I need to run. See you back at base."

Alex's voice came over the microphone, muffled like he was covering it with his hand. "Kiku wasn't going to leave Jimmy. I know it. She would have gone back. Right, Hwan?"

The channel clicked off.

Kiku glanced in the rearview mirror at the headlights gaining on them. "The thin man made it past the oil slick. Hold on." Kiku swung wide into the curve and let off the gas. "Alice, I need you to climb into the back and do exactly as I say."

Alice heard her but kept staring at her shaking hands. People were going to get hurt because of her.

"Alice!" Kiku shook her shoulder. "If we do not find your grandfather, they will kill him. Now climb in the back!"

Alice scrambled over the center console.

"Push the rear panel down."

Alice pressed against the back compartment, and the entire panel folded down so Alice could lie on her stomach.

"Pull out the fabric siding on the left. Grab it and yank hard."

Alice grabbed the fabric and tugged. There was the popping of fasteners, and the panel pulled free. Mounted inside was a gun next to a wide rubber hose.

"Good. Pull the hose out."

"Isn't that for the gas?"

"Yes, but you need to pull it out."

Alice grabbed the hose and yanked, revealing the back of the gas cap.

"Pull the gas cap in. I will slow the car down, and you will shoot the thin man's tires."

"Are you out of your mind? How am I supposed to hit someone's tires when we're going over a hundred miles an hour?"

"You told me that Jack taught you how to shoot!"

"Yeah, but that doesn't mean I'm a sniper queen!"

"I will get you right next to the car. Take the gun."

Alice grabbed the pistol with a very long barrel from its holder on the side of the car. Her hands shook as she clicked the safety off.

"Get ready," Kiku said. "There is a straightaway ahead."

Oh, crap. Oh, crap. Oh, crap.

Alice stuck the barrel out of the side of the car. She closed one eye, but the entire gun blocked the opening. "I can't see anything to shoot!"

"Back up a bit."

Alice's cheeks reddened at the simple suggestion. She scooted back and aimed out the gas cap.

"Get ready!" Kiku slowed down.

The hood of the other car came into view. It was only feet away. So close, Alice could see each LED in the headlight.

Kiku moved their car even closer.

The thin man's tire filled Alice's vision. She pulled the trigger.

The gun kicked up, the muzzle flash blinding her. Smoke singed her nostrils, and her ears felt like someone had placed a bell over her head and struck it with a stack of bricks. Alice stared at the front of the car. Her vision blurred, but she could see Kiku waving at her. Kiku wanted Alice to do something. What that was, she didn't know.

The Demon slid into another curve, and Alice bashed against the side of the car.

Kiku yanked the wheel hard, and Alice rolled over and slammed into the other side.

Trying to escape what felt like being a ball in a pinball machine, Alice scrambled back to the front seat.

Kiku touched her shoulder. She shouted something, but Alice couldn't hear anything.

Kiku jammed the gas pedal to the floor. The Demon roared and shot forward.

The road ahead curved sharply, but the brake lights of Fausto's Corvette were visible in the distance. Fausto had to slow down because of the curves.

Kiku didn't slow. She was speeding up.

The car rocked and shook. Metal groaned, and struts protested as they slammed into one curve, then shot in the other direction toward the next. The tires screamed. Alice felt that the car would fly off the road at any moment.

She shook her head. Her ears popped, and sound was restored.

They flew around a curve that twisted at a ninety-degree angle before turning back on itself, and the Demon pulled right behind Fausto's car.

"I will catch him on the next turn," Kiku said.

Fausto's brake lights glowed, and his car swung wide to the right as he entered the turn.

Kiku hugged the curb and sped up. The muscles in her forearms flexed as she kept her death grip on the steering wheel.

They reached the straightaway, and the cars were almost side by side. Fausto still had the lead, but if Alice rolled down her window and leaned out, she could touch his vehicle.

Kiku shouted, "Hang on!" Then cut the wheel.

Realizing she was still clutching the gun with her left hand, Alice pointed it at the floor and grabbed the door handle with her right.

The Demon's front passenger bumper slammed into the rear quarter of the Corvette.

Alice smashed against the door. Her head dinged off the window with a loud thump.

Metal shrieked. The windshield cracked.

Kiku smiled and hit the gas.

30

When Jack returned to the apartment, Alice's and his bedroom doors were closed. A note on the counter read:

> *Thanks again for letting us stay, Jack. We got you some dinner and left it in the fridge. We took Lady out. I didn't know what time you'd get home. Wake me up if I fall asleep, and we can hang out.*
>
> *Finn*

Jack crept up to his bedroom door, but from the sound of Finn's snoring, his friend was sound asleep. Probably a good thing. Jack wasn't up for talking. He was still trying to get his head around Mark Reynold's theory.

Crossing back into the kitchen, Jack heated a plate of chicken parmesan and ziti. Pouring a glass of water and catching the microwave before it dinged, he headed to his computer desk in the corner.

Saying a quick grace, he kept his eyes closed. Prayer was something that came hard to Jack ever since he was a kid. The asking for something came easy; listening was the part he wasn't very good at. Maybe it was because he always wondered why God would want anything to do with him.

Jack opened his eyes and stared out the window at the night. Could Carl Wilson have changed, or had he fooled everyone into believing he was a different man? From the time Jack could remember, he'd met some of the vilest people on the planet. Pimps, hustlers, and thieves. People who sold their souls and wouldn't hesitate to rob a praying widow in church.

Jack knew evil because he grew up with it.

But he'd also known good.

Aunt Haddie had taken him in as a foster child. She loved him like a mother and taught him with loving actions and tender words. He'd seen the Christian woman straighten out a depressed preacher and bring drunks from the gutter to the shelter. Aunt Haddie always said that the Lord could change anyone.

Jack once believed that. But was he just being gullible? When Tom talked about Carl changing, Jack accepted it as fact. Why? Did Jack want to think people could change for the simple reason he hoped he had?

Lady pressed against his leg, and Jack scratched behind her ears.

Jack remembered the day Aunt Haddie took him home from school after they sent him to the principal's office for fighting. The school didn't know what to do with him. He'd fight anyone—even the kids in the grades above him.

Jack, a scrawny seven-year-old white kid, and his black foster mother stood toe to toe on the back porch like two gunslingers about to draw down. Aunt Haddie grounded him and took away every privilege he had, but the deepest cut was when she said she was disappointed. Then she asked Jack why he wanted to hurt the boy he beat up. Jack had told her he didn't want to hurt him—he wanted to kill him.

Aunt Haddie crouched down and said, “Now I’m disappointed in myself. You’ve still got so much hate in you, Jack. It means I’ve got to show you even more love.”

Jack broke. He cried and cried. Aunt Haddie rocked him with tears running down her face and told him about a man from Galilee who changed her life. She said he wasn’t black like her. And he wasn’t a white man like Jack. He was somewhere in between, because he was a man who belonged to the whole world. And she talked about how God loved the world and her and Jack. Jack believed every word she said. He wanted to believe. He needed to. If not, he felt like all the hate inside would tear him apart.

But now, as a detective, were his beliefs blinding him? Jack knew a hundred guys who went into prison and came out harder, meaner, and filled with rage. Maybe Carl was really like that? So far, Jack only had the word of Carl's granddaughter and Tom, a friend from AA.

Lady laid her enormous head across his lap. She stared up at him with her big brown eyes.

Jack picked up his half-eaten supper and placed the plate on the floor.

As Lady gulped the leftovers down, he patted her back.

“Maybe I am a fool for believing people can change.” Jack wearily rose and moved over to the couch. He flopped down and stared at the books on the coffee table. They belonged to Carl. Jack picked up a red book with a golden shield for a cover and opened it to the first page. Carl had highlighted the introductory quote in yellow.

“Many lose heaven because they are ashamed to go there wearing a fool’s coat.” — William Gurnall.

Jack chuckled. Aunt Haddie always said God has a sense of humor. Maybe being a fool isn’t such a bad thing. Lying back on the couch, he made a mental to-do list for tomorrow when he realized the one thing he forgot to do today.

"Oh, no!"

He jumped back up and darted to his desk for his phone. Sure enough, he had turned the ringer off. Swiping the sensor, the phone blinked to life. Surprisingly, there weren't any calls from Alice. He checked the voicemail and texts, but she had gone radio silent.

"I am so in the doghouse," Jack said, and Lady raised her head. "No offense."

The phone rang four times and went to voicemail.

"Hey, honey. Sorry for calling so late. It's been crazy. I hope you had time to get out and enjoy the day. I'll try again tomorrow. Love you."

Jack hung up and went back to the couch. He smiled as he lay on his back, staring up at the ceiling. What was he worried about? Alice was probably bored out of her mind. Knowing her, she was already asleep.

31

Alice shook her head and rubbed her eyes. The cloud of dirt surrounding the car settled. Fausto's Corvette sat alongside the road, pointed in the opposite direction from Kiku's red Demon.

Kiku leaped out of the car, her pistol in hand.

Fausto kicked his damaged door open and stumbled out. He was yelling in Italian, his hands flying about in all directions.

"Shut up and get in my car," Kiku ordered. "I have questions for you."

Fausto stopped shouting and stared. His lip curled derisively, and he scoffed. "You won't shoot me."

"I may not shoot you, but Z will." Kiku pointed at Alice.

Alice didn't know what Kiku was talking about. She stared at her hand and the gun still clasped in it. Not knowing what to do with the gun after shooting the thin man's tire, she still held on to it. She held it up, careful not to point it at anyone but high enough for Fausto to see.

"She can't shoot me either. I'm a neutral party! I'm protected, like Switzerland."

Alice gave the angry Italian her meanest stink eye. "You're about to look more like Swiss cheese."

Fausto held up his arms.

"Get in my car—now," Kiku ordered.

Fausto hurried over to the Dodge and stared behind the seats at the open back panel. "There's no room. If you have a question, ask me, and let me go."

Sirens sounded in the distance.

"Do you really want to wait here and be arrested?" Kiku asked.

Fausto scrambled into the back.

Alice turned partway in her seat so she could keep an eye on Fausto. She pressed her back against the door but held the gun angled down. Jack always told her never to point a gun at something you didn't intend to kill, and she had no intention of actually shooting Fausto.

Kiku climbed in, and the unlikely trio sped off. She took several side streets, calmly driving the speed limit as if they were going to the store to pick up milk.

"Do you have any idea how much that car cost me?" Fausto, crammed in the back with his knees against his chest, glared at Kiku.

"I will pay you twice that amount."

To Alice's amazement, Fausto thought about it and smiled. "Deal. But you cost me a bodyguard."

"The thin man lives."

"But he failed to prevent you from kidnapping me. So, in addition to restitution for the car, I want your bodyguard. Double for my car, throw in Z, and we are even."

Alice sucked in air. The nerve of the pompous man to talk about her like she was property.

"Do you know why they call her Z?" Kiku asked, glancing into the back seat. "It is short for crazy. Keeping her is like possessing a mad Rottweiler. Eventually, she will turn on you and kill you."

Fausto eyed Alice, who smiled as wickedly as she could.

"I have a better deal for you," Kiku said, crossing through a green light. "Double the price of the car, and I will not inform Takeo that you sold his location to the Russians."

Fausto's pale expression turned chalk white. His rounded eyes left no doubt as to his guilt. "How about we say we are even, and you let me out?"

"Now you are the one who is being generous." Kiku smiled at Alice.

Alice didn't know why. Maybe it was the way the sight of Kiku's pointy canines gleaming in the oncoming headlights made Fausto jump, but Alice chuckled. The momentary burst of laughter made Fausto tremble.

"I'll tell you whatever you want, Kiku. Please. Just let me go," Fausto said.

"Where is Vidal Navarro?"

Alice's nose wrinkled. She couldn't be positive, but from the odor, it smelled like Fausto had wet his pants.

"I can't tell you that. I'll tell you anything else, but I can't tell you that." Fausto's voice was high and shrill.

Kiku clicked on the blinker and changed lanes, letting a car pass them. "Vidal is in town. Where?"

Fausto's eyes darted around the car. He looked at the doors, then the back, and his gaze stopped on the gun in Alice's hand.

"If you want to get out of this car with all the parts of your body still attached, please do nothing foolish," Kiku said.

"I can't cross Vidal. That would be foolish."

"You should not have crossed the Yakuza. Besides, I only want information from Vidal, too. I will not harm him either. Give me the address, Fausto. I want to go to bed."

Fausto hung his head. "He's staying at a place in town. 1141 Bramble Wood Point."

"Thank you," Kiku said.

"You got what you wanted. I'm probably a dead man now." Fausto sighed heavily. "Let me out here, and I'll spend the last of my breath drinking in the night air."

"You have a flair for the dramatic." Kiku smiled. "But do not worry. Once we confirm the address, I will give you a ride home."

Fausto's mouth fell open. He turned to Alice.

Alice's eyes narrowed. She could see it on his face. Fausto had lied to them about Vidal's location.

"Oh, what was I thinking?" Fausto shrugged. "Vidal stayed there on his last trip! He wanted to enjoy the water this time around. He's at 34 Bayview Circle."

"Silly you." Kiku turned right. "Is there anything else you are forgetting?"

"No." Fausto held up his right hand like he was taking an oath. "I swear it on my mother's grave."

Kiku laughed. "Your mother lives in East Boston, Massachusetts, and she is very much alive."

"You are a scumbag," Alice said.

Fausto shrugged. "It's an expression. If my mother were dead, I would swear on her grave."

"Keep it up, and I will give you that opportunity." Kiku laughed and hit the gas.

32

The desert sand blew hot across Jack's face. He knew he was dreaming but was helpless to stop it. In some ways, he welcomed the nightmares. They always had a silver lining.

"Watch your little tootsies!" Chandler yelled as he pulled two long metal ramps out of the back of a camouflaged Army transport and let them fall to the ground.

Jack stared at the space-age vehicle in the back of the truck. It was as large as a soapbox racer, with six wheels, no way to see out, and had an antenna sticking up all along the back.

"What is that?" Jack stepped out of the way.

"A UGV," Chandler replied. He moved his hand, and the vehicle rolled forward. "An Unmanned Ground Vehicle. You control it with your mind."

"Seriously?"

Chandler doubled over, laughing.

Jack punched him in the arm. "Jerk. I've never seen one before. How am I supposed to know how you control it?"

"It's like a big remote-control car." Chandler pointed at a soldier walking at the other end of the UGV. "There's a camera mounted on the front, and Fish controls it from a safe distance. We're going to test it out for recon."

"Fish?"

"He's the new guy. Guess what his favorite thing to do back home is?" Chandler smiled.

"Knitting?"

Chandler laughed again.

"When are we heading out?"

"After we eat!" Chandler grinned as he strode to a tent and held the flap open. "Come on. We need to talk."

Jack followed him inside. Blinded by a bright light, Jack blinked and rubbed his eyes. The desert was gone, and he was back in Darrington, sitting in a booth in a small breakfast diner across from Chandler.

Chandler grinned ear-to-ear as he lifted a fork skewered with sausage, egg, bacon, and a chunk of hash browns. "I already said grace." He stuffed the food into his mouth and smiled contentedly.

Jack bowed his head, and Chandler kicked him under the table.

"Ow. You can't hit me when I'm praying," Jack said.

"Why are you saying grace? You're not eating."

"What?" Jack stared at the dozen plates sitting in front of Chandler. They were heaped with all his breakfast favorites, waffles, eggs, crepes, pancakes—every breakfast item he could think of was there. "Why don't I get to eat?"

"You're getting a belly. Do you want a married guy bod?"

"I'm not getting a gut!" Jack lifted his shirt and patted his toned stomach.

Chandler hit him on the forehead with a piece of biscuit.

"What gives?" Jack wiped his head. "Why aren't you sharing?"

"Because you've got to get moving, soldier. This is your first case. You've waited your whole life for this. Remember what Aunt Haddie said when we were lounging in bed?"

Jack and Chandler repeated the phrase together, "A little sleep, a little slumber, a little folding of the hands to rest—and poverty will come on you like a thief."

They laughed.

"I never could get back to sleep after she said that." Jack slid out of the booth. He glanced back at Chandler and paused. He needed to get going, but he couldn't bear leaving his friend. "I can stay longer."

Chandler shook his head. "You gotta go. I understand."

Jack nodded. The diner became dim and fuzzy.

"Hey, Jack!" Chandler called out. "Tell Finn I said hi, would you? I'm glad he's found someone."

~

Jack sat bolt upright on the couch and rubbed his eyes. The door to his bedroom was open, and so was the guest bedroom. He missed waking up with Alice beside him. He stretched as he walked into the kitchen.

He missed Chandler. They'd been friends and foster brothers since he was little, and now that he was gone, he felt that void every day.

Taking down a water glass, Jack filled it. When he finished drinking, he set the glass on the counter and saw the note.

Sorry our schedules are so diametrically opposed. Annie and I need to finish our report and turn it in today, so we're getting an early start. I didn't want to wake you. We really appreciate your hospi-

tality. I want to take you to lunch and catch up if you're free. Shoot me a text.

Finn

Lady whined and scratched at the door.

"One second," Jack said, rushing to the bathroom himself. He was washing his hands when the door behind him banged open, and Lady stood glaring at him.

"I gotta go, too, you know," Jack said, washing his hands and sidestepping around the dog.

They headed down the stairs and outside to an overcast day. The spring air was chilly, and the leaves, heavy with dew, hung low. The weather was as gloomy as Jack felt without Alice.

Jack texted Ed his plan while waiting for Lady to do her business. Surprisingly, he received an immediate response to his lengthy text. It was so quick; he doubted Ed even read all that Jack wrote.

SOUNDS GREAT. KEEP ME APPRISED.

Jack frowned and stuck his phone in his pocket, taking it out a moment later after receiving a follow-up text.

TAKING SOME PERSONAL TIME THIS MORNING.

"Of course you are. You're probably getting your car detailed. Now that's pressing police business. The fact we have a double murderer on the loose can wait." Jack's voice dripped with sarcasm.

Lady trotted happily over to him and leaned against his thigh.

"Detective Stratton?" A familiar female voice called out, and Naomi Wilson marched across the street directly toward him. She balled her hands into fists at her side, and her red-rimmed eyes blazed with anger. "I stopped by the Sheriff's station, and they said you hadn't come in yet. I doubt you've even started looking for my grandpa!"

"First off, that's not correct."

"Have you found him? Where is he?" Naomi looked around with mock surprise. "Oh, he's not here because you haven't even been looking!"

"Ms. Wilson. I went to your grandfather's apartment. The landlord had recently cleared it out. I have his things upstairs."

"He what? Did he kick my grandpa out of his place? Can he do that? Did you let him do that?"

Jack took a deep breath and tightened his grip on Lady's leash. The gigantic dog was highly defensive of him, and her ears lay back on her head as Naomi yelled. "I also spoke with a friend of your grandfather's at AA. I was going to contact you this morning about something the friend said. This man told me that your grandfather was trying to find a drug dealer—"

"I knew it!" Naomi stuck her finger in Jack's face, then stepped back as Lady growled and pulled against her leash. "I knew you'd think once a junkie, always a junkie. He broke outa that. He wouldn't go back. Never. You and your privileged background don't get that."

Jack forced himself to keep his voice even. "My mother was a heroin addict and a prostitute who abandoned me at a bus station when I was six. I grew up in a foster home next to Hamilton Park. And I'm not looking for your grandfather for you or even for him, although I'd like to find him for both of your sakes. I'm doing it because it's the right thing to do, and it's my job."

The fire in Naomi's eyes cooled to burning embers.

"Your grandfather knew a young man in AA who recently overdosed. Did he ever mention him to you?"

Naomi crossed her arms and nodded. "He said he was my age. He warned me about drugs, but as I said, I'm going into the service. I don't do that crap."

"Did he mention the man's name?"

Naomi thought for a moment and shook her head.

"Your grandfather was upset by his death. I believe he was trying to find the dealer who gave the kid the drugs. Did your grandfather talk about that?"

Naomi stared at Jack. She was close to tears.

"I need your help, Naomi. If your grandfather told you anything, I need to know."

"He wouldn't have talked to him. He couldn't. You know. He couldn't."

"Who couldn't your grandfather talk to?"

"The last day I saw him, Grandpa was upset. He wouldn't say why, but I kept at him, and he asked me to pray about something. After he got out of prison, that's all he'd talk about. Jesus loves me. I should love Jesus. I'm not churchy or nothing, but I told him I would." Naomi stared at the ground.

Lady trotted forward and bumped her.

Naomi sniffed and started stroking Lady's back. She kept her gaze on the dog as she spoke softly, "He said he needed to talk to the guy who put him in prison."

"The police officer? The judge?"

Naomi shook her head. "Some doctor. Not the one who gave him the drugs. There was another one. One that helped the police."

"Why did your grandfather say he couldn't talk to...." Jack's voice trailed off as he answered his own question. "Because it would violate his parole."

Naomi nodded. "Contacting a witness or something. I told him to let it go, but he said God was telling him to do it. I thought it was a terrible idea." Tears ran down Naomi's face and fell onto Lady's fur. "The guy sent him to prison. What would happen if my grandfather showed up on his doorstep?"

"Did he mention this doctor's name?"

"Dr. Mobley."

33

Jack drove slowly across town. His head was spinning. He didn't feel like he was following a trail so much as getting tangled in a spiderweb. This may have been his first official case, but Jack had trained to be a detective since he was a kid. When Jack was twelve, his adoptive father set up a couple of police station tours and ride alongs with Detective Derrick Clark. The detective took a liking to Jack and answered all his questions—and Jack had a lot of them—but he gave Jack an actual picture of what law enforcement was like, warts and all.

Detective Clark also gave him expert advice. Keep moving forward. Don't stop. Even if you're only taking baby steps, keep moving. "If you don't know the next step to take, look at your list, kid. Always have a list. That's the first step. Number one, make a list. Two, take photographs, so you don't forget. Three, interview everyone. Four, collect the evidence. Five, examine the evidence. If you ever get confused, go back over those steps."

Jack sped up. He'd have to call Detective Clark and his father to thank them later, but right now he had work to do.

Dr. Mobley's damaged home was shuttered. Someone had

draped a blue tarp over the missing section of the roof. The police tape flapped in the light rain that now fell. Jack parked in the driveway and hurried up the slick walk. Ducking under the police tape, he clicked on his flashlight and let himself in.

Because of the blue tarp, the room was bathed in an aqua glow. He could have reviewed his body cam footage but seeing a crime scene firsthand did something to his mind that pictures could never achieve.

The place smelt like charred wood and burnt plastic. Jack stared at Dr. Mobley's display cabinet. The certificates from the prestigious colleges lay broken on the floor. Even the award his mother had given him was gone—all of that work and now nothing to show for it.

A dripping sound came from the kitchen. A gust of wind sent the tarp rippling, giving the living room an undersea feel as the blue light danced all around. The key to the explosion that killed Dr. Mobley was the cap on the propane tank. If someone swapped it out, one of the neighbors may have noticed something.

Jack slipped out of the house and back to the car. Dr. Mobley's home was situated on the only buildable lot on the road. Ed had uniformed officers interview the few surrounding neighbors at the end of the street. Maybe if Jack widened the search area, he'd find someone who saw something.

Three hours later, Jack was giving up hope. He'd stopped by almost every house on the road and only had one left. No one had seen anyone or anything suspicious. Half of the people he questioned didn't even know there was a home further up the mountain until they saw it on the news.

Jack rang the doorbell, and dogs barked inside.

A moment later, a young woman cracked open the door as one black, and one yellow Lab yipped and pranced, trying to see who it was.

"Can I help you?" she asked.

"I'm Detective Jack Stratton with the Sheriff's Department. I'm investigating the explosion up the road at the house on the hill. Do you have a moment to answer a couple of questions?"

"Certainly. I'm Judi Moore. Such a shame. It was a beautiful home. I'd pass it on my walks with my dogs."

At the mention of "walks," the dogs flipped out. They barked, pushed, and barked some more.

"Hold on a sec." Judi held the dogs back, slipped out the door, and quickly closed it behind her.

Jack glanced at her very pregnant belly. "Congratulations."

"Thank you. My first." Judi cradled her tummy. "Twins."

"Wow. Double congratulations."

"My husband is a twin, and so am I."

"You could have had quadruplets."

Judi rolled her eyes. "Twins is hard enough. Do you have kids?"

"No. I just got married."

"I'll give you a heads-up on what comes next. Everyone, and I mean everyone from your best friend to your dentist, is going to ask you when you're going to have kids. The pressure is brutal. I swear my mother-in-law sabotaged my pills, but now I wouldn't have it any other way."

"Do you know what you're going to have? Besides the obvious answer—babies."

"Nope. We wanted that part to be a surprise." Judi wrinkled her nose. "I swear being pregnant affects my brain. I fogged on what you were asking me."

"I'm investigating the explosion at Dr. Mobley's house. Did you see anything suspicious earlier in the week? A person or vehicle that you didn't recognize?"

Judi opened and closed her mouth. She bit her bottom lip and shook her head. "No. Nothing."

"Ms. Moore, this is an active murder investigation. If you know anything, we can use your help."

Judi cupped her hands together. "He was murdered?"

"That's what I'm looking into. Did you know Dr. Mobley?"

She shook her head. "I'd see him when taking the dogs for a walk. He'd be inside and wave as we'd go by."

Jack waited.

Judi rubbed her left hand with her right. She gave a one-shoulder shrug. "It's probably nothing. The man could have been a friend. But the day before the explosion, I was on my walk. There are never cars up there, so I let my dogs off the leash, but that morning, this car came barreling around the corner and scared the wits out of me."

"Did you see what kind of car it was?"

"It was part of that local ride thing. They have the blue-and-yellow $7 ride signs. That was part of the odd thing. A few minutes later, the driver came by again. Before, there had been a man riding in the back seat, but the driver was alone now. He slowed to apologize, and I said it was my fault for not having the dogs on a leash. He admitted he was driving too fast."

Jack had to keep himself from asking her to get to the point and let her keep telling the story in a natural flow.

"After he drove off, we kept going up the hill, and when we got to the top, I saw that man who the taxi driver had dropped off. But the man hadn't gone into Dr. Mobley's house. He was staring at it. When he saw us, he started walking in the opposite direction, but there's nothing up there. It was so strange, I turned around and went home."

"Can you describe the man?"

"On the tall side and thin. He wore a sports jacket. I'm unfamiliar with sports, so I couldn't say the team."

Jack forced himself to slow down and not ask any leading questions. "Did you notice any specific details about the jacket?"

Judi's nose wrinkled. "It was blue, red, and yellow. Mostly blue. And it had a red letter C on the back. Does that help?"

"It does. You said the man was tall and thin. Do you remember anything else about him?"

Judi exhaled. "He was African American, but my telling you that has nothing to do with the color of his skin. I'm not prejudiced. I hear about someone calling the police on someone because of that, and then it goes on social media. Protestors show up outside your house—"

"I get it." Jack nodded. "You're simply relaying that his actions were suspicious, not him."

"I didn't say suspicious. But they were strange. Very odd."

Jack held out his business card. "Thank you very much for your time. If it's okay, I need to stop by later this afternoon and ask you some questions."

"That'll be fine. I'm not due for another three weeks, so you have some time."

"Have a nice day." Jack marched back to his car. He wanted to show Judi a photograph of Carl Wilson he had on his phone, but if he only showed her Carl's picture, a good defense lawyer could say it prejudiced her objectivity. Jack needed to wait until he could put together a photo lineup. That was another thing Detective Clark had taught him.

"Remember, Jack. Never forget that catching a bad guy is only half the battle. Later, twelve people are going to be reviewing your work. Dot every I and cross every T. That's how you win the war."

34

Before Jack could put together a photo lineup for Judi Moore and the taxi driver, he needed to make two other stops. He had two working theories regarding the murder and needed to look into both of them.

His first destination brought him into the heart of downtown Darrington. The city center had turned into a bit of a technology hub. Companies specializing in computer chips, robotics, and software engineering flocked to Darrington for the ready pool of candidates from White Rocks Eastern College. Some complained that the companies were mainly interested in the cheap labor provided by interns. Mandatory internships created a constant supply of eager, low-cost, disposable workers.

Eagle 247 Technology had taken over one of the Flagg buildings—two steel and glass office towers that sat opposite each other on main street. The northern building was five stories tall but fifty yards wider, while the southern was seven stories and narrower. A newspaper article had recently dubbed them Bert and Ernie because of the green initiative the companies had launched. They'd erected gardens on top of both buildings, and if you viewed them from a distance, you could see the resemblance to the *Sesame Street* characters and their wild hair.

Jack strode through the front door and was surprised to see two armed security guards and a row of four metal detectors. Jack approached the guard sitting on a tall stool.

With all the eagerness of someone repeating a speech for the 3,423rd time, he said, "All visitors must place all metal objects in the provided containers. No cameras, cell phones, or electronic devices of any kind are permitted on Eagle 247 Technology property. If you do not wish to store your belongings in your car, please use the bags provided for your use."

At the mention of giving up his phone, Jack felt like an addict being asked to quit cold turkey.

A woman holding a tablet hurried over to him. "Welcome to Eagle 247 Technology. How can we assist you today?"

He flashed his badge. "I'm Detective Jack Stratton with the Darrington Sheriff's Department. I'd like to speak with Sabrina Hall."

The woman's mouth stayed open. She took a shallow breath, angled her head, and appeared ready to say something, but just stared at him. Jack felt like he was watching her shuffle through a deck of canned responses, loading one, then deciding she shouldn't say it and searching for another.

"One moment," she muttered and hurried several feet away. The woman's tablet's screen flashed to life, and she spoke in a hushed tone to someone. Smiling, but obviously flustered, she turned back to Jack. "May I ask why you wish to speak with Ms. Hall?"

Jack raised his voice. "It's regarding a homicide investigation."

The woman nodded rapidly, spoke in hushed tones to whoever was on the tablet screen, then came back over to Jack.

"Could you please wait in the guest area? Someone will be right down."

Jack approached the metal detectors. Both guards stood, feet wide apart, shoulders back, arms crossed and tight-lipped smiles. Internally, Jack groaned. Most security guards were good people, but like any group, you had a few morons. These two looked to fit that bill—policemen wannabes who, when given the slightest opportunity for power over a person in the very position they wanted, took it to extreme measures.

The larger security guard gave Jack the same speech as before, but this time with an added zing to it. "All visitors must place all metal objects in the provided containers. No cameras, cell phones, or electronic devices of any kind are permitted on Eagle 247 Technology property. If you do not wish to store your belongings in your car, please use the bags provided for your use."

"I have a service weapon," Jack said, removing everything from his pockets. "I'll need you to sign for it and make certain it's locked up."

"We know how to do our job," the second guard said. "Here." He held out a tablet for Jack to sign while the other guard turned to a cabinet and opened a locker, using both a code and a fob.

Jack stepped through the metal detector, and it binged.

While the second guard ran a wand over Jack from head to toe, the first guard stood and stared.

The wand beeped at Jack's waist. "It's my shield. It's not coming off." Jack's eyes narrowed. He'd been accommodating, but taking off his badge wasn't an option.

Both men stepped aside.

Jack marched over to an area that held couches, coffee machines, water, and snacks. He didn't sit down. Without his gun, body camera, and phone, he felt off balance, like a carpenter without his tools.

The minutes stretched on until Sabrina Hall strode through the lobby and headed his way. The tall, blonde woman wore a beige, open suit jacket with a blush top and diamond hoop earrings. Her hair was pulled back in a tight bun. There was a confidence in her stride that made Jack stand at attention.

"Detective Stratton?" Sabrina said, her voice throaty, sultry even. She held out a hand and shook his with a firm grip and maintained eye contact. "Sabrina Hall. Let's talk in my office."

"I appreciate you meeting with me." Jack followed her back to the elevators.

"Please forgive all the James Bond security. Unfortunately, it's standard in the industry."

"What exactly do you do here at Eagle?"

Sabrina pressed the elevator button, and her eyes met his. "I see you've decided to take the coy approach, Detective. I took a moment to read up on you on the way down. The youngest detective in the county's history. Decorated veteran. You also captured the Giant Killer and saved your own wedding by stopping a serial murderer. With a résumé like that, you didn't come here all wide-eyed and naïve. I'm sure you did your homework."

Jack grinned. "You're very direct or, as my father would more politely put it, you say what you mean and mean what you say."

The elevator doors dinged and opened.

"It's how I run my business. And everything is business." They got into the elevator. Sabrina swiped her card and pressed the button for the top floor. "How was the Caribbean?"

Jack raised an eyebrow.

"You're still tan, so you went somewhere warm. Your parents live in Florida, so I ruled that out, leaving the number-one honeymoon destination for Americans."

"I take it you're a Sherlock Holmes fan?"

"More Doctor Watson. I have a theory that he was really the

genius at solving the cases, but when he wrote them up, he was modest and gave Holmes the credit."

Jack nodded. "A humble doctor. Finding one would be more of a mystery."

Sabrina laughed. "I take it you're not a fan of deductive reasoning?"

"You realize that as a detective, I use deductive reasoning day in and day out. But it is not foolproof. You're correct in my honeymoon destination, but I could have gone to Italy."

The doors opened. "True." Sabrina said, smiling and nodding at a woman sitting behind a large marble-topped desk. "I prefer the term calculated risk." Again, she flashed a disarming Mona Lisa smile.

They walked down a hallway whose walls were covered with framed awards and newspaper articles. Still photographs had been printed out from various shows Sabrina had been featured on. Sabrina appeared on everything from tech shows to talk shows and even late night.

"You have a busy entertainment schedule," Jack noted.

"Advertising. Pure and simple. I'm not an extrovert by any means, but I'll do the dog-and-pony shows if it gets Eagle's name in the press. Coffee?"

"I'm good, thanks."

Sabrina shoved open the double doors and strode into a corner office with a spectacular view of the city. The back walls were filled with the biggest smart boards Jack had ever seen. Her desk was average sized, with only a monitor on top and two chairs in front of it. Other than that, the space was empty.

"I'm a minimalist. Visual clutter bothers me to no end." Sabrina surprised Jack again by sitting on one of the chairs in front of her desk and offering the other to him.

"You can't beat the view," Jack said, taking a seat.

"As long as you don't look over my shoulder."

Jack's eyes traveled to the taller building across the street.

"I have to admit," Sabrina said, smiling, "that after the Enterprise nicknamed it Ernie, it is growing on me. Pun intended. What can I do for you, Detective?"

Sabrina had positioned the chairs, so they were almost knee to knee with one another. Now that she leaned in, he could smell her perfume. He didn't know its name, only that it smelled expensive. She teetered at the very edge of Jack's personal space. It was a rapport-building tactic Jack had learned in an interrogation class, but now that it was applying to him, it had the opposite effect.

"I'd like to ask you some questions concerning an automated delivery system recently pitched to you."

Sabrina's lips pressed together, and she inclined her head toward him the way a mother looks at a child when they ask a stupid question. "You'll need to be more specific. We receive hundreds of solicitations regarding projects worldwide every month."

"Dr. Samuel Mobley and a team from WRE created an unmanned, automated, aerial delivery system. Either he or someone from his team made a presentation here."

Sabrina crossed her legs, laying both hands palm up on her leg. She closed her eyes.

Jack sat there as an awkward silence grew. She looked like she was meditating, but Jack never had someone he was speaking to spontaneously break into meditation.

Her eyes fluttered open. A shudder ran up her back, and she smiled pleasantly. "My apologies. As you said, I can be rather direct, but I'm trying to be less brutal when I speak honestly. There's very little I can say regarding Dr. Mobley without my lawyers present. He's threatened several lawsuits and made a number of highly inflammatory accusations." She stood up and stepped closer to him. Her thigh brushed his and she gazed down at him. "Do you mind if I walk while we chat? It helps me remain calm."

"Knock yourself out," Jack said. He'd read in one article that the CEO was delightfully quirky, and Sabrina definitely did not fit the mold for the traditional head of a company.

"I need to make something perfectly clear from the start. We at Eagle have never seen a presentation of the project nor reviewed any pitch nor materials regarding it. The whole thing never saw the light of day because it didn't pass the first hurdle —the ownership of rights was in question."

"Why would you think that Dr. Mobley didn't own the project?"

"Because two other people showed up with identical packages. All three claimed to be the rightful owners of said project."

"Who were the others?"

Sabrina stopped pacing and cradle her chin with her hand. "Dr. Navi Patel and Dr. Yan Chen, I believe."

"There was a fourth party involved in the project."

Sabrina shrugged. "Those were the names passed along to me. Who was this other individual?"

"Oscar Chambers."

"The name isn't familiar." Sabrina touched her ear and said, "Please look up a visitor named Oscar Chambers and send all contact logs to me."

"But the two others met with you?"

"Not with me directly. They spoke with one of the VPs. I'll forward that material to you, including dates and times. What is your email?"

Jack handed her a business card.

Sabrina placed it on a small plate on her desk. A light glowed beneath his card and she pressed her ear again. "Send all contact logs regarding Dr. Navi Patel, Dr. Yan Chen, Dr. Samuel Mobley, and Oscar Chambers to Detective Stratton's email."

"I appreciate that."

"In matters where it is possible, I believe in full disclosure." Sabrina picked up her phone off the desk. She touched the screen twice, read something, and shrugged. "Oscar Chambers was given an introductory tour of the lower level. That's the tour that we give to potential interns and school field trips. They get a goodie bag and a free soda, and we get PR. No one spoke with him regarding a project nor accepted any materials from him."

"Are you certain about that? His roommate said he came here to pitch the project."

"Anyone can walk through the front door. Not everyone can pitch a project. The only reason someone spoke with the others is because of their standing at WRE. Eagle and WRE have a long commitment of cooperation, and if tenured doctors want fifteen minutes, we'll give it to them."

"You mentioned that Dr. Patel and Dr. Chen didn't speak with you but spoke to a VP. Did you speak with Dr. Mobley?"

"Not at first. Dr. Mobley initially spoke with the same VP. Elizabeth Hasting, I believe. I spoke with him personally on a later visit."

"Why was that?"

"Dr. Mobley dropped off his package a day before the others brought theirs. The following day, Dr. Mobley was in the lobby creating a scene and making all kinds of unfounded accusations. I spoke with him in the seating area where I met you to defuse the situation."

"Did you?"

"I thought I had." Sabrina sighed. "I even provided him with my email, which proved to be a mistake. He's been barraging my account almost daily, although I have to say it's been pleasantly quiet today."

"Dr. Mobley is dead."

Sabrina turned to stare at Jack. "Another example of the

weakness of deductive reasoning. I hoped he had gone on vacation."

"No. And Dr. Yan Chen was killed yesterday morning."

Sabrina paled. She crossed to the chair and sat down. "Killed? Murdered? Both of them?"

Jack nodded.

"Well, if whoever killed them did so because of the project, it was in vain. Eagle will never consider it now." Sabrina's eyes narrowed as she gazed at Jack. "What a waste of human life and possibly a great project. I was curious to hear that pitch."

"You never heard about the project from any of them?"

"Not a chance," Sabrina said. "Procedure dictates that all pitches be vetted beforehand. Before speaking to anyone, we do everything to avoid legal problems. We don't have plausible deniability; we have provable deniability that will hold up in any court."

A chime sounded on the desk.

"I apologize, Detective. I have another engagement that I can't reschedule." She stepped forward and once more offered her hand. "I've attached my personal contact information to the emails I had forwarded. Please feel free to reach out if you have questions or if you're still curious about what we do here."

Jack's skin tingled as her thumb brushed the back of his hand. "Thank you for your time." As he headed back to the elevator, he tried to organize this latest development. Motive, means, and opportunity was a mantra Detective Clark had drilled into Jack's head.

But if the others couldn't sell the project, did that remove their motive? Or did it expand the list of suspects? The project seemed on life support. Maybe someone from outside the group of four wanted to pull the plug.

35

Jack waited for the manager of A. G. Maxwell Insurance in the deserted lobby. Four chairs sat on each side of the small room, with a water cooler beside the window that overlooked the parking lot.

An older man with thinning hair combed over his bald spot stepped out of an open doorway and motioned Jack over. "You must be Detective Stratton? I'm Peter Ryder. Pleasure."

"Good afternoon, sir. Do you have a few minutes?"

"Of course. Come in." Peter led them to a small, cramped office with stacks of papers and boxes everywhere. "Excuse the mess. We're trying to get everything digital, but the paper stacks keep growing. You said on the phone that this is about Dr. Mobley's policies?"

"Yes. Did Dr. Mobley hold both life and home insurance through you?"

"He did. It's one of the reasons I feel so badly about what happened. I tried to caution Sam not to go through with it. I was worried something would happen." Peter moved a box of papers off a chair for Jack, then sat behind his desk.

"You cautioned Dr. Mobley not to go through with what?"

"Downgrading his policies. He dropped his life insurance and cut his homeowner's policy in half. If he'd lived, the payout of the house wouldn't be enough to repair it."

"Dr. Mobley had no life insurance?"

"None with us, and we'd held the policy for over thirty years. Sam was a friend. I tried to convince him to keep the policy. I went so far as to offer him a loan, but he opted to cancel. He would have dropped the homeowner's insurance but couldn't because of the mortgage company."

"His house was mortgaged?"

"Twice. He overextended himself."

Jack cleared his throat. "Dr. Mobley worked at the hospital and the college, correct?"

"For years." Peter put both elbows on his desk and wrung his hands. "Sam was obsessed with an idea for this high-tech project. He said it was real Star Trek stuff. He'd go on and on about it."

"You mentioned Sam was a friend. Did you two talk often?"

"About once a month, we'd meet for lunch or coffee."

"And Sam said it was his project."

"Oh, it was definitely Sam's baby. It was his dream. He came up with the idea years ago and recently got all fired up over it. But some dreams can turn into a money pit. Sam poured money into it. I tried to get him to slow down, but he said his mother always told him to shoot for the moon. If he missed, he'd hit the stars. I didn't have the heart to tell him that some rockets blow up on the launchpad. What happens to his work now?"

"I suppose that would depend on the will. Who had been the beneficiary of his life insurance?"

"A cousin in New Hampshire. I can dig out the details if you want."

"Yes, please." Jack handed him a card. "Send me everything you can."

“I will. It could take a few days.”

“That’s fine, but the sooner you get me that information, the better. Were you the one that put the tarp over Sam’s house?”

“My son and I did. We didn’t go inside or touch anything.”

“That’s fine. It was nice of you. Thank you for your time.”

Jack showed himself out of the office. The spring air had warmed, and the sun made an appearance. He was almost to his car when he spotted Finn and Annie parking their car a few spaces over.

“Hey, Finn!” Jack waved.

Annie waved and grinned broadly.

Finn’s eyebrows pulled together, and he slammed the door after getting out. “What are you doing, Stratton?”

From his clipped tone to the tightness of his eyes, Jack didn’t know why Finn was upset, but he clearly was.

“I had to check on Dr. Mobley’s insurance policy.”

“Really?” Finn limped slightly as he marched forward. “And you don’t think of asking me first? You know this is the company Annie and I work for, right?”

Annie started signing something to Finn, but he kept his stare locked on Jack.

“Yes, but I didn’t want to jam you up.”

“You say you didn’t want to jam me up, but you come here without talking to me? Does that make any sense?”

“It does. I didn’t even tell Peter that I knew you. All I did was ask what policies Dr. Mobley had and who was the beneficiary.”

Annie tugged on Finn’s sleeve. The two signed back and forth, and Annie’s smile disappeared.

Finn turned back to Jack, still clearly agitated. “I wouldn’t go to your work without talking to you first.”

“If it didn’t have anything to do with me, I wouldn’t care.”

“It does have to do with me!” Finn snapped.

Annie walked back to the car and got in.

"Great. Just great." Finn ran his hand through his hair. "Now Annie's mad at me."

Jack held up both his hands like he was surrendering. "I apologize. I didn't think—"

"You didn't think about me. You get to live the dream I wanted, and you can't even throw me a bone." Finn limped back to his car.

Jack's phone buzzed in his pocket. He reached to silence it when he noticed the text was from Annie.

Please forgive Finn. We had to view the pictures from the morgue. I think seeing the injuries to Dr. Mobley triggered Finn.

Like a punch in the gut, Jack winced. The explosion had torn Dr. Mobley's body in half and left behind only his shattered legs. Of course, that could traumatize Finn. An RPG had blown off Finn's leg. Before it happened, Jack had never seen a man so full of life. Finn was the guy who was always in motion. Running, climbing, jumping, Finn didn't stop. And, like Jack, Finn's goal was to be in law enforcement. But the RPG ended those dreams.

As Annie backed out of the parking lot, Jack watched his friend. Finn sat in the passenger seat, staring out the side window. He didn't even glance in Jack's direction.

Jack hung his head. Everyone Jack had served with in Iraq came home broken if they came back at all. For some people, the missing limbs, burns, and scars made their injuries easy to see. But the invisible wounds of war often cause the most pain and go undetected, leaving the veteran to suffer alone.

The human spirit can endure a sick body, but who can bear a crushed spirit?

36

Alice sat at the coffee table in the Airbnb kitchen, watching Jimmy devour a pile of fast food. His right ear was bandaged, but he seemed uninjured from the accident.

"Where are the other guys?" Alice asked.

"Upstairs. I'm not really a gamer." Jimmy mumbled between bites of french fries and onion rings. "And it's kind of Hwan and Alex's bonding thing."

"How's your ear?"

"Not bad. My plan worked brilliantly. I took out almost all the other racers. Besides crashing, I'm happy with it. I never thought the car would catch on fire as fast as it did."

"Gas and oil tend to do that."

"Tell me about it." Jimmy slurped his shake. "Can I ask you a question? How'd you meet up with Kiku? Are you like mobbed up?"

"No." Alice blushed. "A while back, Kiku came looking for my husband's girlfriend. Former girlfriend. She was kidnapped, and Kiku helped my husband find her."

"Really?" Jimmy pointed a French fry at her. "Is your husband named Jack?"

"Yes. Do you know him?"

"No. But I've heard of him. He's developed a bit of a reputation."

"That sounds like my husband."

"Kiku said he would have made a good ronin. That's a masterless samurai."

"Jack has a bit of an issue following orders. Do you know where Kiku went?"

"No idea. She may be checking if Fausto's people are looking for him."

Alice rubbed her forehead.

"Do you need some aspirin?"

"I need my head examined. I'm now party to a kidnapping."

"Oh, don't worry about it." Jimmy dunked a fry into a pool of catsup.

"Kidnapping is a felony."

"From the way I figure it, you've already committed four or five felonies. Besides, Kiku will let Fausto go, and he won't tell the cops."

"Really?"

"No way. Fausto would never go to the police. He'll send someone to kill you."

Alice went back to rubbing her temples.

Jimmy's smile faded. "You know Kiku woulda come back for me."

Alice stared at the table. Maybe Jimmy said that to make himself feel better, but if Jimmy had seen the look in Kiku's eyes, he wouldn't believe what he'd just said.

"She woulda," Jimmy repeated. "I can't tell you how many times she's saved my butt. I owe her my life."

"I became too focused on my mission this time." Kiku's voice from the doorway made them both jump. Kiku walked in front of Jimmy and bowed. "Gomen nasai."

Jimmy stood up so fast that he almost knocked the chair over. Jimmy bowed even lower than Kiku had.

Kiku handed him an envelope. "I should never have asked you and Hwan to help with this."

The fat envelope in Jimmy's hands crinkled as he felt it.

"That is all for you." Kiku smiled. "It is time for you, Hwan, and Alex to return home."

Jimmy shook his head. "You still have to get to Vidal."

"I will not involve you three anymore. Takeo will be furious that Alex was here, let alone an active participant. You will leave in the morning. Now, I need to speak with Alice privately."

"Sure." Jimmy jammed the envelope into his belt, shoveled his food back into the bag, picked up his shake and the bag, and hurried out of the room.

Kiku pulled up another chair.

From the living room, Jimmy screamed, "Oh, my freaking word! Wow!" He rushed back to the doorway and bowed so low to Kiku that Alice thought his head might hit the floor. "Osoreirimasu! Osoreirimasu!"

"Do not waste it on something frivolous," Kiku said.

"I won't. No way. I'm going to invest it!" Jimmy smiled so wide his face was practically glowing. "One word—Lamborghini." Jimmy raced out of the room and thundered up the stairs. "You guys aren't gonna believe this, but I'm buying a Lambo!"

Kiku shook her head and leveled her gaze at Alice. "I owe you an apology as well."

"No, you don't. I shouldn't have gotten you involved in this."

"It was I who came to you. Do not forget, I also have a personal stake in this."

"What is it? Are you looking for other information from Vidal?"

"No." Kiku reached across the table, her hand hovering over Alice's before she withdrew it and set both hands in her lap.

"You must know this. You are my friend—one of the few people in the world I have ever called that. But I must get this information. It means everything to me, and I will do anything to get it."

Alice nodded.

"I say this to you because I need to make something clear. No matter how much I care for you, I cannot turn to the right or the left or go back. I must see my mission through. If it comes to choosing between my mission and you, there is no choice."

Alice squared her shoulders. She didn't have many friends, and now, one of the few she did told her if it came down to her mission or Alice, Kiku would let her die. "I understand."

Kiku stood.

"Do yourself a favor, Kiku. If something happens, whatever you do, don't tell Jack you helped me. You could hand him twenty of those envelopes you gave Jimmy, and he'd still come after you."

37

Jack lifted the crime scene tape and pushed the gate to Dr. Chen's yard open. With the dogs shipped off to animal services, the silence was unnerving. Being alone at the run-down house where a murder had occurred gave him the creeps.

Jack's shoes crunched the gravel as he approached the home. Since his childhood, crime had fascinated him, and so had crime's aftermath. He wasn't a superstitious man, but after many cases of violent crimes, people often claimed the site was now haunted.

Jack stepped onto the front porch step. A gentle breeze sent the grass swaying like waves at sea, but the wind also brought the faint sound of groaning. It was nothing but trees. Jack quickly dismissed the idea of it being anything other than his overactive imagination.

Was it only that?

Seeing how Jack believed that when a person died, they went to either Heaven or Hell, he didn't believe in ghosts. Some stories he heard rang true. And if it wasn't a ghost haunting a place, what was it? Something showed up after the scene of a violent crime. Maybe that something was a demon? Could evil be like nuclear waste? Does it leave a residue that draws them like garbage attracts rats?

Jack stepped onto the porch, the wood groaned, and the front door creaked open. Wisps of cold air licked out of the house and brushed his face. An icy shiver ran down his spine. Feeling like a kid standing at the top of the cellar stairs and staring into the darkness, Jack's first instinct was to run in the opposite direction.

But Jack wouldn't run.

Demons be dammed.

Drawing his gun, he breached the door.

The home was as cluttered as he remembered it. Dr. Chen's next of kin had been notified, but they hadn't cleaned up the blood. The sickly sweet smell of death drifted out from the kitchen.

The profound silence strained Jack's ears to hear anything. No dogs barked. Nothing moved.

Jack started moving. It only took a minute to sweep the house and ensure he was alone. He strode into the kitchen, holstering his gun, and stared down at the dried blood that marked where Dr. Chen had bled out.

Mei had completed the autopsy this morning and sent Jack the report. Dr. Chen's cause of death was five 9mm rounds to the chest. Jack had initially thought the wounds were large caliber because of the size of the damage, but he was mistaken. The cluster of bullets was so tight that the bullet holes overlapped.

Whoever the shooter was, they were a marksman. Even at close range, considering the kick of the gun and the movement by Chen as he was shot, the spread should have been larger. Jack didn't know if he could have pulled off so many shots with that tight cluster.

"I doubt even Kiku could do it." He said the words aloud and felt like he'd just shouted in a library.

However, the shooter's proficiency wasn't the biggest question on Jack's mind. Something else bothered him even more. Mei's report continued with another odd fact—the height of the gun when fired. An average-sized man stood 5'9" while a woman was 5'4". Eye level was two inches lower. Considering the surgical nature of the strike pattern, you'd expect the trajectory of the bullets to be fired from a shooter's stance and, therefore, at eye level.

But Mei estimated they held the gun at the height of three feet. It's possible that the shooter crouched down, but why? And why did they come to the back door?

Jack walked through the house and out the front, shutting the door after him. He slowly and methodically walked the perimeter of the fence, staring at the barbed wire and chain link, searching for any foreign material or opening. By the time he made a full circle, he was convinced the shooter hadn't gone under the fence or over it.

It wouldn't matter, anyway. They'd still have to get past the dogs even if they went through the gate. The pack was loose.

He stood in the middle of the driveway, staring at the house. The sun poked out from behind the clouds, blinding him. Shielding his eyes with his hand, a warm gust of wind wafted across his face as he scanned the windows for any sign of movement. Two steps led to the little front porch. Examining the ground, Jack circled to the right. He followed the same route as the day before and stopped at the tree where he took cover.

The path led straight to the back door.

No steps.

Jack smiled. "That's how the shooter got past the dogs."

38

"How? How is Stratton doing this?"

I hold the sight to my eye and watch as Stratton races to his car. Exuberance is written all over his stupidly handsome face. He must have figured out something.

What?

I aim the rifle, using the passenger door as a rest. Because I parked at the far end of the field, there isn't any way I can make the shot while Stratton is running. I'm no sharpshooter.

The crosshairs of my scope shift as I focus on the driver's side of his car. I try to slow my breathing. I can do this. It will be the longest shot I've ever tried, but I can do it.

Stratton yanks open the door and slides into the seat.

My crosshairs rest on the side of his head. I let my breath out.

Slowly.

Calmly.

The metal of the trigger is cold to the touch.

Stratton jerks toward the passenger seat, reaching for something.

My finger eases back.

I repeat the process. Breathe in. Slowly let it out.

He's started the car.

Squeeze the trigger.

The butt of the rifle kicks back against my shoulder. Firing from inside my car without ear protection, I feel like someone popped a balloon inside my head.

Stratton's car is moving.

I press my eye against the sight.

He's driving away, a triumphant smile still plastered on his face.

I chamber another round, but it's too late. If I missed that first shot so badly, and Stratton didn't even hear it, what chance do I have of hitting him while driving?

Stuffing the rifle in the back seat, I toss my jacket over it. With a few key presses, the monitor on the dash comes to life, and I can see Stratton speeding back to the main road.

Jamming my car into gear, I push the gas pedal to the floor. Dirt and gravel ping off the undercarriage as I race down the dirt road. Holding onto the steering wheel with my left hand, I open the glove compartment with my right. Taking out my pistol, I release it from its holster and let it drop to the floor.

Stratton has reached the main road. He's driving fast but doesn't have his emergency lights on. I can catch him, and he must be stopped. If not, he'll ruin everything.

A red pickup truck pulls in front of me. I pump the brakes and beep.

The driver flips me off.

Oh, how I want to pull alongside him and put a few rounds into his head.

What am I thinking? No. The lack of sleep is getting to me. I couldn't risk that.

I swerve over the yellow line and see that Stratton is pulling away. I start to pass the truck when I remember the tracker I put on his car.

Slow down!

I hit the brakes as the truck turns to the right, and the driver yells something out the window at me, followed by some more obscene gestures.

I rub my hand down my face. It's trembling. Is that why I missed?

Stratton zips through the yellow light. I speed up, running the red.

My eyes dart up and down the street. Are there any police around? Did they see me? What about Stratton? Did he notice?

Fool! Slow down!

I'm risking getting caught. Why?

"Stupid! Stupid! Stupid!" I slam my fist against the steering wheel as I shout.

I don't know why I'm so sure, but Stratton has figured something out. I know it! And I have to kill him. Everything inside me is begging for me to do it.

The light in front turns red.

Stratton rolls to the white line, and I stop behind him.

This is my chance. I can pull alongside him and pull the trigger until he's dead.

But what if I miss?

I stare at my shaking hand. Why now? Normally it's steady, isn't it?

Do it. Drive forward and finish him.

No! If I kill him now, the police will descend on the scene. If I had only killed him at Chen's, I could have hidden the body, but not now.

The light changes.

Stratton drives forward. He reaches up and pulls down his rearview mirror.

He knows. Somehow, he knows that I'm following him.

I turn right. I can't risk being discovered. So what if Stratton found something at Chen's? Figuring out who killed Chen is one thing. Catching me is another story entirely.

I need to wait. I have to get some sleep, but how? Every time I close my eyes, I see his face, and when I dream, I kill him repeatedly. I should have triggered the propane tank earlier. That was my first mistake.

Why did I wait?

It doesn't matter. Not now. I need to get to sleep.

The alarm on my phone tolls a loud beep three times.

Sleep will have to wait.

Someone else has to die.

39

Back at the Sheriff's station, Jack stood in front of a giant whiteboard with a dry-erase marker in his hand. He had commandeered the classroom to lay out the case to Ed, who sat in the front row sipping a latte and typing on his phone. Other than the two of them, the room was empty.

"I'm confused," Ed said without looking up from his phone. "How does the junkie work into all this?"

"If you got off your phone and paid attention, it might help clear things up for you," Jack said.

"I'm taking notes."

"Sorry," Jack apologized.

Ed set the phone down on the desk, and Jack snatched it up.

"You're not taking notes. You're texting the car place!" Jack shouted.

"I'm thanking them for getting my car back to me so quickly. That is a note." Ed snatched his phone back.

"Get off your phone and listen to the whole thing, okay? I still need to run the photo lineup with Carl Wilson past the neighbor and the taxi driver, but I'm certain Carl went to Dr. Mobley's house."

"What's his motive to kill the doctor? To steal drugs?" Ed asked.

"Carl had an ax to grind with Dr. Mobley. I spoke with Detective Mark Reynolds, and it turns out that Dr. Mobley was an informant on the Sweet Sally bust that sent Carl to prison. It's possible that the killer hired Carl to set the device on the propane tank."

Ed sipped his coffee. "That's what I was thinking."

The Sheriff's warning to play nice with Ed rang in Jack's ears. He swallowed down his sarcastic remark and took a deep breath.

"But that still leaves us looking for the person who hired Carl," Ed pointed out.

"Right, that's why we need the warrant to get into the robotics lab at White Rocks."

Ed sat up in his chair. "I don't want you to think I'm caving to political pressure here, but do you know how touchy that is? Before I go asking for anything at the college, I want to make darn sure it won't blow up in my face."

"Then say I requested it. I'll take the hit if I'm wrong."

Ed eyed Jack suspiciously. "Explain it to me again."

"You remember how the dogs acted when we came to the house, right? They freaked out and went into guard mode. Whoever the shooter was, they'd have to get by those dogs."

"Maybe they had a werewolf like yours."

Jack grinned. "No one's got a dog like mine. So, the shooter would have to have another way in. And check this out." Jack quickly sketched the door and a person standing in front of it. "This would be the height of an average shooter. Mei's report said the gun was held at this level." He drew a red line at a forty-five-degree angle.

"Maybe the killer shot from the hip? Or they were crouching down?"

"Not with that tight of a shot group. There's no way anyone could be that accurate."

Ed puffed out his cheeks and exhaled. "Are you saying it was a little person? Or a kid?"

"No." Jack cleared his throat to cover his laugh.

"Then who?"

"Not a who. ADA."

"What's an ADA?"

"An Automated Delivery Assistant. Dr. Patel has one in the robotics lab."

"You mean that lunar lander-looking thing?"

"We used UGVs in Iraq. Unmanned Ground Vehicles. They're the same as ADAs, just bigger. It would be easy to modify ADA's arm to hold a pistol, especially for Dr. Patel, who also owns firearms."

Ed stood up. "So you think Navi sent her robot in? That's how she got by the dogs." Ed scratched the side of his chin. "But why not drive the thing to the front door?"

"The front of the house has steps," Jack said.

Ed clapped both of his hands to the sides of his head. "Now it all clicks. But what about the other guy? Is Oscar in on it?"

"I don't know, but we have to treat him like a potential target. I sent a patrol car to pick him up. We need to bring him to the station for his protection."

Ed pointed at the whiteboard, took out his phone, and took a picture. "This is good."

"I typed up the warrant request and sent it to you," Jack said.

"I'll send Morrison an update. Good job, Jack."

Jack followed Ed out of the room, but when they reached the branch in the hallway, Ed stopped.

"It may be better if I speak with Morrison *mano a mano*. You know what I mean? That way, he'll be a little more relaxed. You said it yourself. We're talking about WRE, and Bob's an elected official. Not that politics would sway his opinion, but trust me on this one."

Jack didn't trust Ed not to screw this up, but despite his better judgment, he nodded. If Ed shot himself in the foot or stuck his foot in his mouth, Jack could always explain the reasons for the warrant to the Sheriff later.

Ed snapped his fingers, patted Jack on the back, and strolled over to the Sheriff's office with a spring in his step.

Jack headed to his locker. If they fast-tracked this warrant, he'd want to be wearing his vest.

Jack ran down the mental list of defects of body armor.

The vest is only bullet-resistant. Larger-caliber and high-velocity bullets can still perforate the plates. The vest only covers vital organs. It doesn't make you invisible or impenetrable.

He created the list in his head when he first got to Iraq. He made it after the first firefight. They lost three men that day, and four were wounded. All of them wore vests and felt invincible when they reached the battleground, Jack included.

That night, after he got back, he felt about as powerful as a blade of grass. Ronnie Johnson had gone through boot camp with Jack. They'd trained together for months, eaten at the same table, slept in the same barracks, and become friends.

Ronnie was the first to fall. They were walking down a street, and Ronnie stumbled back a step. He stared at Jack with an odd look on his face. "Didn't hurt," he said before dropping to his knees.

Dead.

The sniper's bullet hit him between plates and pierced his heart.

People aren't bulletproof.

Neither are veterans.

"Jack?" Officer Kendra Darcey called to him, but she sounded very far away. "Are you okay?"

Jack closed his eyes, exhaled, then looked around.

Kendra stood beside him, her blue eyes rounded in concern.

He gave her a quick nod. "Everything's under control."

"Congratulations on the promotion. You deserve it." Kendra smiled. The four-inch scar that ran from the corner of her chin to her eyebrow stood out. Only a few people knew how she'd gotten it, and Jack was one of them. While walking with her enormous dog, the dog spotted a coyote and bolted after it. The retractable leash snapped and caught her in the face, and the whip mark never healed quite right.

But that wasn't the kind of story that earned a rookie cop respect. She told Jack she got it in a fight with four guys during a bust, but he knew it was a lie. He called her on it, but he also gave her a way to tweak the truth and make it sound cool: She was injured training a K-9 unit. They became good friends after that.

"Thanks. Are you starting your shift?" Jack asked.

"About to. What's up?"

"I'm hoping Morrison comes through on a warrant. I can't think of anyone I'd rather have covering my back. You want in?"

Kendra nodded rapidly, sending her blond ponytail bobbing. The twenty-six-year-old was an all-around athlete and an adrenaline junkie. "Hell yeah, I got your six. Is this a standby to standby, or should I get full battle rattle?"

Jack chuckled at how quickly Kendra, former Army, slipped back into grunt speak. "Suspect is armed and considered dangerous, so gear up."

"Full battle rattle it is!"

Jack patted her on the back as he exited the lockers, grateful she didn't ask about his zoning out.

Sheriff Morrison met him in the hallway, with Ed at his side. "Hey, Jack. I just met with Ed, and his theory is solid, so I've fast-tracked the warrant. He suggested we pull you in at this point to plan how to execute it. I trust your judgment but still want you to run it by me before implementing it."

Jack nodded but stopped listening after the Sheriff said it was Ed's theory.

"Good." Bob clapped Ed on the shoulder. "Great work, Ed. Fantastic job."

The muscles in Jack's back tightened, setting off a chain reaction. He lifted his chin and flexed the muscle along his jaw.

Ed took a step back. "I had to rush to explain things to him. But don't worry about it, buddy. I promise I'll let him know that this was a team effort. I'll make sure he knows your contribution."

My contribution? You spent your time getting your car fixed while I did all the work, and now you want all the credit?

Jack didn't trust his voice not to scream in Ed's face, so he pressed his lips tightly together.

"Trust me." Ed smiled as he slipped past Jack. "After we bring in Navi, I'll explain everything to Bob."

Jack cracked his neck and rolled his shoulders, forcing himself to let Ed's credit stealing go. They were going after an armed shooter suspected of killing two men. Jack had to focus on that.

If Jack didn't get his head in the game, he might not be coming home.

40

Jack waited by himself in his car outside the technology center, tapping the folded warrant against the steering wheel. He wanted to notify the campus police, verify Dr. Patel was in her office, and head in to arrest her. But Ed insisted on stopping by the administration office to alert the dean, Lorina Chaffin, before serving the warrant. Ed wanted to give her a personal explanation before potentially causing a campus scene.

The compromise was that Jack would wait at the tech center in case someone tipped Dr. Patel off, and she tried to flee. But that meant that Kendra and the rest of the backup officers had to remain out of site to not alert the doctor.

Jack's phone buzzed. He was hoping it would be Alice, but it was a call from Ed.

"It went great," Ed said in a deeper than normal voice. "Dean Chaffin gave us permission to execute the warrant. I'm on my way with her and will set up a command op center in the parking lot."

Jack hated non-military people trying to sound like they knew what they were talking about. He didn't have the time or patience to explain that you either had a command center or an op center, and you couldn't just smash the terms together, hoping they sounded good.

"Did the dean verify that Dr. Patel is in her office? Her car is not here."

"Yes. Her secretary—" Ed covered the phone, and Jack could only hear muffled voices— "sorry, her assistant checked, and yes, Dr. Patel is in her office right now. The robotics lab is empty."

"You're sure?"

There was another moment of muffled dialogue before Ed spoke again. "They're sure. Roger. Over."

"I'm on it." Smiling, Jack shoved open his door and clicked on his microphone. "Kendra, is everybody in place?"

"We are ready, steady. Are we a go?" Excitement filled Kendra's voice.

"Green light. Move in and meet me out front."

Jack jogged up the steps and waited on top for Kendra and the other officers to respond. He wanted to keep things as secure as possible without escalating the situation. It was always a balancing act. If he brought too few people, critics would say he was under-prepared. If he brought too many, the same critics would say the police were storming the college.

Jack didn't care about the politics of policing. He decided based solely on safety.

Kendra pulled up out front with Officers Brian Hicks and Lamar Goodman. Hicks was a good cop with nearly ten years of service. Goodman was a rookie.

Jack had Goodman and Hicks wait at the top of the stairs. Two people showing up to question someone was intimidating enough. Four cops coming to talk to you would make anyone panic.

Kendra followed Jack inside and up to the second floor. Jack opened the door to the lab. No one was inside, but the hum from all the electronics sounded like a beehive. In the room's corner, the ADA sat plugged into a charging station.

While making his way to the storeroom door, Jack's curiosity got the better of him. He glanced at the ADA as he passed by, moving over to get a close-up view of the robot. The lights on the back blinked a steady beat of green flashes. The robotic arm was retracted, hiding the grip Jack had noticed earlier.

Jack squatted down, stared at the tire tread, and broke into a broad grin. A piece of gravel was embedded in the tread of the middle tire. That would be a huge win if they could match the rock in the ADA's tread to the stone driveway at Dr. Chen's cabin. If anything, it showed that someone had taken the robot outside the lab.

Standing up, Jack signaled Kendra he was heading to the rear door. Kendra fell in behind him, her hand touching his shoulder to let him know exactly where she was. They moved as one. They had previously trained together when Jack was an officer and, like two dance partners, fell right back into sync.

"Sheriff's Department," Jack called out as he opened the door.

Jack checked the right side of the hallway while Kendra scanned the left.

Clear.

Dr. Patel's office was the first door on the right. Jack stopped before the entrance, using the wall as cover, and waited for Kendra to place a hand on his shoulder.

Jack knocked twice.

No one answered.

He listened. The hum of electronics sounded like the angry bees were still swarming around the hive, but no other sound came from the office.

"Sheriff's Department," Jack called out as he opened the door.

The room was empty.

Kendra swore.

"Bathrooms," Jack said, backing out of the office and heading to the only other doors in the hallway.

They repeated their informal breaching procedure in the women's room. It, too, was deserted. They checked the men's room just in case, but no one was there either.

Jack clicked his microphone. "Ed, are you there?"

"I'm in position," Ed said.

"Dr. Patel is not here," Jack said.

There was a muffled conversation. "The dean's calling her secr—assistant now. Hold on."

"Hold on?" Kendra mouthed.

"Goodman, Hicks, meet us on the second floor," Jack ordered.

Jack and Kendra headed back through the robotics lab and out into the main hallway.

Jack waved Goodman and Hicks over while he waited for an update from Ed.

"I asked that secretary to call over there. I swear I did," Ed said. "But now she's saying she just checked the schedule, and Dr. Patel was supposed to be in her office."

Jack clenched his hands. "I need everyone to fan out and look for Dr. Patel. Goodman, you stay with the thing that looks like a lunar rover in the next room. Don't let anyone near it. Hicks, take the third floor. Kendra has this floor, and I'll take the first." As everyone headed in separate directions, Jack relayed their movements to Ed. "We're going to clear this building. Get a car over to Dr. Patel's house."

"Will do. That secretary totally screwed this up."

"What matters now is finding Dr. Patel before she's in the wind," Jack said.

While the others rushed to follow Jack's orders, he headed for the stairs.

"Oh, my, oh, my." Ed whistled. "Look who just drove into the parking lot. If it isn't the good Dr. Patel."

"Wait for us, Ed," Jack said.

"This ain't my first rodeo, Jack. Besides, I think she sees me."

Jack sprinted forward. When he reached the top of the stairs, the aquarium-sized windows gave him an unobstructed view of the lot. Dr. Patel's blue sedan was slowly circling the parked cars.

Ed ran forward and stopped directly in front of the sedan with his arm outstretched. The warrant in his hand flapped in the breeze like some impotent magic wand.

Jack's legs pounded like pistons as he thundered down the stairs. He sprinted across the foyer, his arms jolting as he shoved the front doors of the tech center open.

The engine of Dr. Patel's car roared, the rear tires spun, and the car raced forward.

Ed tried to run, but it was too late.

The front bumper of the car crashed into Ed's legs. He slammed onto the hood, his body cracking the windshield as he windmilled over the vehicle. Ed's body landed on the tar with a sickening thud.

The sedan skidded to a stop. Through the shattered windshield, Jack caught of glimpse of Dr. Patel behind the wheel.

Jack drew his service pistol. "Freeze!"

The car's tires spun, spewing smoke and rubber into the air. Not knowing if Dr. Patel would back up and run over his injured partner lying on the road, Jack fired.

Bullets ripped through the windshield. The sedan rocketed forward. The car swerved, clipped a silver sports car, and rounded the parking lot's exit.

Jack dropped the magazine from his gun and slapped a fresh one into place.

The doors behind him smashed open, and Kendra raced out.

"Call in an ambulance. Ed's down," Jack shouted. "I'm going after Patel." Sprinting for his car, Jack glanced into the parking lot.

Ed was lying on his side and wasn't moving.

Jack yanked open the door of his cruiser and started the engine. Ramming the car into drive, he unleashed the power of his Charger, and the chase was on.

Hitting the lights and grabbing the microphone, Jack spoke calmly as his speedometer raced toward triple digits. "This is Detective Stratton heading west on Franklin following a blue, two-door sedan. License plate 546-RO80. Vehicle has front and side damage. Involved in officer assault. Request backup."

While dispatch relayed his information, Jack pulled up the GPS. A turn a quarter mile ahead forked toward the college observatory or a residential neighborhood. The road to the observatory was a dead end, but once Dr. Patel took that right, Jack would have to follow policy and slow down.

Jack pinned the gas pedal to the floor. He loved to drive fast, and now he had a reason to. Ahead, he caught sight of the sedan. Dr. Patel sped toward the fork in the road but cut left to Jack's surprise.

"Suspect has turned south on Ash Valley," Jack relayed into the mic.

Why did she turn left?

Jack's foot eased slightly off the gas. He had her boxed in. He could wait for backup.

Unless she was headed for the observatory to take a hostage, which was a leap, but other than that, Jack couldn't think of any reason someone familiar with the route would head toward the observatory. It was a dead end.

Jack sped back up. The Charger slid into the first windy curve and clung to the road. He smiled. The new tires were a wedding present from Tank, another squad mate with an odd sense of humor, but they were certainly coming in handy now.

The road to the observatory twisted and turned around the sheer drop-offs. Some sections had guardrails, but at this speed, they would do little to prevent him from plummeting to his death.

Through the trees, Jack saw the sedan slam on its brakes and skid to a stop. The reverse lights clicked on. The sedan turned around and stopped.

Jack stopped too. He had been in a head-on collision once; he didn't want to do it again. "Suspect has changed direction. Now headed north on Ash Valley. I'm blocking her in."

"Backup on its way."

Jack shoved open his door, and he heard the sirens. They were close. Probably Goodman and Hicks, but they wouldn't be here in time to help him.

Jack grabbed the shotgun from the console and got out of the car.

The sedan's tires spun, sending smoke billowing out behind the car. It shot forward, barreling down the hill.

As a police officer, Jack had made an oath to protect and serve. As a husband, he'd made a vow to grow old with Alice. There wasn't any way he would let Patel keep him from doing that.

With his car sitting at an angle, he moved behind the front wheel to use the engine block as cover. Taking a shooter's stance, Jack readied the shotgun.

Sweat rolled down his back.

The sound of the sedan racing around the turn grew louder.

Sun warmed the skin on the back of his neck. It gleamed off the windshield of the oncoming car and sparkled.

Jack fired a warning shot.

The car headed straight for him.

Jack's finger rested on the trigger. He slowly let the air out of his lungs.

The car jerked to the right, the tires screeching like a hawk swooping in for the kill as they dug into the tar. A piece of the broken fender fell off and clattered along the road.

Jack shifted his sights, but the sedan wasn't headed for him. It barreled straight into the guardrail. The car's front bumper crumpled back into the tires. The guardrail bent, and the car sailed over it. For a moment, it looked like it was flying. It was surreal as it cleared the treetops, defying gravity for a few seconds.

Then its nose tipped down, and it fell like a stone.

Branches snapped, metal shrieked, and glass shattered.

Jack raced over and stood on the edge of the cliff. Fifty yards below, the car lay on its roof, the wheels still spinning. The impact crushed the vehicle, and, seeing how the airbags deployed when the car struck the guardrail, there was no way Dr. Patel survived. Jack tipped his head up, stared at the clear sky, and prayed that Ed would.

41

Jack waited on a bench outside his partner's hospital room in the hallway. Because he had fired his service weapon in the line of duty, he hadn't been allowed to come directly to the hospital to check on Ed. Instead, he spent two hours getting interviewed, processed, and giving his report of the shooting. Kendra confirmed Dr. Patel was in the car, and she was deceased, but until the fire department removed her body from the wreckage, he didn't know if any of his shots struck her.

Jack exhaled and let his head tip back until it rested against the wall.

Three doctors were dead. And for what? Money? Pride? Probably a combination of those things. What a waste.

Jack stared down at his steady hands. He was a little surprised at that. Maybe he hadn't shot her. He only fired to save Ed's life. She tried to kill Ed when she hit him the first time. There was the distinct possibility that she would have put the car in reverse and driven over him again.

Still, she was dead. Jack became a cop to save lives, not end them.

"How are you holding up?" Sheriff Morrison asked.

Jack snapped to attention. He'd been so preoccupied with his own thoughts he didn't hear him approach. "I'm fine, sir. How is Ed?"

"Broken fibula and a concussion. He'll be out of commission for a while but should make a full recovery. I didn't have the heart to tell him about his car."

"What about his car?"

"You know the one Dr. Patel sideswiped on the way out of the parking lot?"

Jack's lip curled. "I thought Ed's was red?"

"He just had it painted silver." Morrison gave a tight smile. "You two did great work on this. With Ed sidelined, I'm counting on you to wrap everything up."

"I'm concerned about Oscar Chambers. We've yet to contact him."

"Oscar showed up at his apartment to pick up some things, and uniforms spotted him. He's fine."

"Did they bring him in? I wanted to question him. He lied to me about trying to sell the project to Eagle 247 Technology."

"There's no reason to question him now. Dr. Patel killed Dr. Mobley and Chan."

Jack raised an eyebrow.

"Don't give me that look, Stratton. Come on. I brought you on the force to make my life easier, but the look on your face is telling me the opposite is about to happen."

"There are still unanswered questions, sir. Carl Wilson could be involved and..." Jack's voice trailed off. He couldn't put his finger on what bothered him, but something was there. "I want to speak to Mei. Can you have her fast-track the autopsy on Dr. Patel?"

Bob rubbed his temples with his thumb and forefinger. "I will, but can you please explain to me why? And let me be straight with you. I know it was you who connected the dots of Dr. Chen's murder back to Patel."

"Whaaat? Ah—" Jack put his hand to his mouth to stop the sputter.

"Ed just admitted it to me. I don't know if it's because he's on morphine or some other reason, but he's in there baring his soul. So why, if you're the one who figured out that Patel was the killer, do you still want to bring in Oscar Chambers for questioning?"

"Detective Clark taught me never to rule anyone out. Until I'm one hundred percent convinced, I'm not going to. Something bothers me."

Morrison reached into his pocket and took out a small cylinder. He emptied the contents into his hand and popped them into his mouth. "Antacid." He explained. "I've got a bad feeling I'm going to need to pick up more."

"So, I can keep digging?"

Morrison nodded. "Do what you think is right. It's your investigation now, Jack."

42

Alone in his apartment, Jack stood at the kitchen counter, carefully removing mug shots he printed at the station. Lady sat on the couch, chewing on a weird piece of wood, watching him.

"Witness lineups are the worst thing." Maybe to break the silence, or perhaps because he was lonely, he said the words aloud. "You stand there, staring at the witness because you don't want your eyes to give away who you think the suspect is."

Lady stopped chewing for a moment and stared at him.

"The only picture I have of Carl Wilson is a mug shot, so I've got to pick other photos where the guy is in a mug shot. Why, you ask? So some snarky defense attorney doesn't say I'm prejudicing the witness. They could still try to twist things and say I'm subliminally telling the witness that a criminal committed the act, but since I don't have another photo, what can I do?"

Lady went back to chewing.

"I'll want to say to the defense lawyer, well, maybe my being a detective and asking the witness if they saw this guy at the scene of a homicide gives away the fact that I think he's a criminal too, but that lawyer will cut me off, and the judge will say blah, blah, blah. Detective Stratton, please stick to the question."

Lady hopped off the couch and trotted over to the door.

Jack's heart skipped a beat, hoping it was Alice.

A moment later, someone knocked, dashing his hope.

Making a mental note to pick up a door camera, Jack checked the peephole. Finn stood outside, staring straight ahead.

Jack opened the door and held out his hand. "Hey, buddy. I'm sorry again."

Finn swatted Jack's hand away, stepped forward, and hugged him. "Shut up, Stratton." Finn clapped him hard on the back, then let go. "I'm a moron. You've been nothing but good to me, and I go off on you like that? I'm the one who's sorry."

"Don't just stand in the hallway apologizing. Come in."

Finn stood his ground, staring at the carpet.

Lady trotted behind him and nudged him with her head.

"Did you train the beast to do that?" Finn walked in, and Jack closed the door.

"Where's Annie?"

"She's down in the car making hotel reservations. There was a car accident at the campus. The insurance company wants us to look into it."

Jack exhaled. "Why don't you call Annie to come on up? You two are sleeping here. And before you argue, you need to hear me out. I need information about that accident. I was there." Jack headed into the kitchen. "You want a drink?"

"A water would be great. I'll text Annie." Finn said as he typed on his phone.

Lady took her wooden dog toy off the couch, and Finn sat where it had been. "Your werewolf is not only well trained but quite polite."

"That would be Alice's influence."

Finn stroked Lady's head. "I didn't mean any of that garbage I said. I saw you and freaked out. Not because of you." He stared at his prosthetic and chuckled lightly. "Do you know I thought I was tapping my foot? They call it a phantom itch. Your mind tricks you, and you think the part you're missing is still there."

Jack let the silence stretch on. He'd give Finn all the time he needed to gather his thoughts, or he'd remain silent if Finn wanted to stop talking. When it came to PTSD, Jack knew he wasn't the only one with it.

"My life is finally turning around," Finn continued after a moment. "My job is great. And I really, really like Annie. Seeing you there made me think something went wrong. I freaked. It was like something was hitting me, and I was helpless to stop it. I thought I was going to lose everything all over again. Do you ever feel like that?"

Jack brought Finn a glass of water. "Today, as a matter of fact. I thought I was going to die."

"Did you freeze up?"

Jack took a long drink, some water spilling onto his chin. He wiped it off with the back of his hand. "No. I fired four rounds."

"I have no idea how you can put yourself back into that situation." Finn set his water glass down. "Is that what caused the car crash?"

"I don't know if I hit the driver or not. I fired, she took off, and I gave chase. She drove toward the college observatory, then turned back around. I set up a roadblock. I don't know if she tried to go around my car and lost control, but it looked like she had purposefully smashed through the guardrail."

"Let me get Annie up here so we can record your statement," Finn said.

The water in Jack's glass sloshed out as he flung his arms wide. "You can't do that! I'm not talking on the record. This is an officer-involved shooting. You can't—"

"I won't. I won't." Finn stood up and put both hands on Jack's shoulders. "Brother, I won't. If you say all that was off the record, I won't ever mention it again.

"All I'm saying is anything I tell you on the record has to come through my delegate and the Sheriff. I'll help you, but let me clear it with them first."

Jack ran his hand through his hair and shook his head. "Sorry. Guess it was my turn to freak out."

"No worries. I get it. We should wear those 'combustible under pressure' warning labels plastered on gas cans." Finn chuckled.

Lady trotted over to the door. Someone tapped lightly.

"It's Annie," Finn said.

"Come in!" Jack shouted.

Finn patted his back as he walked past. "She's deaf."

"Sorry again!" Jack shook his head. "My day for being a moron."

Finn opened the door.

Annie stood in the hallway with a bright smile. She signed something to Finn, who gave her a thumbs-up.

"What did she say?" Jack asked.

"She wanted to know if I apologized for being a jerk."

"I didn't say jerk." Annie rubbed Lady's neck.

"She swore like a sailor," Finn said.

Annie stood up and playfully swatted his arm. "I did not, either."

"Are you two hungry?" Jack asked.

"You remember that training mission when Tank accidentally brought expired rations?"

"Yeah, I was ready to eat my socks by the time they hauled us out. Chicken and rice?"

They both nodded.

Jack started cooking while they unpacked. Once they were done, Finn began going over the accident report while Annie volunteered to take over the cooking. But Jack would hear nothing of it.

"No. You're my guests. Please help Finn. Look at the poor rooster pecking away. He needs all the help he can get!"

Annie laughed, gave a little wave, and crossed the room.

Finn and Annie sat side-by-side as they read the reports.

As Jack watched them, his heart ached for Alice. *Where was she? When was she coming home?*

"You okay, buddy?" Finn called out.

Jack flipped the chicken in the pan. "I'm fine. Hope you like your chicken a little crispy."

"I do," Annie said.

"You're incredible." Jack set down the spatula and started taking out plates. "From how far away can you read lips?"

Annie shrugged.

"If she can see your lips moving, don't say any secrets," Finn said.

Annie elbowed Finn in the ribs.

Finn signed something.

Annie shook her head and signed something back.

"This is not fair," Jack said. "I can tell something is going on, but not what." He shut the burners off.

Finn's lips pressed together. He glanced at Annie, then said, "You don't have to answer this, but I wanted to ask one question about the car accident. Was Dr. Patel sitting in the driver's seat with her hands on the wheel?"

Jack scrunched up his face, pretending to concentrate. "No. She was driving with her feet, I think. What kind of question is that? Of course, she was driving with her hands. How else would she drive?"

"It was a self-driving car, so we need to make certain," Finn said. "Welcome to the future."

"Hold on!" Jack's hands flew to both sides of his head. "When she was at the police station, the car pulled out of the space and to her by itself. I thought they could only do something like that and stay in their own lane like high-end cruise control. Are you telling me they can drive-drive?"

"Dr. Patel's car is a brand new model. It was very sophisticated. But if you saw her driving with her hands on the wheel, then she was driving."

Jack stopped in the middle of the living room, trying to picture the scene. "Her front windshield broke when she hit Ed, and I caught a glimpse of her in the driver's seat. I fired. The car came forward." He closed his eyes. "I couldn't see the wheel then or her hands."

"What about later?" Finn asked. "You said you set up a roadblock, and she drove straight at you."

"The sun was behind me, and it bounced off the windshield." Jack's mouth fell open. "I don't think her hands were on the wheel! She was in the driver's seat, but her arms were at her sides."

"The car wouldn't drive off the road by itself, would it?" Annie asked.

Jack shook his head. "No. Not unless someone else was controlling it." He grabbed his keys off the table, snatched up his phone, and raced toward the door. "I've got to go. Oscar Chambers is still out there, and so is the killer."

43

Alice paced the bedroom floor as she texted Jack. She was now officially avoiding speaking to him. He had a built-in lie detector, and she felt so guilty she'd be sure to set it off. How long was finding her grandfather going to take? She left thinking it would be a few days, but now Kiku wanted to perform recon tonight.

They rented an Airbnb identical to the Airbnb next door. Both homes were enormous, expensive, waterfront properties right on the beach.

"Wear a bathing suit," Kiku called out from her bedroom. "Or something that shows a lot of skin."

"I don't think I packed anything like that," Alice said.

A moment later, Kiku, wearing a dark jogging outfit, walked into Alice's room carrying two outfits on hangers. One was a bikini, the other short shorts and a crop top.

"Ah," Alice pointed at the clothes. "Where are we going, and what are we doing?"

"You are going for a walk on the beach."

"And why do you want me to do that half naked?"

Kiku crossed her arms. "You sound like you do not trust me."

"During your last plan, you offered me up as a prize." Alice looked at the ceiling. "Speaking of which, is Fausto still upstairs?"

"Yes. I just checked on him. He is sleeping."

Alice pressed her lips together and raised an eyebrow.

"Besides being tied to the bed, he is fine. And to answer your other question, in order to find out if Vidal is next door, I need to draw his security detail's focus away from me."

"And onto me, half naked and walking down the beach?"

"I would prefer that you strut. Get dressed, please."

Alice wasn't sure if Kiku added the please out of sincerity or if she noticed Alice bristle at being eye candy. Holding up the skimpy outfits, Alice settled on the shorts and top.

Kiku met her at the back door, clicking on a fanny pack.

Alice was about to joke about her looking like a soccer mom until she realized that Kiku probably had a gun inside.

"You are beautiful bait," Kiku said.

Alice frowned and tugged at her shorts. "What am I supposed to be doing out there? It's kinda late to be picking up shells."

Kiku glanced around the kitchen, marched over to the counter, and picked up a complimentary bottle of wine the host had left and a glass. "We will keep things simple. Here." She handed the items to Alice and then took a beach towel off the rack next to the door and draped it over Alice's shoulder. "All you need to do is find a spot in the light from their house and sit and drink."

"Just sit and drink? Isn't that odd?"

"Look off to the sea. Be a mystery. The men will wonder what you are thinking, and that is what I want."

"That's a little weak motivation."

"We are not filming a movie. You sit on the blanket. Once I

am in place and you have the security detail's attention, you will go for a swim."

"A swim? In what?"

"The bikini I gave you. That is the purpose of the two outfits. You will remove the shorts, and the guard will call others to see you."

"You have a really low opinion of people."

"Jack once told me of a 911 call from the Dayside Apartment Complex regarding a possible kidnapping. It took 1 eleven minutes for an officer to respond. On a different day, from the same complex, someone reported a drunk, woman skinny-dipping in the pool. Six police cruisers showed up in under three minutes. A fire truck arrived soon after—all like moths to a flame."

Alice rolled her eyes and stomped back to the bedroom to change again.

Fifteen minutes later, she was sitting on a beach towel, staring out at the ocean and drinking a glass of wine. She was halfway through the first glass when she pulled her knees up to her chest and wrapped her arms around her legs.

The warm, salty air made her think of the Bahamas and Jack's powerful arms cradling her to his broad chest. She'd never been happier, and now that everything was going so perfectly, she risked screwing it all up by lying to him. She'd never lied before—

That was a lie, too.

Alice hadn't told Jack when Kelly, his old girlfriend, had cheated on him. He'd been deployed to Iraq then, and Chandler had just been killed. Alice and Michelle decided it was best to wait to tell Jack. Even so, she'd felt guilty withholding the truth. Alice wasn't doing that now. Now she was straight-up lying.

She gulped down her glass and poured another. But what could she do? He just started his new job. And his first case is a murder investigation. She wasn't telling him for his own good, right?

Down at the water's edge, couples strolled hand in hand. Young and old took advantage of the moonless night, stopping to kiss as the ocean lapped their feet.

The minutes stretched on. Alice finished her second glass and stared down at her phone. What was taking Kiku so long?

She poured herself another drink, and the bottle had run dry. Cocking one eyebrow, she shook the bottle, but it was empty. "I thought these things hold like five glasses." The wineglass Kiku had picked out was big, but could Alice have drunk the entire bottle?

Alice sipped her last glass as she searched the internet for the answer.

"I was right. This bottle must be extra small or something." She finished her drink, and the phone in her hand vibrated.

"Do not turn around," Kiku said. "All eyes are on you. Go for a swim."

Alice stood up and swayed like a tourist on the deck of a ship. Following Kiku's orders, she didn't look behind her, but the sound of laughter floated in the breeze. Stripping down to her bikini, she slid down her shorts, pulled off her top, and a wave of dizziness and shame washed over her.

She stumbled toward the water, eager to hide beneath the sea. The cold water sent chills racing up her body. She strode deeper, and she dove in.

No sooner had she gone under that she came up sputtering and splashing back to the shore.

The swim was a bust, but she was Kiku's distraction. Alice had no idea if Kiku would do anything more than recon, but she couldn't put her friend in danger or let her down. Alice did her best Baywatch slow-motion jog back to her towel on the sand but didn't pick it up. Instead, she made a show of using her hands like a squeegee to wipe the water off her legs, arms, and torso.

Having been infatuated with Jack since she was a young teenager, Alice had never had a boyfriend. She had no clue what to do to attract a man, let alone how to deliberately use her untapped sex appeal to distract several. Scenes from movies and TV shows of women posing and tossing their hair flashed in her muddled mind. Alice wondered if anyone would actually do that.

The wine made her head fuzzy, and she leaned slightly forward, shaking her hair and then tossing it back.

The men's voices from the house grew louder.

Her display was working! She didn't feel sexy at all, but she was a distraction. Now she had another problem. She wanted to run back to the house and use the bathroom.

"Alice?" A familiar voice called to her from the direction of the water. "We thought that was you."

Alice gasped and grabbed the large beach towel, knocking over the empty wine bottle and glass. She hurriedly wrapped the towel around herself as she stood trapped in a nightmare. Standing before her were Ted and Laura Stratton. Her new in-laws.

Short and heavy-set, Ted Stratton commanded your attention. Maybe it was the years of teaching math or how he carried himself, but when her father-in-law entered the room, the focus always shifted to him.

Alice's mother-in-law was a small, slender woman with hazel eyes, which were now rounded in concern as she stared at the empty bottle of wine.

"Why, hello." Alice swallowed. "What are you doing here?"

"We were about to ask you the same thing." Ted smiled, adjusting his glasses. "Is Jack with you?"

"He's working." Holding the towel to her chest, Alice picked up the bottle and glass. "I'm so proud of him. I didn't want to disturb him. He's already on a big case!" Her last words came out far louder than she intended.

"We're very proud of him, too." Laura took Ted's arm. "Is everything all right between you two?"

"Fine! I've never been happier. Your husband, I mean your son, who is my husband, is the best son you could have." Alice smiled as her feet shifted in the sand.

Ted and Laura exchanged a nervous glance.

"Did you drive here, Alice?" Ted asked.

"No. I'm staying there." Using the wine bottle as a wand of sorts, she pointed at the enormous seaside Airbnb.

"You rented that?" Laura stepped closer to her husband. "For just yourself?"

"No. My friend rented it. I never would stay in someplace so expensive. I don't even know how much they spent. Looking at it from here kinda puts it in perspective. You know?"

"Oh, a friend from the wedding? Do we know them?"

"Yes, I think you might. I don't mean to seem impolite, but I was ready to race back to use the restroom."

"We'll walk with you." Laura pulled on Ted's arm, and the three hurried toward the house.

"And what are you doing here?" Alice asked, hoping to change the subject while doing her best not to zigzag.

"We decided to take a little romantic seaside getaway," Ted said.

"That's nice. Are you staying close by?"

"We've got a little place more inland," Laura said.

Alice jogged up the back steps, pulled the slider open, and pointed at the kitchen table. "Make yourselves at home. I'll only be a minute." Trying to stay upright on the slippery tiles, Alice held onto the wall as she sped to the bathroom.

Oh, no. Oh, no. Oh, no.

Nothing could be worse than being found drunk, in a bikini, on a beach by your in-laws while your new husband was busy working and didn't know her whereabouts. On top of all that, they must think she's blowing their money on this huge rental.

After finishing up, washing her hands, and rinsing her mouth, Alice darted for her room to change. "There's water in the fridge!" she called out. "Help yourself to anything!"

Pulling on the most modest dress she could find, Alice strolled back into the kitchen.

Ted and Laura sat side by side, looking more like two judges at a parole board hearing who was about to pass judgment.

"Alice." Laura pulled the chair beside her away from the table. "Would you mind if we had a little chat?"

"Perhaps I should step out," Ted said, rising.

"Actually…" Alice stared at the back door as if Kiku would appear at any moment. "There's something I need to do. I left my friend back on the beach, and I should get back."

Laura took Ted's hand. "We want you to know that you can talk to us about anything, Alice. You're family now. Is something going on between you and Jack? The first year of marriage can be a challenge."

"You can say that again," Ted said, quickly adding, "It wasn't for us, but for some people, it's challenging."

Laura shot him a sideways glance. "It was for us, too. Marriage takes a lot of give. It's not easy, but we want you to know that we're here to help."

Upstairs, something banged.

"Is your friend here?" Laura asked.

Alice closed one eye and tried to concentrate. Kiku was on the beach. No one else was here—except Fausto!

"Maybe?" Alice jumped up, and the room spun. "I'll be right back."

"Do you want me to come with you?" Ted called after her.

"No, thanks!" Alice raced down the hallway, grabbed the railing, and took the stairs two at a time. She rushed to the bedroom. A muffled conversation in Spanish came from within.

Alice jerked the door open.

Fausto was gagged with his hands tied to the headboard, but his legs were free. He shifted halfway off the bed, so his left leg was on the floor. A TV on the wall played a soap opera.

Panicking, Alice picked the lamp off the dresser and raised it over her head.

Fausto mumbled something through the gag and shook his head. Like a horse counting, he stomped on the floor with his left leg. His bare foot was inches away from a television remote.

"Get back on the bed!" Alice whispered, holding the lamp like a bat.

Fausto pulled his legs onto the mattress.

Alice snatched the remote off the floor and handed it to him.

Using his thumb, Fausto changed the channel to a soccer game and relaxed.

"Be quiet!" Alice said, setting the lamp back down.

Fausto nodded. With his right hand, he flashed her a thumbs-up, and his attention went back to the TV.

Alice slipped out of the room and dashed back down the stairs. She was woozy and out of breath as she hurried into the kitchen. "I left a window open. Sea breeze."

"We've been talking," Ted said, taking out his phone. "If you think it will help, I can call Jack."

"No!" Alice blurted out. "We're good. Really. This is just a complicated situation. I can't talk about it right now." Alice took Laura's outstretched hand. "I need to ask you both a favor. Please don't tell Jack you saw me."

Ted crossed his arms. "I can't do that, Alice. That boy's my son, and I promised him two things the day we brought him home. One, I'd always love him. Two, I'd never lie to him."

Alice shook her head. "You don't understand. I just mean,

don't tell him right now. Wait until I get home. He just started this job, and I don't want him to worry or put in for time off. You know Jack. He would drop everything and drive here if you told him where I was."

Ted and Laura looked at each other, a silent conversation taking place between them.

"It sounds like you're keeping secrets from Jack," Laura said.

"Who is this friend of yours?" Ted asked. "Are they in trouble?"

Alice took a deep breath. She couldn't tell them about Kiku, or Jack would go through the roof.

Footsteps in the hall startled all three. "Mr. and Mrs. Stratton." Kiku smiled as she strolled into the kitchen. "What a pleasant surprise."

"Oh, you're the friend," Laura exhaled and seemed to relax somewhat.

"Yes. I apologize for the mystery. I am dealing with a personal issue, and I asked Alice not to say anything to Jack about it."

Ted grimaced and didn't uncross his arms. "If I can help, I will. But I can't lie to Jack."

Laura placed a gentle hand on his arm.

"No, Laura. I made a promise to our son. I won't break my word for Kiku, Alice, or you."

"Can you just wait until I get back?" Alice pleaded. "Two days. That's all."

Laura squeezed Ted's arm.

Ted stared at Alice for what seemed an eternity. She held her breath, praying he'd give her that time.

"Two days," Ted said. "After that, I have to tell Jack where I saw you and who you were with."

44

Jack stood on the front step of Oscar Chambers's apartment and pounded on the door.

The living room light snapped on, and a moment later, Oscar's roommate, Jim Parson, peeked out the window. Seeing Jack, he jerked the shade shut.

Jack stared at the knob, expecting it to turn. Instead, the light inside blinked out. Jack pounded again. "Police! Open the door, now!"

The light turned on once more, and the door opened a crack. Jim's eyes were bloodshot, and he reeked of marijuana. "No one's home."

"You are."

"I mean besides me."

"I don't care if you've been smoking dope. I need to speak with Oscar right now. Where is he?"

"I wasn't smoking anything."

Jack stepped forward, and Jim backed up. The door swung open, revealing the messy living room. "You've got two choices, Jim. I drug test the large bong on the coffee table, and the little plastic bag next to it you'll claim is oregano and arrest you."

"Or?" Jim asked, rubbing his nose.

"Or you tell me where Oscar is."

"I don't know. Honest. I swear. Is he in trouble?"

"He's in danger, Jim. Three of the people who worked on the project with him are dead."

"Dead-dead? Killed dead? No way!"

"D-E-A-D," Jack said each letter as if giving the stoner a lesson.

Jim's hands went to the side of his head, and he started rocking back and forth. "Oh, man. He said everything was cool now."

"When did you see him last?"

"A couple of hours ago. He stopped by to get some stuff and then headed out."

Jim's recount matched what the Sheriff told him outside Ed's hospital room. Uniform was done with questions, but Jack was far from through. "What stuff? Drugs? And like I said, I don't care about the drugs. I'm trying to find Oscar."

"I rolled him a couple of joints. Small doobies." Jim held up his hand with his thumb and forefinger pinched to emphasize the narrow width. "He grabbed some clothes and split. He didn't say where or with who."

"Try to call him."

"Okay. Okay."

Jack followed to a door at the end of a hallway and into a bedroom that looked like a clothes and junk food wrapper bomb had gone off. Jim shoved a pile of clothes off a chair in front of the computer and wiggled the mouse.

"What are you doing?" Jack instinctively checked his watch. It was almost 11. "I need you to call him."

"I lost my phone. I'm gonna try a video call."

While Jack waited ankle-deep in the pile of laundry covering the floor, Jim tried to get the computer to work. After several failed attempts, Jim shook his head. "I think I gotta reboot and reinstall the app."

"I don't have time for that. Do you have that app that finds your phone?" Jack's eyes lit up. "Is Oscar's computer here?"

"It's in his room."

"Can you get into it? Do you know the password?"

"Yeah. Why?"

Jack dragged Jim out of the chair. "Because Oscar may have that app on his computer. If he does, we can find his phone."

"Oh," Jim nodded as he crossed the hall to a tidy bedroom. "How is that gonna help us call Oscar? Won't he have his phone on him?"

"Just log in, okay."

Jim powered up Oscar's computer and got to the main screen. Jack was about to sit down but realized if Jim did all the work, Jack could honestly say in court he had nothing to do with it, so he remained standing.

Jim double-clicked a little radar symbol.

A map appeared, and on the left-hand side of the screen, two devices were listed:

OSCAR'S COMPUTER — HOME

OSCAR'S PHONE — DARRINGTON. TODAY AT 10:37 PM

Jack stared at the large gray box on Winston Chapel Avenue.

"I don't know where that is," Jim said.

Jack patted him on the back. "I do. Good job, Jim. Lay off the dope, or it'll rot your brain."

~

Ten minutes later, Jack skidded to a stop in front of the Willow Park Apartments. The upscale residential units had a doorman during the day and security at night. Because of the time, it was a security guard who met Jack at the front door.

Jack flashed his badge. "I'm Detective Jack Stratton with the Sheriff's Department. I'm looking for Oscar Chambers. He's about six feet tall with wavy, dark hair. Hold on." Jack pulled out his phone and pulled up Oscar's social media site and a picture. "Have you seen this guy?"

The older guard reached into his pocket and removed his reading glasses. "I've seen him before, but not tonight. I started at 11:00, so he may have come in before I arrived."

"Do you know who he comes to see?"

"No. He's usually alone."

"Can I see the registry? It's important."

"I don't see any problem with that."

Jack followed the guard over to the desk. There were fifty units in the ten-story building, and his hope faded as Jack scanned the list of names. A quick scan didn't reveal anyone with the first name of Oscar's girlfriend—Bree—and none of the names beginning with B were even close.

"No luck?" the guard asked.

Jack shook his head. He could always pull the fire alarm or go door to door, but either tactic would make Morrison go ballistic. Just as he was about to give up, a familiar name jumped out at him—Sabrina Hall.

"Bree must be B-r-i. That can be a nickname for Sabrina, right?" Jack pondered aloud.

"I think so. But that's such a pretty name. Why would you shorten it? Have you seen the movie? Not that remake. The real one with Bogie, Hepburn, and Holden. I fell in love with Audrey the moment I saw her."

Jack nodded. To him, Alice had the same beguiling beauty as Audrey Hepburn. Pushing his longing for his missing wife aside, Jack headed for the elevator. "Do you need to come with me to 1001?"

"The penthouse?" The older man shook his head and took out a book. "I think I'll keep my head down and say I handed off responsibility to law enforcement."

"Smart man." Jack headed into the elevator and up to the top floor.

The carpeted hallway, accented with paintings and sculptures, screamed high-end and expensive. Considering Sabrina's position as CEO, that wasn't surprising. One thing that made Jack pause was that if Oscar and Sabrina were seeing each other, the age gap would be vast. Not just double digits, but she was twice his age.

He knocked on the door and waited.

After a few moments, a winded and smiling Sabrina Hall opened the door wearing a light pink bathrobe. "Detective Stratton. I must say that I'm surprised that you stopped by so late. To what do I owe this pleasure?"

"I need to speak with Oscar Chambers."

Besides a slight tightening around her lips, Sabrina's expression didn't change. "Why would he be here, Detective?"

"You must be a fantastic card player," Jack said, "But you just made two mistakes that tell me you're lying. I don't care why, but I need to speak with him—now."

"He's not here, nor has he ever been."

"The three other people involved in Dr. Mobley's project are dead."

"Yes." Sabrina leaned against the doorframe, her fingertips absentmindedly stroking the wood. "And I heard you caught the killer. Congratulations!" Her voice rose dramatically. "Another notch in your gun, Detective."

"Dr. Patel may not be the murderer."

Sabrina's smile faded.

Jack's eyes traveled over her shoulder, but he couldn't see far into the darkened apartment. "That's why I need to speak with Oscar—now."

Sabrina straightened up. "Are you here to warn Oscar or question him?"

"Both," Jack admitted. "Have him come out, or I'll have to call in for a warrant."

Sabrina shook her head. "I'm sorry, Detective, but he's really not here."

Jack shrugged and took out his phone.

Sabrina sighed and stepped aside, letting the door swing open. "You are quite obstinate."

"Some people say it's part of my charm."

Sabrina's penthouse was spectacular. The modern furniture had a European feel, and the apartment appeared ripped from the pages of Architectural Digest. A bottle of wine and two glasses sat on the sleek coffee table. The oversized couch faced the windows overlooking the city.

"So you're only partially lying," Jack said, facing Sabrina. "I take it Oscar left?"

She nodded but said, "I'm not saying anything."

"Do you know where he went?"

"Again, I'm not acknowledging he was even here, so I would check his apartment if I were you."

"So you have been dealing with Oscar. Did he try to sell you the project?"

"It's late. I am tired and have had a few drinks, so I am going to bed. Good night, Detective."

"Good night, Ms. Hall."

Jack didn't debate pressing her. She hadn't lawyered up, and there was nothing to gain by pushing the issue now. But one thing was sure. After he talked to Oscar, he needed to have a long chat with Bri.

45

Jack woke up bleary-eyed and wanting to go back to bed. After leaving Sabrina's, he'd gone to Oscar Chamber's apartment and come up empty. He tried in vain to track Oscar this morning. Jim Parsons may have told Oscar that Jack was using Oscar's phone to follow him, or Oscar figured it out. Either way, the tracking feature was now off.

Finn and Annie had left before he got up. Jack hurriedly got ready, taking a shower and grabbing a couple of hard-boiled eggs and a protein drink for breakfast. Grateful for his ever-present dog sitter, Jack dropped Lady off at Mrs. Stevens's and checked his phone for messages from Alice.

Zero voicemails. One text.

LUV + MISS U HOPE ERYTNGS GRT! CALL U PM XO

Why had his wife taken off? Was marriage not what she expected?

He tried to shift focus to his list instead of his woes. Grabbing his keys and the manila folder off the table, he headed for his first stop of what he expected would be a very long day.

Jack drove with the windows down, the wind washing over his face and drying his damp hair. Carl Wilson was missing, and Oscar Chambers was actively ducking him. Why? The fact Oscar didn't want to speak to law enforcement rocketed him to the top of the suspect list, but something about Oscar made it hard for Jack to believe he was a stone-cold killer.

But then, why was he on the run?

Jack turned onto the road leading in the campus's direction and sped up. Oscar wanted to sell the project to Eagle 247. Seeing how he was at Sabrina Hall's last night, it would appear he was positioning himself to do just that, along with other perks that went beyond the traditional business deal.

Stopping in front of Jodi's house, Jack snatched up the manila folder and headed up her walkway.

Despite it being eight o'clock in the morning, Jodi answered the door fully dressed, broom in one hand, a rag in the other, and still extremely pregnant. She smiled and said, "Nesting." As if that explained it all.

"Like a bird?"

"More generic mothering." Jodi blushed. "I want to make the house a home, if you know what I mean."

"I do. This should only take a moment. I put together a series of pictures I need you to look at. Take your time, and try to pick out the man you saw dropped off by the taxi outside Dr. Mobley's house."

Jodi leaned the broom against the wall and balled the rag in her hands.

Jack opened the folder, and her finger went straight to Carl Wilson's picture. "That's him."

"If you need more time, that's fine."

"Nope. That's the man. I'm certain of it. I'm good with faces."

"Thank you. Please initial beneath the picture of the man you have identified." Jack handed her a pen.

"If you think of anything else, please let me know," Jack said as she scribbled her initials.

"I will. Here's your pen. Now it's back to cleaning!"

"Thank you for your help. I'll see myself out."

Jack got in his car and drove straight from Jodi's to Seven Dollar Taxi. The ride service charged $7 within certain boundaries and advertised rides to medical appointments, assistance with groceries, and safe bar pickups. According to the website, the taxis were parked at Mike's Auto.

After speaking with the manager of the auto repair business, Jack discovered they also ran the taxi service. It grew out of their courtesy shuttle amenity. The manager checked his log and told Jack that Sid Beecher was the driver that day, and he was out back now, cleaning the cab.

Jack cut through the auto shop and out the rear door.

Three different vehicles were painted a bright yellow and blue with $7 RIDES emblazoned on the side. Two were sedans, and one was a minivan. A man in his late forties with close-cropped hair, tan skin that had seen too much sun, and sunken eyes shut off the vacuum he was using and stared at Jack as he approached.

"You a cop?"

"A detective. Jack Stratton with the Darrington Sheriff's Department."

"Look. I just drive. I didn't buy the girls any booze and didn't let them drink it in the van."

Jack didn't know what he was talking about, but when someone started discussing a possible crime, he was more than willing to listen. "Why don't you start at the beginning?"

"Ask Billy in dispatch. He sent me out to pick them up—five girls from The Pistol. Do you know the club out on Westmooreland? These girls are three sheets to the wind. Laughing, falling, screaming they're on top of the world, then two of them puke in the back." He points at the minivan he's cleaning, and Jack gets a whiff of the odor.

"Then what did you do?"

"I dropped them all off at the first girl's house. They pitched a fit and said they would call you guys and their boyfriends. Hell, one even said she was getting her daddy. I don't give a flying rat. I wasn't going to end up driving one drunk girl alone. Not gonna happen, so I dumped them all safe and secure at the first house."

Satisfied with his story, Jack nodded. "That clears that up. I have a question regarding a fare you took earlier in the week to 21 Mountain View Bluff."

"That the joint that looks like the hotel California? The house on the cliff?"

"That's the place."

"Yeah, I went there. Dropped off some nut job."

"Why would you call him that?"

"He was one of those religious wackos trying to cram their faith down your throat."

"What did he say, exactly?"

"He invited me to his church."

"And?"

"And what? That's all, but where does he get off telling me I need to go to church?"

"He said you needed to go?"

"Not exactly. He just asked, but you know what that means. I guarantee he was the type that thinks he's better than everyone else. I should've given the tip back."

"Did he say anything else?"

"No. I told him I drove a cab, not a talk show. If he felt like talking to someone, wait for a telemarketer to call him. It's not my job to entertain him. He can buy some earbuds. What do I look like, Britney Spears?"

Jack pulled out a new photo lineup sheet. "Please take your time looking at this. Can you identify who the man was?"

Sid scratched his chin and stared at the page for a few minutes. "I don't want to sound racist or anything, but this is hard. Like I said, I didn't talk to the guy. I don't even like looking at fares. And I mean any ride. I'd pick up someone blue if they have green in their pocket, know what I mean?"

The more Sid spoke, the less Jack liked him. Because of the task at hand, Jack kept his mouth shut.

"That one." Sid pointed to the photo of Carl.

Jack clenched his fist. He had double confirmation that Carl had been to Dr. Mobley's. "I'll need you to initial underneath the photo of the man you identified."

"You dropped that man off at 21 Mountain View Bluff when?" Jack asked as the taxi driver initialed the paper.

"Six days ago."

"Did you see him go inside?"

"I don't wait for them. He paid, and I left. That's the way it works."

"Where did you pick him up from?"

"Outside the Willamina Inn."

Jack handed him a card. "Thank you for your time."

46

Jack's next stop brought him back to the morgue. He stood next to Mei, staring down at the corpse of Dr. Navi Patel. Her body lay naked on a metal gurney. She had three obvious bullet wounds in her chest.

The blood pounded in Jack's ears, drowning out Mei's voice until it sounded like she was shouting at him from the end of a long hallway. His mouth was so dry he couldn't swallow. His thumbs dug into his thighs, and he locked his knees to keep his legs from shaking.

He blinked and relived what had happened just before the shooting. He raced down the tech center stairs. Shoving the door open, he watched as the scene unfolded in slow motion. Ed tumbled through the air, his body striking the tar with a loud smack.

Tires skidded. The car came to a halt.

Jack had to do something.

Ed lay on the ground, injured and helpless.

Jack drew his weapon.

The reverse lights on Dr. Patel's car glowed brightly. She

shifted in reverse, intent on running over Ed as he lay wounded on the tar.

Jack's finger touched the cold metal of the trigger. He pulled. The gun roared and kicked in his hand. He let the barrel settle down, adjusted his aim slightly, and squeezed the trigger again.

Once. Twice. Three and four times. He kept pulling the trigger until the car stopped. That's what he was trained to do. Fire until the threat is neutralized. He fired four bullets. He had no other choice.

Or did he?

Could he have fired a warning shot?

If Dr. Patel hadn't heeded the warning, Ed would be dead.

Could he have shot the engine or the tires?

Cars can still drive on flat tires.

Was there anything else he could have done?

"Jack?" Mei gave his arm a gentle shake. "Are you all right?"

"Fine." Jack looked around the room as if he'd awoken from a dream. "I'm sorry. I, ah," He cleared his throat. "Did you say the cause of death was the gunshots to the chest?"

"No." Mei stared at him, concern marring her brow. "The victim was already deceased when she was shot."

Jack's eyes widened. "What? Are you certain of that?"

"A hundred percent. It was a short time between Dr. Patel's death and being shot, but she was definitely dead before the bullets struck her. I am working on a time of death, but I believe she may have died ten minutes, give or take a few, before the gunshots." Mei pointed at the center chest wound. "This bullet penetrated her heart, but there is not an excess of blood in the cavity wall. If she'd been alive, the blood would have filled the void. Another indicator that she was deceased prior to the wounds is minor pooling in her lower extremities. That indicates she died, and someone placed her into a sitting position."

"What killed her?"

"I've ruled out cardiac, pulmonary, and vascular causes. It was most likely an overdose. I found no puncture marks. I will let you know when the toxicology report comes back."

Jack's hand went to the back of his neck. The cool metal of his wedding band on his skin made his eyes narrow. He was still getting used to wearing jewelry, but the unfamiliar touch was welcome now. "You're certain it was a drug overdose?"

Mei crossed her arms. "I believe I said most likely, Jack. The tox report may reveal that she was poisoned. I must say that I'm taken aback. You've never questioned my findings before, Jack. Why now? Do you think I'm unqualified to be the Chief Medical Examiner?"

"Not at all. I think you're brilliant, Mei, and I can't tell you how much I appreciate your fast-tracking everything for us."

"Then why are you looking at me like I'm from another planet and questioning everything I'm saying?"

Jack waved his hands in front of himself like a referee stopping a play. "I'm sorry. My job is to ask questions, in this case, I'm questioning everything. Here I am looking at three bullet holes I put into someone, and you tell me that the person I believed I shot and killed was dead before I shot her."

"I understand this is a lot to process, but I don't understand why you're surprised by my findings."

"Because that means Dr. Patel was driving the car after she died."

Mei chuckled and stared at Jack like she was waiting for the punch line. "That would be impossible."

"I know. Now I need to figure out how someone made the impossible possible."

47

Jack leaned back in his cubicle chair and stretched his arms toward the ceiling. His phone buzzed with a call from Finn.

"Talk to me, buddy," Jack said. "Did you get anything from Dr. Patel's car?"

"These new models come with an EDR. That's an Event Data Recorder. They're kind of like black boxes for airplanes."

"Do they just record speed and braking?"

"No. These are very sophisticated. They record everything."

"Dr. Patel wasn't actually driving the car." Jack slid forward to the edge of his seat. "It shows that, right?"

"That's where things get complicated. Really complicated. We'll have to send it to the manufacturer, but I'm certain legal will want a backup made of it first, and I don't know what that will involve as far as time is concerned."

"You're losing me, Finn. I'd assume the log would show that the car was in manual or self-driving mode."

"Normally it does, but on the report, the readout for that entry is N/A."

"How is that possible?"

"Technically, it's not. And it gets weirder. Someone installed new software into the car's system two days ago, but there hasn't been an update from the manufacturer. All the usual data regarding the update is blank."

"Is it possible that someone hacked the car and was driving it remotely?"

The silence grew on the other end of the line. "I can say that someone installed foreign software. What the purpose of that software was or what it enabled someone to do, I don't know."

Jack felt like he was in court watching an expert witness testify. "Is it possible..." Jack rubbed his forehead and searched for the correct way to phrase his question. "Is the car capable of being driven remotely? I watched the car drive out of a parking space and stop in front of Dr. Patel, but I need to know if someone outside the car could steer it around."

"I've seen demonstration videos of people doing that. So yes, it is possible."

"You're the best! Now I owe you two dinners."

"You owe me nothing, buddy. I'm glad I can help. I'll let you know as soon as I get more info."

"Thanks again. Talk to you soon." Jack grabbed his notebook and pen and headed for Sheriff Morrison's office. Knocking on the door, Bob waved him in, smiling broadly.

"From the look on your face, I can tell you're upset, but let me tell you, you have no reason to be." Bob motioned for Jack to take a seat. "I'll get the credit sorted out. I'm sure they're going to run a second article."

Jack remained at attention. "I'm not tracking, sir."

Bob steepled his hands and rocked in his chair. "The reporter for the Enterprise embellished Ed's role in the arrest and failed to mention you. I'll call Martin Brenner, the editor, and let him know of your part in cracking this case." Bob grinned broadly. "I do have to tell Martin to tone down the headlines. The Enterprise looks less like a newspaper and more like a tabloid daily." Bob handed Jack the front section of the newspaper.

They printed the headline in two-inch bold letters—Mad Doctor Killer Made House Calls. The article named Dr. Patel as the murderer of Dr. Mobley and Dr. Chen. Accompanying the piece was a large photograph of Ed, giving him credit for making the arrest.

"I'll fix it," Bob said. "They'll print a retraction, and everything will be okay. The mayor is over the moon, too. I spoke with her this morning."

Jack flashed a sympathetic smile.

Bob stopped rocking in his chair. "That look on your face tells me you're not in here to discuss who gets credit for the collar."

"I don't want credit for saying Dr. Patel was the killer. I never said that. Do you remember our conversation at the hospital? I said that something was bothering me, and you said it was my investigation and I could keep digging."

Bob opened his drawer and took out a bottle of antacid. "I said that, but forensics matched the gravel found at Dr. Chen's house to the robot's tread in Dr. Patel's lab. Now you want to tell me that Dr. Patel didn't kill Chen?"

"I don't know if Dr. Patel used the robot to kill Dr. Chen. She may have."

Sheriff Morrison's eyebrows bunched together, and he leaned forward in his chair. "You realize that you're contradicting yourself."

"I'm not, sir. These are the facts we have so far." Jack flipped open his notebook. "The day before the explosion at Dr. Mobley's house, Carl Wilson, my missing person subject, took a cab out there. A neighbor and the cab driver both confirmed it. I don't know why Carl went there, but it's possible he was the one who installed the modified cap on the propane tank."

"Why would he do that?"

"A few years ago, Dr. Mobley was working with our narcotics unit, and his testimony helped put Carl Wilson in jail. Carl could have been seeking revenge for himself, or someone could have hired Carl to do it."

"Do you have any leads to Carl's whereabouts?"

"None. He's in the wind."

"And what about Dr. Chen's murder?" Bob asked. "Do you have any evidence of Carl's involvement?"

"No. But someone drove the robot to Dr. Chen's and operated it remotely."

"Something like that could give anyone a solid alibi. How technical do you have to be to control one of those things?"

Jack looked down at his notes. "To quote one expert I spoke with, not technical at all. You could control a robot like that with a video game controller and fire the weapon with the push of a button. And everything about the shooting points to the killer using ADA." Jack read from his notes. "The angle of the gun would match the height of the robot. The tight grouping of the bullets would be consistent with a machine firing the weapon. And it also explains how the killer got past the pack of dogs."

"You're certainly not going to hear an argument from me about any of that. Everything you said makes perfect sense. Dr. Patel created the robot, correct?"

"Yes, sir. And I'm not ruling out the possibility that Dr. Patel killed Dr. Chen and Dr. Mobley, but someone else killed Dr. Patel. Mei finished the initial autopsy. Dr. Patel died prior to my shooting her. She is waiting on a tox report."

"Are you trying to tell me a dead person drove that car?"

"A dead woman was behind the wheel but wasn't driving."

Bob opened his drawer again and took more antacids.

"Are you supposed to take so many?" Jack asked.

"Probably not, but right this second, my stomach acid feels like molten lava burning a hole in my gut." The sheriff munched the chalky tablets. “I thought a self-driving car meant you could take your hands off the wheel and eat a sandwich. Eyewitnesses said it took off like a rocket and drove like a madman. You want me to believe someone else was controlling it?”

“Someone changed the car’s software the day before the accident. The black box log showed it wasn’t in manual operation, nor was it in automatic mode. The tech nerds will have to analyze more, but all those facts point to one thing.”

“A killer is still out there.” Bob exhaled.

Jack nodded. “Sorry to ruin your morning.”

“Ruin it?” Bob shook his head as he picked up the newspaper, crumpled it, and threw it into the trash. “Don’t look at it that way. You may have saved my tomorrow. We didn’t take these jobs because they’re easy. We took them to do the right thing. I meant it when I said that to you in the hospital. Now do me a favor. Go stop this guy before they kill again.”

“Working on it. Right now, Oscar Chambers is both my prime suspect and next potential victim. He’s the last living member of the project group.”

“Do you have any leads on his whereabouts?”

“His roommate used a program on Oscar’s computer and tracked him to Sabrina Hall’s apartment. She’s the CEO of Eagle 247 Technology. She admitted he was there, but he’d left before I arrived. I’m going to talk to her again now.”

Bob’s expression turned grim. “We already have one officer in the hospital. Be careful, Jack.”

Jack stood up and grinned. “Aren’t I always?”

48

Jack paced the lobby of Eagle 247 Technology. There were six security guards on duty this morning, and everyone had to go through the metal detectors and was patted down. The extra security created a backup in the line that now unfurled out the door.

A woman in a black business suit approached Jack. "Detective Stratton, please come with me."

"The lobby is a little crowded this morning." Jack fell in step beside her as they walked to the elevator.

"We sometimes have high-security drills." The woman smiled pleasantly. "I'm certain it's nothing to worry about."

"Seeing how you've tripled security, someone is definitely worried." Jack stopped outside the elevator. "You know three people who came here to pitch a project are now dead?"

"What?" The woman quickly stepped back off the elevator. "Who was killed?"

Jack walked to the back of the elevator foyer, and the woman followed him. "I didn't catch your name."

"Tahirah Nadeau. I'm one of Ms. Hall's assistants. I wasn't made aware of any threats."

"That's troubling. I would think your boss would have mentioned something for your own safety." Jack opened his phone and pulled up a photograph of Dr. Mobley. "Do you recognize this man?"

Thirah nodded rapidly. "Yes. He showed up here a few times. He was very agitated. Is he the reason for the additional security?"

"No." Jack switched to a photo of Dr. Chen. "What about him?"

"He was here, too. He met with Ms. Hall."

"Are you certain?" Jack glanced down at his body camera to check if it was on, but security had him remove it and place it in the lockbox along with his gun and phone.

"Yes. I brought him coffee. He came last week."

"And you're positive he spoke directly with Ms. Hall?"

"Absolutely."

"What about her?" Jack showed the picture of Dr. Patel.

"Yes. That's Dr. Patel. Same thing, different day. She met with Ms. Hall, but she had tea."

"Again, you're positive?"

"Yes. There has to be a record of it with security." Thirah clicked on her tablet. "I made the appointments myself."

"What about him?"

"Oscar Chambers." Thirah rolled her eyes. "He came bearing a bottle of Ms. Hall's favorite wine. I don't know how he talked security into letting him bring it along, but he did."

"When did Oscar meet with Ms. Hall?"

Thirah's finger tapped the screen. Windows opened. She swiped left, then rapidly pressed the screen a few times. Frowning, she closed the window and started again, ending her endeavors with the same frustrated expression on her face. "The meetings aren't listed anymore. I know I put them all in the schedule, but something must have gone wrong."

"That's okay, Thirah. I'll ask Ms. Hall about it myself." Jack handed her a business card. “I will have further questions for you. Do you have a card?”

Thirah removed one from the leather binder holding her tablet.

“Thank you.”

After she handed the card to Jack, her tablet beeped, and Thirah frowned. “Ms. Hall is expecting you.” She typed a quick message, and they headed back to the elevator.

Once they reached the top, Thirah escorted Jack to the office, let him in, and closed the doors behind him. Sabrina was alone, sitting in her chair behind her desk.

“Was there a problem on the way up?” Sabrina asked.

“Not at all. You have this place running like a well-oiled machine.”

Sabrina smiled without showing her teeth.

“Thank you for seeing me. I have some further questions for you.”

“Of course.” Sabrina pointed to a folder on her desk. “That is my official, on-the-record response.”

Jack crossed the room and picked up the folder. Inside, printed on heavy paper, was a one-page legal document. At least Jack assumed it to be legal, considering the letterhead contained the names of two different law firms and several lawyers were referenced at the bottom.

“In summary, Detective, although I’ve met with Oscar Chambers in my office here at Eagle, it had nothing to do with business. We didn’t discuss the details of any technical projects and the like. It was all pleasure, I assure you. Surely in your line of work, you’ve encountered office dalliances, Detective. You’ve likely had a few of your own with your handsome face.” Sabrina scanned Jack from head to toe like a lioness eyeing her next meal and licked her red lips.

The temptress had planted a seed that bloomed in Jack’s mind. Marissa. Jack fought back the memory of his on-the-job tryst with the gorgeous tattoo artist while a cop on the beat. If that massage table could talk, he'd have had to shoot it.

"I have no stories to tell." Jack shook his head without breaking eye contact.

"And neither do I." Sabrina smiled victoriously. "My legal counsel has advised me not to answer any of your questions without those questions first being presented to said counsel."

"So you're refusing to cooperate?"

"Not at all."

"You're refusing to speak with me directly and forcing me to run all my questions through two law firms first, and you call that cooperation? I have another word for it. Stonewalling."

"That's if you want my answers on the record." Sabrina crossed her long legs and folded her hands in her lap. Even with them tightly entwined, Jack noticed her fingers trembling.

Jack leaped through the crack in her beautiful veneer. "I want to help you, Sabrina, but if you don't tell me what's going on, I can't." Jack pulled up a chair and sat. "Talk to me."

Sabrina's foot bounced. "When you came to my apartment the other night and asked me if Oscar was there, you said that I made two mistakes that told you I was lying. What were they?"

Jack stared at the CEO. Her gaze was intense, but he was used to seeing people hide fear. He'd ridden in enough transports, helicopters, and police cruisers with men and women heading into situations with a high probability of someone dying to know how to read the signs. Sabrina was acting tough, but something scared her, and it wasn't Jack.

Maybe that's why she's still talking to me, even though her lawyers told her not to.

"You didn't react to my question. You masked your expression, thinking that it would make it appear like you were neutral. It didn't. You should have been surprised I even asked if Oscar was there."

"And the second?"

"You asked me why Oscar would be in your apartment. You answered my question with a question, not a denial. That's suspicious. Innocent people deny a wrong question. Your guilt got the better of you, and you wanted to know how I figured out he was there. You wanted to see my hand."

"How did you know?"

Jack touched the side of his head. "I've got a wireless plate in my head that picks up radio signals from the moon's dark side."

Sabrina chuckled. "You are very, very good, Detective. Now, let me speak off the record."

Jack nodded.

Sabrina smiled. "You and I both know nothing I truly say is off the record when speaking to law enforcement. My lawyers drilled that into my head this morning. But I know about deniability. If this were ever to reach court, which I assure you it will not, I would categorically vow that this conversation never took place. It will be my word against yours."

Jack shrugged. "So far, three people are dead. You've tripled your security, and it's you that's sweating. So, on the record or off the record, I agree with you that the way things are going, odds are you won't live to make it to court."

"Me?" Sabrina straightened up, her watch clicking off the hard surface of her desk. "Why do you think I should be worried?"

"Because you're worried, which means that you have a reason to be. I don't know what that reason is yet, but I know that you've been lying to me. And if you're willing to lie to law enforcement, you're willing to lie to anyone. So why don't you start telling me the truth?"

"I had nothing to do with those people's murders."

"Convince me."

"How? I'm sure if you gave me the various times they were killed, I'd have an alibi."

"I'm sure you'd come up with alibis, too. You must have a lot of people who would vouch for you."

Sabrina crossed her arms, but the corners of her mouth ticked up. She may have been worried, but she also liked a thrill. "You are a man of little trust."

"I don't trust anyone, especially someone who's repeatedly lied to me. Why don't you start with the truth? You met with Doctors Mobley, Chen, and Patel personally."

"Yes. I did."

"And all three pitched the project?"

"The 30,000-foot view. A ten-minute spiel. I hardly paid attention."

"But you certainly paid attention to Oscar. In more ways than one, it seems."

Sabrina leaned forward and stared at Jack, her brown eyes peering from under thick, long lashes. "Men have been doing the same thing for decades, and no one casts a stone. So I saw some wide-eyed MIT, water-polo-playing stallion and decided to ride him." She held up a hand. "I confess to that indiscretion, off the record, but that's where my involvement in this whole thing ends. I led Oscar on to get into his pants. He was my best cardio; I hate going to the gym—nothing more. When it comes to that drone project, do you have any idea how many similar proposals we receive? Dozens every month. I certainly wouldn't kill for a project I had no interest in."

Jack twisted his wedding band. Either Sabrina was a brilliant actress, or she was telling him the truth. "If that's the case, why are you so nervous? Why all the extra security?"

Sabrina's eyes fluttered to the ceiling. "Oscar is the last man standing. Who do you think has the most to gain from this project? Not me. Check with my legal team. I may be CEO, but I made Eagle 247 Technology a public company. I couldn't touch Sam Mobley's design now that it is such a hot potato."

Jack glanced over Sabrina's shoulder at a darker spot on the horizon outside. The gray clouds looked like rain, but something was off about that spot. It was heading in the opposite direction of the other clouds. It was moving toward them.

"I thought Oscar was some greedy, stars in his eyes, kid, eager to make the big deal. But he got weird quickly. He thought he was some sort of golden boy, the next Musk or Gates. He even said that he wouldn't let anything stop him and after Dr. Patel was killed...." Sabrina slapped the desk with her palm. "Are you listening to me? He gave me the creeps. He—"

"Move!" Jack grabbed her arm and yanked her from her chair.

Something slammed against the window.

Sabrina gasped. "Was that a bird?"

Jack shook his head and pointed. There were more dark spots. Whatever hit the window, there were more of them coming.

Sabrina exhaled and smiled at Jack. "Now it's my turn to tell you not to worry. These windows are a polycarbonate mix. They're bulletproof."

A loud bang echoed through the office as another object struck the glass. But this time, the pieces didn't fall harmlessly to the ground. A gray blob that resembled clay remained.

A muffled explosion shook the window. Smoke and fire flashed, only to be swirled away in the wind.

A two-foot section of the window had thin cracks running through it like a spiderweb.

Sabrina reached under her desk. "I have a safe room." She hurried over to the far wall.

The dark objects moved closer. What appeared to be one large mass was actually dozens of drones, all heading toward them.

Sabrina grabbed the door handle to the safe room, but it didn't budge.

Another object hit the window, but the clay-like blob fell

away a moment before it exploded. Still, the cracks in the glass were growing.

"It won't open!" Sabrina swore as she ran to the main office door, but it, too, was locked.

Jack picked up the chair and brought it down on the handle. The chair back broke, but the handle didn't budge.

"Call security and see if they can open it from there," Jack said.

Another drone shattered against the window, leaving behind the gray clay. A moment later, it exploded. The window shook. A large crack ran the entire length of the glass, and a small crater appeared.

"The line is dead!" Sabrina glared at the telephone.

"What are the walls made of?" Jack asked.

"Concrete. We're trapped."

Jack moved behind Sabrina's desk. Lowering his shoulder like a linebacker, he shoved the desk against the interior wall. Jumping up, Jack ripped off the cover to the air vent. It was small, but she could make it.

"You can fit!" Jack helped Sabrina up onto the desk.

A loud explosion rocked the room. Smoke, dust, and fire shot through a small opening blown into the window.

"You can't." Sabrina grabbed his arm.

"Try to get the door open from the other side." Jack grabbed her waist and hoisted her up until she could grasp the sides of the vent's hole.

Sabrina wiggled her way into the air shaft. She shouted something, but between another explosion and the echo, Jack couldn't hear what she said.

Jack jumped off the desk. The top was thick wood, but judging from the window, it would do little to protect him from the explosions. Staring around the room, he didn't have many options. The drones were striking the window at evenly spaced intervals. Every ten seconds, another drone made impact.

Racing to the far corner of the office, Jack peered out. Three stories below him was a roof. He'd never survived a fall that high, but it was his only option.

Grabbing a knocked-over box of tissues off the floor, he stuffed his ears with them before tying his shirt around his head. Moving as he developed a plan, he jumped back up on the desk and ripped down three ceiling tiles. Above those tiles was solid concrete, but they had used the space between the tiles to run the data lines for the office computers.

Jack grabbed the cables and started pulling.

Ceiling tiles rained down as another drone smashed into the glass.

The explosion was deafening, even with the tissues and shirt around his head. He dropped to the floor and shoved the desk into the corner. Flipping it onto one end, he used it as a shield while he coiled the cable at his feet.

Shrapnel peppered the desk as another drone showered clear, plastic chunks from the window into the room.

Could the cable bear his weight? Would he make it out the window before a drone hit?

Questions and doubts about his plan swirled through Jack's mind as he tied off the end of the cable around the desk and the other end around his waist.

Another drone exploded. A large chunk of glass punched through the desk and missed Jack's head, coming so close it blew back his hair.

Ten seconds.

Jack darted out from behind the desk and sprinted for the window.

The explosion had blasted a hole slightly larger than his shoulders through the glass. A line of ten more drones headed straight for the office in the sky beyond.

Jack dove through the window like a lion leaping through a flaming hoop in the circus. The cityscape spread out before him. He twisted in the air, rotating onto his back. Holding the multicolored lifeline in both hands, he fell with his face raised toward the sky.

The clouds had cleared, and a bright blue spot shone through the gray. It was beautiful.

Alice.

He pictured her smiling face and regretted not calling her this morning. Now, would he get the chance?

God help me, please.

The line continued to play out. He was falling, speeding up as he plummeted toward the other roof three stories below.

The cable jerked tight around his back, and he swung toward the building. Momentum pulled him toward the concrete. He bent his legs to absorb the impact. He hit about as hard as if he'd been parachuting.

The cable played out again. It dragged against something, slowing his descent, but he didn't stop. The ground rushed up toward him.

Had he left too much slack?

He needed to slow down even more. The cable jerked tight. Pain raced up his sides as it yanked up around his arms. The line snapped.

Jack landed on his feet. His knees came up so fast his right knee struck him in the forehead. His eyes watered, and everything blurred, but he rolled with the impact. Like a gymnast sticking the landing, he stood triumphantly and lifted his hands over his head.

"Thank you, God!"

He raised his eyes to the heavens.

Above him, the desk tipped out of the shattered window and plummeted straight at his head.

Leaping out of the way, Jack belly-flopped onto the roof.

The desk crashed onto the spot he'd been standing, sending splinters in all directions.

He lay on the tar roof, trying to catch his breath. Most of his body hurt, but nothing felt broken. He picked himself back off the ground and limped for the entrance to the building. He needed to make sure that Sabrina had gotten safely out.

Then he was going to track down Oscar Chambers. And when he did, for the first time in Jack's law enforcement career, he hoped someone resisted arrest.

49

Alice paced the floor as Kiku stared out the window at the house next door.

"Not to rush you or anything," Alice said, "but I only have two days before my father-in-law tells Jack. And one of those days is almost gone. Is Vidal next door?"

"He is. But so are two guards. If you want me to hurry, I am open to suggestions. I must overcome their security system, sneak past the guards, and convince Vidal to give me the information."

"Isn't that what you do?"

"That is the end result. Careful work and planning should form the basis of any operation. I know Vidal's bedroom is on the third floor, facing the water. Scaling the exterior to the balcony is not an issue. The issue is the alarm system."

"Can't you just disarm it?"

"It is a sophisticated system connected to the internet and monitored remotely off-site. That is an assumption, considering the same company holds both rental properties."

Alice felt a hot glow start in her belly and blaze through her system. She bolted for her bedroom. Opening her laptop, it was hard to type with her fingers shaking so much. She pulled up a map of the street they were on.

Their rental house was 1927 Wave Crest Lane. She scrolled over to the home next door. Its address was 1929.

Biting her lip, Alice clicked the network button. Besides her phone and her current connection, no other networks were listed. Undaunted, she unplugged her laptop, picked it up, and headed back to Kiku's bedroom. She hurried over to the other window on that side of the house and opened it.

"What are you doing?" Kiku asked.

"Checking on something." Alice clicked the network button again and smiled.

Kiku crossed over to her. "They say over time, married couples look like each other. I did not think it happened so fast, but the grin on your face reminds me of Jack. What have you come up with?"

"Let me make sure it works first." Alice grabbed hold of the nightstand, dragged it over to the window, and then set the laptop on it. Her fingers flew across the keyboard as she typed, opening multiple programs while she worked.

Kiku stood beside her, silently watching.

After a few moments, Alice closed the window. "Okay. This room should be almost identical to Vidal's, right?"

"Yes."

"Please open the balcony door. And be prepared," Alice quickly added. "The alarm is on." Alice swung her laptop around so Kiku could see the screen and the security program for the home.

Kiku opened the door.

A warning light flashed on the monitor, followed by a timer counting down.

Alice pressed a few buttons. "I'm entering the alarm code." The timer disappeared, and the yellow light turned green.

"Now." She pressed a few more keys. "Close the door, wait for a second, and open it."

Kiku closed the door and, after a moment, opened it.

The alarm stayed off.

Alice smiled triumphantly. "Yes!"

"Congratulations, Alice. You can control our system. But will you be able to hack theirs?"

"Already have." Alice danced a little jig.

"How could you have cracked their security so fast?" Kiku's tone was a mix of wonder tinged with skepticism.

"It was easy because the same people rent out both homes. The network password for our system is lovingmystay1927. 1927 is the address of the house. The address next door is 1929, and so is their code."

"You are brilliant. Are you positive you can shut off the alarm next door?"

"One hundred percent. The wi-fi signal is a little weak, so I need to put my laptop in the window, but I can connect and access it fine."

"I will go get dressed." Kiku smiled. "Great work. Now, you should be able to make it home with Jack still none the wiser."

50

Jack replayed the video on his computer monitor a dozen times. He'd recorded the footage of Dr. Mobley's house with his body cam when he and Ed first interviewed Sam. Maybe he was missing something that Dr. Mobley said, but Jack couldn't shake the feeling that Carl's disappearance and the murders were connected.

Why was Carl at the house? Jack wanted to believe that Carl had changed in prison, and he was trying to track down the dealer who gave the drugs to Carl's friend, who had overdosed. Jack still hadn't been able to track down the name of Carl's friend who had died. In the last two months, there'd been a half-dozen people that fit the description, but most of them were on the street. With the limited time and resources Jack had, he needed to focus his attention on Carl.

Jack stared at his notepad and circled the question—Why was Carl at Dr. Mobley's house? Maybe because Dr. Mobley had cooperated with the police in the drug sting that landed Carl behind bars, Carl went to ask for Dr. Mobley's help.

Or Carl remained bitter about the arrest. Had he planted the device that caused the propane explosion? That explanation was more feasible, but it didn't explain the other deaths. Unless Oscar discovered Carl's hatred for Dr. Mobley and hired him to do the killings?

The idea made Jack sit up straight.

"That works for me." Jack stood. "What about you, Lady?"

His dog, lying on the couch, didn't lift her head. She lazily opened her eyes and immediately closed them again.

"Oh, come on! It's plausible!" Jack walked as he worked out the theory in his mind. "Oscar could have known that Dr. Mobley was a police informant. Oscar is a schmoozer. He's no killer. But he could have discovered that Dr. Mobley put some very bad people away and reached out to them for help. That—OW!" Jack swore and grabbed his bare foot.

The sole of his heel was indented but not bleeding.

Jack picked up a curved, mahogany-colored piece of wood with Lady's teeth marks in it. "Stupid thing is hard as a rock. How do you chew this?" He stared at the toy but didn't recognize it. "Where did you get this?"

Lady continued to ignore him.

"Did Annie get it for you?"

Finn and Annie were out at a movie, so he couldn't ask them.

The wood was smooth as glass, but hard as concrete. His eyes narrowed. Jack marched over to his phone and took a picture of the toy. The reverse image search turned up nothing for dog toys, but it identified the wood and where it came from —Tanzania and the root of a coffee wood tree.

His grip tightened on his phone case as he speed-dialed his wife. Only one person would give Lady such an exotic chew toy.

The phone rang twice before Alice picked up.

"Hey, handsome hubby!" Alice sounded happy. "Great news. I should be home soon."

"That's wonderful. How's Kiku?"

Alice gasped. "I can explain. Don't flip out and whatever

you do, don't come here. Everything's under control. I was going to tell you. I can't believe your father didn't give me two days! He promised."

"MY FATHER KNOWS WHERE YOU ARE?!?!" Jack held the phone at arm's length as he shouted. "Hold on! My father knows you went with Kiku and didn't tell me?!"

"You didn't talk to your dad?"

"No, but I'm going to have a little conversation with him right now."

"Oh, no. I'm so stupid. I, ah, I thought you… How did you figure it out?"

"That doesn't matter. What does is that you and my father have been lying to me."

"Not lying. I just didn't tell you because I knew you'd want to come with me and you just started the new job. I didn't want to ruin that, but Kiku knows a guy, who knows a guy, who knows where my grandfather is."

Jack's anger cooled. Alice had lost her entire family but recently found out her grandfather might be alive. If Kiku might know where he was, Jack wanted nothing more than Alice to find him. "You talked to your grandfather?"

"Not yet. But Kiku is going to speak to the guy who knows the guy tonight about where he is." Alice sighed. "I'm so sorry."

"Not telling me is still a lie."

"I know that now. I realized it before I ran into your father."

"So my father knows, *and* he didn't tell me?"

"It's not like that, Jack. I bumped into your dad. He and your mom are on a mini-vacation to the coast and—"

"My mother knows, too?!"

"Yes, but please let me explain. Your dad told me flat out he was going to call you. He said that he promised you he would never lie to you. He told me that, Jack. I begged him to give me two days. He didn't want to, but he relented. He said he's never lied to you and even though he loves me, he's going to tell you he saw me in Florida with Kiku."

"Yeah, right."

"It's true, Jack. He said he'd give me two days to tell you and if I didn't, not me, not your mom, not Kiku, not anyone could stop him. Please believe me. I lied. For that I'm so sorry, but I would never forgive myself if I did anything to harm you and your father's bond."

Jack hung his head. A two-day warning to do the right thing sounded like something his father would say. "Put Kiku on the phone."

"She's not here. She went to go talk to the guy."

"Do you need me to come there?"

"No! Really. She's just going to talk to the guy and then we're going to see my grandfather. I'm perfectly safe."

"You're with Kiku! The last time I saw Kiku before the wedding, she had me arrested."

"She only did that so she could get away from the police. And she apologized."

Jack rolled his eyes. "Are you kidding me? I'm looking at the patched bullet holes in our walls now. Not to sound like a movie trailer, but wherever Kiku goes, danger isn't far behind. I can get on a plane..."

Jack's voice trailed off as he watched the video still playing on his computer monitor. He and Ed had finished the interview with Dr. Mobley and the house exploded. Jack dragged Ed to safety and had just rushed through the open front door.

Smoke rose from the kitchen and flames crackled above the broken wall and flickered against the now visible skyline. At the base of the center island, sticking out of the debris, was a pair of brown leather shoes and tan pants. The blast obliterated the upper torso.

A flash of flame filled the screen.

Jack rewound the video ten seconds.

"Are you still there?" Alice asked.

Jack's focus was on the monitor as he let the video play. He tapped the space bar, freezing the video on a shot of Dr. Mobley's cabinets.

"Jack?"

"I'm here," Jack said, a smile spreading across his face. "Can you and Kiku handle the situation with your grandfather?"

"Yes, we can. I promise."

"Great. I love you."

"I love you, too. Just to make sure, you're not coming to Florida, right? You're going to stay and work on your murder case?" Alice said.

"As a matter of fact, I'm heading out right now. I think I solved it."

51

Alice sat at the upstairs window, staring at the house next door. It had been almost an hour since Kiku had disappeared out the back door and into the night. Even knowing that Kiku would cross the backyard, Alice never saw her do so. She kept vigil until her eyes burned and finally gave up.

Now she sat there monitoring the security system of the other house. She had disabled everything but still watched the system in case she missed a motion sensor or someone manually turned it back on. The only way for the guards to know the system was offline was to check the panel, which Kiku assured Alice they wouldn't.

A pang of guilt gnawed at her gut. Jack had yelled but then settled down when he realized that the reason Alice went with Kiku was Alice's desire to meet her grandfather. She tried to convince herself that if Jack were in a similar situation, she would've been just as understanding, but that was a lie. She would've been disappointed in Jack and ticked off.

Alice closed her eyes. What did Aunt Haddie call these times? Teaching moments. All Alice could do now was what

Aunt Haddie drilled into all of her foster kids' heads: If you mess up, fess up and move on.

The icy touch of steel on her neck made her gasp.

"Shh. If you make a sound, I will kill you," a man whispered.

Alice slowly turned her head.

The thin man, Fausto's bodyguard, held a gun with a long barrel to her neck.

"Where is she?" he asked.

Alice's mind raced. Should she bluff? Lie? Make him look somewhere else? "Taking a bath," she blurted out.

He held a finger to his mouth and stepped back, motioning her to rise.

Alice slowly raised her hands.

The thin man waved her toward the door with his pistol.

Alice stared at the weapon. She wasn't Kiku or Jack. There was no way she'd be able to knock it out of his hands or take it from him without getting shot. She started for the doorway.

The bathroom was at the end of the hall. The door was closed. If he made her go through first, perhaps she could slam the door into him.

The barrel of the gun jammed into her back and prodded her forward.

Alice's bare feet didn't make a sound on the soft carpet. As they passed the bedroom where they kept Fausto, the TV's sound escaped into the hall from under the door.

The thin man poked the gun into Alice's back again.

She winced and stopped. Her odds of trying to take on the thin man by herself were slim. If he freed Fausto, she'd have no chance of fighting them both.

The thin man angled his head as he stared at the bathroom. He was listening. Without warning, he grabbed Alice by the hair, whipped open the door to Fausto's room, and shoved Alice through.

Alice fell sprawling onto the carpet. She was about to scramble to her feet when she noticed Fausto's cowboy boots on the floor at the end of the bed. She raised herself on her left elbow and grabbed a boot with her right hand. Holding the boot tightly to her chest, she collapsed onto the floor.

Fausto started making grunting noises.

The thin man strolled over to the edge of the bed. He must have removed Fausto's gag because Fausto began shouting something in Italian.

"English," the thin man said.

"You have no idea how glad I am to see you, my friend!" Fausto chuckled. "Did you bring more men? Where is Kiku?"

"I was hoping you could tell me that."

"Me? I don't know. They've kept me locked in this room. Ask the girl you shoved in here. She must know."

"I did. She lied. So you don't know where Kiku is? Pity."

"What do you mean? Why are you looking at me like that, mi amico?"

"There is a sizable bounty on Kiku's head. I intend to collect, and I don't wish to split it."

"Split? I don't want any part of it. You keep it. All of it!" Fausto's voice rose. "Seriously. You know me. I did nothing to earn it. I have no claim to it."

"You are the one who led me to her," the thin man said.

"What are you talking about? How could I have led you to her?"

The thin man shoved his gun into his shoulder holster and grabbed Fausto's wrist.

"Ow! What are you doing?"

"Taking back my gift to you."

"My watch? Why?"

"I like to keep tabs on my employers in case they're watching me." The thin man laughed. "Get the pun? Watching me? The watch is how I found you. And once I collect the bounty for Kiku, I no longer have to bow and scrape at your feet for your crumbs."

"What crumbs?" Fausto said. "I paid you well. I gave you bonuses."

"You threw me a bone now and then, but I was still a dog. Face or chest?"

"Put the gun away! Let's talk this over."

Alice inhaled. The thin man was going to kill Fausto unless she did something. It was true Fausto was a mobster. Even so, she had to do something. Cradling the cowboy boot to her stomach, she gripped the top loop tightly and slowly crouched on the balls of her feet.

The thin man stood with his back to her, his holster empty.

Alice swung as hard as she could. The boot arched through the air, the heel connecting with the side of the thin man's face.

His head jerked to the left. He stumbled but kept his grip on the gun.

Alice pulled back her arm to strike again.

The thin man darted sideways, his arm rising, the barrel moving toward her.

An enormous shadow appeared on the wall. Someone else stood in the doorway behind her.

Alice's eyes widened. The person charging into the room was too big to be Kiku.

The thin man spun to confront this new threat. He raised his arm and screamed in pain as a tire iron slammed onto his forearm. Shrieking, he dropped the gun, which bounced twice and disappeared beneath the bed.

Ted Stratton stood there with a triumphant grin, an old tire iron grasped in his hands. "Put your hands on your head!" he ordered.

The thin man lunged forward, tackling Ted and knocking them both to the floor.

The two men wrestled, twisting and turning, but the thin

man got the upper hand. He rolled Ted onto his back and pinned Ted's right arm, which still gripped the tire iron, to the carpet.

Alice kicked the thin man on the side of his head. It sounded like she'd struck an unripe melon with her foot.

The thin man swayed to the side but didn't fall over.

Alice kicked again.

The thin man blocked it, grabbing her leg and flinging her backward into the bureau.

Alice's head slammed into the wood. Stars filled her eyes, and her vision blurred.

Ted struggled to pull his arm free.

The thin man reached down and yanked something from his boot. He raised his arm, the blade of a large knife gleaming as he held it high, ready to thrust down into Ted's chest.

Laura Stratton burst through the doorway, a baseball bat in her hands. She swung hard and fast, catching the thin man in the center of his chest.

The thin man didn't make a sound as the blow knocked him onto his back. He started rolling back and forth, looking like a fish gasping for water. His mouth opened and closed, but he didn't make any noise.

"Oh, dear Lord, I killed him!" Laura cried.

Ted grabbed hold of the chair and pulled himself up. "He's still moving. Hit him again."

"He's not breathing!" Laura held her hands to the side of her head. "Do something, Ted!"

"Give me the bat! He was going to shish kabob me, and he hurt our girl!"

The thin man gasped, coughed, and curled into a ball on the floor.

"Oh, thank the Lord." Laura handed the bat she was holding to Ted. "Don't hit him again. He's had enough."

The thin man reached for the knife.

Kiku sprang through the door, her foot pinning the thin man's arm to the floor.

The thin man glared up at her.

She struck him in the temple with her pistol.

The thin man slumped to the floor.

Kiku gave a slight bow to the Strattons. "Thank you for your assistance. I will take it from here."

52

Jack dialed with one hand as he sped across town. His mind was racing, but it was like driving through a storm of thoughts. His wife was in Florida with Kiku and looking for her grandfather. But how bad could it be if his parents were there? Still, Alice should have given him the who, what, and where just to be safe. With Kiku, anything could happen.

Hopefully, Alice was on a need-to-know basis, bored out of her mind, sitting in a hotel room and waiting for Kiku to locate her grandfather. And if something went south, his father would let him know.

Oscar's voicemail picked up again. Jack didn't bother leaving a message. He'd left several already, all saying the same thing—"Your life is in danger. Call back immediately and go to the nearest police officer."

Another idea flashed into his head. He pulled up Oscar's background check and called the one person who might convince him to turn himself in, whether Oscar was a victim or the criminal—his mother.

The phone rang three times before a weary woman answered.

"I apologize for the late call. May I speak with Brenda Chambers, please?" Jack said.

"Speaking."

"My name is Detective Jack Stratton, and I'm with the Darrington Sheriff's Department. We believe your son Oscar is safe, but we must speak to him immediately."

A torrent of frantic questions poured out of her mouth. "Was there an accident? Was he drinking? What happened?"

"Who are you talking to?" a man in the background asked.

"The police," Brenda whispered.

"Brenda, I need you to listen to me." Jack kept his voice calm. "We want your son to come to the police station immediately."

"He'll do no such thing." The man, presumably Nate Chambers, said as he took the phone. "If you've got questions for my boy, I want him talking to his attorney."

"That's his right, sir. But you need to get him someplace safe first. Right now."

"What is this all about?"

"Three people who worked with him on a project have been murdered. We believe Oscar may be the next target."

Nate gasped. Brenda sobbed.

"Call him," Nate said. "Pull yourself together and call him right now!"

Jack calmly explained to the worried father everything he could without jeopardizing the case. He'd rather err on protecting human life, but there was still a good chance that Oscar was the killer.

"My wife is calling him. Once we get off the phone, I will too."

To Jack's surprise, the father was dealing with this news remarkably even keeled. Typically, the parents would be so upset you couldn't understand what they were saying.

Brenda's sobbing came closer to the phone. "He didn't pick

up! I left a message, but why wouldn't he pick up?"

"It's going to be all right, Brenda. We'll get through."

"Nate, if you hear from him, no matter the conversation, please let me know."

There was a long silence as Jack waited for the father to respond. He checked the phone. The call hadn't disconnected. If Nate was debating about telling him something, the last thing Jack would do was interrupt.

"Do you believe my son is mixed up in this somehow?"

"There is always that possibility, but we can sort everything out once he's safe. That's the important thing. If Oscar got involved in the wrong thing, he needs to listen to you and talk to us. Can you do that for me, Nate?"

"I will. Please—" Nate's voice broke. "I'll call him now."

The phone disconnected, and Jack shoved it back into his pocket. He sped along the windy roads and past the cliffside homes until he reached the burned-out shell of Dr. Mobley's house.

Turning on his body camera, Jack headed inside. He flicked on his flashlight, the beam casting a sharp circle on the wall as he swept the room. Jack had no reason to believe that anyone would be there, but the habit drilled into him by the military and the police had become part of his DNA.

Picking his way across the debris, Jack stopped at the shelf in the living room. Frames and awards had fallen off the wall and lay on the floor. There was a lot of water damage caused by the spray of the firemen's hoses, but it contained the flames in the kitchen.

Using the fireplace poker, Jack sifted through the remnants of Dr. Mobley's life until he was sure that what he was searching for wasn't there. His flashlight beam gleamed off a torn open white envelope. Jack pulled it from the damp pile and carefully removed the letter.

Peter Ryder, the manager of A. G. Maxwell Insurance, had

written to Dr. Mobley asking him to reconsider lowering his insurance coverage. Peter also expressed concern for his friend, saying he had a nagging feeling that something terrible would happen.

Jack removed an evidence bag from his pocket and sealed the letter up.

His phone rang. Jack laid the bag and flashlight on the shelf and quickly answered after reading the caller-ID—Oscar Chambers. He set the call onto speaker so his body cam would record the audio.

"Detective Stratton?" Oscar's voice sounded thin and scratchy. "Can you hear me? Hello?"

"Where are you?" Jack hurried out of the house and began jogging for his car.

"I had nothing to do with the murders. I wouldn't kill anybody. This whole thing is crazy. When Dr. Mo's house exploded, I wasn't sad. I was kinda happy, which is totally, totally wrong, but he was making my life hell on earth. But I didn't kill him or Yan or Navi. I swear it. I swear it on my mother's life."

"I believe you." Jack chose his words carefully. "Right now, you're in danger."

"I know! They're all dead! I don't know why, but I'm the only one left! It's nuts. You have to think I did it, but I didn't kill them, and now the real killer will come after me."

"I can protect you, but you have to tell me where you are. Where are you, Oscar?" Jack yanked his car door open and got in.

"I'm at this creepy hunting cabin a friend of mine from high school's dad owns. It's perfect for a horror movie. I know I'm gonna get an axe in the head."

"Give me the address, and I'll come and get you."

"There is no address. It's a bunch of logging trails. I don't even know if I'm at the right cabin."

"Do you have your car?"

"Yeah." Oscar sighed. "I'll come to you. Okay? But you need to promise me two things. First, I think Sabrina Hall may be a target. She's the CEO—"

"Of Eagle 247 Tech. I know. Someone tried to kill her this morning, but she's safe."

"What?" Oscar shouted. "Bri? Where is she?" From the sound of his breath, Oscar was running.

"She's safe. You need to come directly to the Sheriff's station."

"I will but I need to warn her— I'll come— once I—"

"Don't go over there. Go to the Sheriff's station. Oscar? Can you hear me?"

The call went dead.

Jack swore and hit redial. The call went straight to voicemail, so he hung up and dialed Nate Chambers.

"Did you speak to Oscar?" Nate asked, hope in his voice.

"Yes, but we were disconnected. Oscar said he was staying at a high-school friend's father's hunting cabin. Do you know who that would be?"

"A hunting cabin? No." Nate covered the phone, mumbled something to his wife, and said, "Brenda doesn't know anyone either. We'll start making calls."

"Great. Do that and get back to me."

Jack hung up and called dispatch to send another unit to Sabrina Hall's. Sheriff Morrison had already stationed a car outside her penthouse, but Sabrina had insisted on using her security.

If Oscar went to Sabrina's apartment before turning himself in, he'd be doing the killer a favor. Now the killer could take them both out at the same time.

Jack started the engine, flicked his emergency lights on, and hit the siren. Despite the noise, he powered down the windows and let the wind and adrenaline invigorate him. The few cars on the road moved out of his way, and he made it across town in under twenty minutes.

An empty police cruiser was parked out front of Sabrina's building. Officer Donald Pugh was chatting with a large man dressed in black slacks and a black T-shirt, smoking an e-cigarette. Donald wasn't the brightest star on the force, but he was a good guy.

"Hey, Jack!" Donald waved and smiled. He was Jack's age and height, but Jack had twenty pounds of muscle on him. Donald was the type who never could seem to gain weight, even if he wanted to. He pushed his hat farther up his sandy brown hair. "This is Trevor Simion. He's working security for Ms. Hall. He covered the President once."

The man crossed his arms and puffed his chest out. "It was a contract job. Mostly for FLOTUS."

"That's code for the First Lady," Donald said excitedly.

Jack nodded, unimpressed. A contract job for presidential security meant he was a guard at some venue where the President spoke. Trevor would have been seated in a hallway or stationed at a bathroom door while the Secret Service handled the real details.

"I have to ask, given that there was an attempt on Ms. Hall's life this morning, why on earth has your outfit not relocated her to a safer location?"

"I'm not at liberty to discuss her reasoning, but rest assured, we advised her to do so."

"I need to speak with Ms. Hall. Oscar Chambers is on his way here," Jack explained.

Trevor shook his head. "No can do. The doctor gave her something to sleep. She just sent her assistant home and went to bed."

"I didn't ask." Jack started forward.

Trevor reached out and put a hand against Jack's chest.

Donald stepped somewhat between them. "I, ah, I wouldn't

do that, Trev. Not if you like using that hand."

Trevor let go. "I'm just following orders. Let me call my boss."

Jack nodded. He was in muddy waters. Legally, he couldn't barge into the apartment. Two minutes later, an older man with a bald head and powerful build strolled out the front door. "Detective Stratton?" He shook Jack's hand. "Bill Bliss. I'm head of security for Ms. Hall. Is this regarding Oscar Chambers?"

"It is. He may come this way."

Bill shook his head. "No, sir. He called Ms. Hall at twenty-three past midnight. She told him she was okay, and he stated he was going to the Sheriff's station to speak with you."

"Did you talk to him?"

"No, sir. But Ms. Hall relayed the information to me as I requested she do regarding all outside contact. I can say the information put her at ease. She finally took the prescribed sleeping medicine and went to bed."

"I'd like to hear this from Sabrina."

"That's your right. Tomorrow." Bill lifted his chin. "No offense, sir. I'm following orders just like you. She doesn't want to be disturbed. It will take a warrant to get me to stand down."

Jack eyed the man. He was a Marine through and through, and the last thing he wanted to do was bust him for doing his job.

"I give you my word, sir." Bill stood at attention. "Ms. Hall is fine. I have a man outside her door, and I'm going back up as soon as we're done. If you ask me, I think you'll find Oscar back at the station, hiding under your desk."

Jack nodded. "I called in another unit, and they'll be stationed out back. Donald, let me know if anyone else goes in or out."

"Will do," Donald said.

Jack hurried back to his car. He needed to get to Oscar before the killer did.

53

Alice paced in the living room while Kiku and Jack's parents spoke in the kitchen. Could things get any worse? Her new in-laws catch her drunk on the beach dressed in a teeny-tiny bikini. Then she admits to lying to their son. Now they find a guy tied up in her bed and another trying to kill everyone he can get his hands on.

I've really done it this time. Aunt Haddie said if you tell one little lie, you've put out the welcome mat for the devil to come calling. What can I say to get out of the mess I've made without telling more lies?

Alice stared at the wall, and no explanation came to mind. She couldn't tell them the truth. For one, she'd be breaking Kiku's trust. Two, they'd have her start at the beginning—ransoms, traitors, and feuding foreign factions. It'd take a month to bring them up to speed. Three, they wouldn't believe it. Four, it would put them in even more danger.

And what was Kiku going to do to Fausto and the thin man? Kiku didn't let people go. She sent them home in boxes. The thin man said he would kill them all, but what had Fausto done besides be an arrogant blowhard?

The felonies Alice had committed, illegal possession of a firearm, drag racing, and breaking and entering, paled compared to kidnapping and double murder.

Forget explaining things to Jack's parents. What was she going to tell him?

The door to the room opened, and Jack's parents hurried in. Laura and Ted rushed over and wrapped Alice in a bear hug.

"You are the sweetest girl in the world," Laura said.

"Kiku explained everything," Ted said. "She also said you told Jack where you are and what you're doing."

Alice glanced over their shoulders at Kiku standing in the doorway.

Kiku made a forward circling gesture with her hand and smiled.

Alice didn't know if the motion meant to go with it, but seeing how she had no other choice, she hugged them back and said, "Thank you for understanding."

"I hope you're not upset with us stalking you," Laura said. "But we were worried after we ran into you on the beach."

"I promised Jack at your wedding that we'd love you like a daughter." Ted smiled. "And part of my parental rights is keeping tabs on you."

Laura squeezed Ted's hand. "We love you, Alice. Ted came running when we saw that man sneaking into the house."

"You did, too." Ted placed one arm around Laura's shoulders and the other over Alice's. "But you need to promise us something, Alice. We have a few Stratton decrees chiseled in stone, and it looks like my son failed to tell you what they are."

Laura took Alice's hand. "One, no matter what you do, we will always love you."

"Two, let someone know, no matter how much trouble you are in. A cord of two, three, or four is much harder to break."

Kiku cleared her throat.

Ted nodded. "You two need to get going, and we'll let you. Promise me you'll be careful?"

"And call us as soon as you can." Laura kissed her on her tear-stained cheek.

"I will," Alice said and sniffled. She was still unsure what Kiku could have possibly said to her in-laws to not only garner this positive reaction but for them to be all right with her continuing on the quest.

Kiku held the door open. "Thank you for understanding the situation and our need for expedience."

After Kiku showed them out, Alice followed her back into the kitchen.

"How did you do that?" Alice asked, amazed. "What did you tell them?"

Kiku poured herself a large glass of water and sipped it. "The most important thing to realize about your in-laws is that they are the people who raised your husband. They poured into Jack parts of who they are and shaped him into the man he is."

"I understand that. They're two of the best people on the planet."

Kiku raised her glass in salute. "Agreed. So I simply told them the truth."

"Everything?" Alice's mouth fell open.

"All of it. They are far tougher than they appear."

Alice walked over to the sink and poured herself a glass. "What now?"

"We have to hit the road. We will take Fausto and the thin man with us. Fausto will ride shotgun, and the thin man will be in the trunk."

"Did you kill him?" Alice spilled water down the front of her shirt.

"No. Per your request. But I have turned the thin man over to Fausto. His fate is no longer our concern. That, along with saving Fausto's life, will satisfy Fausto's pride and provide ample restitution for his car."

"Did you find where my grandfather is?"

Kiku smiled. "Vidal was more than accommodating."

Alice eyed her suspiciously.

Kiku chuckled. "And to answer your unasked question, he is still breathing. Now pack. In a few hours, you will meet your grandfather."

54

Jack poured himself another coffee in the Sheriff's Department break room. In some ways, he was glad that they'd switched to a machine that made single cups, but after waiting here all night in vain for Oscar Chambers to show, he yearned for that pot of coffee that some old-timer made so strong your spoon would stand up.

"Have you been here all night?" Donald Pugh walked into the room and headed straight for the vending machine.

"Yeah. Oscar was a no-show. Anything at Sabrina Hall's?"

"No. But she must have woken up. Her assistant came back about an hour after you left. Oh, crud. Someone took all the bear claws." Donald frowned.

"There are free donuts on the counter." Jack pointed next to the refrigerator.

Donald stared at the vending machine like a young guy picking out an engagement ring. "Nah. I want something sugary."

Jack rolled his eyes. For him, a glazed donut was a sugar bomb. "Won't that keep you up?"

"Hope so. Working a double." Donald made his selection

and proudly held up a frosted cake and a candy bar. "Buy one, get one free! Lucky day!"

"Unless you're the vendor."

"Cost of doing business." Donald strutted over to the counter and picked up two Styrofoam cups. "You know what I miss? Ned's coffee. Rocket fuel, I used to call it. He'd put like half a bag in. "

The speaker on the ceiling crackled to life. "Detective Stratton, please call dispatch. 10-54. Detective Stratton, please call dispatch. 10-54."

Donald's smile faded.

Code 10-54. Discovery of a dead body.

Jack stood on the side of the road, staring down at Oscar Chambers. Oscar lay on his back, his arms outstretched, and his gray eyes were staring at the lightening sky. A drainage ditch ran along the side of the road. Oscar had slid halfway down, making him invisible from anyone driving by. Three gunshots riddled his torso. Unlike Dr. Chen's, these bullets were scattered.

Climbing up the bank, Jack headed to the ambulance, where a young woman in shorts and a T-shirt sat sipping water and talking to the paramedics. The officer on scene had provided Jack with some of the details regarding the jogger who found the body.

"Tillie Haymond. I'm Detective Jack Stratton. I need to ask you some questions."

"Of course." Tillie started to rise unsteadily to her feet.

"Why don't we sit and talk?" Jack sat down next to her.

Tillie nodded. "Thank you. I feel horrible. It was terrifying."

"Let's start with how you got here." Jack stared up and down the long, deserted road. In either direction, there wasn't a house for a mile.

"I live over on Hillcrest." She pointed west. "My house is next to the reserve, and I like to run the trails."

"Do you usually run this way?"

"I vary it up, but at least once a week. I take the trail first, then switch to the road for sprints."

"So you came down that fire road?" Jack pointed to the gravel road leading off into the woods.

Tillie didn't answer the question. Her eyes fluttered, and she gulped air.

"Take your time. Have another sip of water."

Tillie held the bottle in both hands like a child and drank. "There was a car on the trail. It's down before the first turn. No one was in it."

Jack glanced at Donald, who stood listening a few yards away.

Donald nodded and walked toward the fire road.

"I thought it was weird. If the driver wasn't in the car, where were they? I've never seen a car parked there before. I almost turned around, but I thought I was making up an excuse for not working out. I ran wide around it and made it to the road. Because of the sprints, I stopped to tighten my sneakers." Her lips twisted in relived horror, and she covered her mouth. "He was lying there. I knew he was dead because of his eyes. They were open!" She sobbed and covered her face with her hands.

One paramedic came over and motioned for Jack. "Her blood pressure is through the roof. I called the hospital, and they agreed we should take her in to give her something to calm down."

"Do you have all of her contact information?" Jack asked, handing a card to the EMT, who nodded. "I'll send a uniform over to get a full statement once she calms down. Thanks."

After the ambulance pulled away, Jack walked over to the other police officer on the scene, Anakin Fletcher.

"Anakin, I need you to wait there for the M.E.," Jack said. "I'm going to look for Donald and the vic's car down the fire road."

"Sure thing." Anakin popped a mint into his mouth and held one out to Jack, who gladly took it. "We haven't informally met. Everyone calls me Skywalker."

"I heard, but I wanted to ask if you were okay with that first."

"Because I'm Wampanoag? It's not like people are calling me he who walks on the sky or anything. It's a Star Wars thing. I like it. Besides, it beats Fletch. Fletcher's the name my like great-great-grandfather picked, anyway. Native Americans didn't have last names. That's kind of a European thing. So, Skywalker is totally cool."

"All right." Jack unwrapped his mint, popped it in his mouth, and grinned crookedly. "It makes me feel like Han Solo."

Jack walked a dozen feet down the road and stopped beside a large rock. Shoe prints had matted down the grass in front of it, and half a dozen cigarettes had been snubbed out on the rock.

Jack photographed the potential evidence and started on again. Further down the trail, a car was parked, and Donald stood beside it. The car faced Jack, telling him everything he needed to know.

"It's Oscar's," Donald called out as Jack approached. "I called in the plates, and they were a match. I haven't touched it, but it's empty inside besides a couple of take-out bags and drinks."

Jack pulled on a rubber glove and tried the door. It was locked.

Donald moved next to Jack. "Why did the guy stop here? Do

you think someone blocked him in? You know, like a mob hit?" Donald's voice rose, filling with excitement.

Jack pointed at the ground. "It rained yesterday afternoon, but there are no tire tracks between us and the road. No other car was here."

"Then why did he stop?"

Jack's microphone clicked on. "Detective Stratton?" Skywalker said. "The M.E. is here."

"Please tell her I'll be there shortly."

"You met Skywalker?" Donald grinned. "Check this out." He cleared his throat and changed the tone of his voice to an English accent. "It's over, Anakin. I have the high ground. Don't do it!"

Jack stared, unsure what Donald meant.

"Oh, come on! The Phantom Menace? Obi-Wan versus Anakin? It's a pillar of cinema."

"Right up there with Casablanca. I need you to keep going down the road into the woods. Oscar told me last night he'd been staying at a hunting cabin. When you find it, call me."

"Can't I drive?"

"I don't want to ruin any tire impressions. Walk along the edge and keep an eye out on the road as you go."

Donald huffed. "Looking for a cabin in the woods is like something out of a horror movie."

"I thought you liked movies?"

"Movies, yes. But that stuff happens in real life too. Have you heard about the girl who lived? Four people were killed at a cabin in Marshfield ten years ago, and only one girl lived. That's the stuff that freaks me out."

"You have a gun, Donald."

"They're useless against ghosts!" Donald laughed and made a face. "Shoot. What movie was that from?"

Jack shrugged. While Donald walked away talking to himself, Jack headed back to the road.

Mei and three other techs were busy taking pictures and measurements while Skywalker watched out for motorists.

"Good morning, Jack." Mei smiled, then switched to a serious face. "Sorry. I have to remind myself to appear more stoic when I'm out in the field." She nodded curtly. "Detective."

Jack didn't know what to say. On the one hand, he'd rather have her smiling, but on the other, he understood public perception. The average person doesn't see death up close. EMTs, law enforcement, and the coroner especially deal with it on a day-to-day basis. But struggling to keep from falling into an abyss of despair by trying to act somewhat normal was perceived by the public as irreverent.

"I was going to stop by your office this morning, Dr. Lai. I need you to run a vaccine titers test on Dr. Mobley for me. Can you please fast-track it too?"

"I have to finish here, but afterward, of course."

"Wonderful."

"What are you looking for?" Mei asked.

"The second killer."

55

Alice rang the doorbell; certain her knocking knees were making an equal racket. The apartment complex was run down and needed a paint job. The Florida sun had faded the bright pastel colors until they blended into a jaundiced yellow.

A lock clicked open, followed by a chain rattling, and then something metal banged against the tile. The door swung open, and an old man with a barrel chest, who, despite his age, stood tall, stared down at her. His gray hair was thick, and his brown eyes were large and filling with tears. He said something in Ukrainian that Alice didn't understand.

"I don't speak Ukrainian."

"I must be dead," the man said in English. "My Kaya Kukla. I would know those emerald eyes anywhere."

Tears streamed down Alice's face. Her little brothers used to call her that. Andrew would shout, "Kaya!" and Alex would respond, "Kukla!" It meant "little doll."

"Hi, Grandpa."

Andrew swept his granddaughter into his arms and squeezed her so hard she could barely breathe. He carried her into the apartment, closing the door with his foot. Singing some odd song, he twirled her round and round. Between the spinning and squeezing and not breathing, Alice got light-headed.

"Grandpa! Please put me down. You're killing me."

Andrew set her on the floor, laughing and wiping his eyes. "How is this possible? The news reports said everyone in the car was killed."

Alice explained how a hitman drove the dump trunk that killed their family. The words tumbled out as she explained being swept up into the foster care system and eventually coming to live with Aunt Haddie.

Andrew's wrinkles grew deeper and darker. His hand balled into a fist. "Had I known you lived, I swear I would have never stopped looking for you. All these years, I thought you were dead."

Alice squeezed his hand. "It doesn't matter now. I've found you."

Andrew's jaw hardened, and he stared at the door. A shotgun lay against the frame. "Does anyone else know you are here? Anyone? Even my brother?"

At the mention of Uncle Alex, Alice swallowed. "I'm so sorry, Grandpa. Your brother is dead. He wanted to find you for the money. He was going to kill my husband to make Jack tell him where you were, but Yana shot him."

"Yana? His own daughter?" Andrew covered his eyes with his large hand and muttered something in Ukrainian. "It is a blessing that my poor mother did not live to see the day. Alex was always a greedy man. But his own daughter? Terrible. And for nothing. There is no money."

"Uncle Alex said you stole millions from the government."

"I didn't take a single kopiyok. To secure loans, the government had to say they had financial reserves. I've never understood the banking system, but there were no reserves. The government needed money to run to support the people. They lied to get the loans. It was a lie we hoped would not see the light of day."

"So you took the blame?"

"The truth always wants to come out. It would have crushed our country if the financial systems had found out the truth. We need to keep the secret. And then another enemy rose. The Russian mob, led by Cade Novikov, wanted me to support his candidate. I refused."

"So they killed Nana?"

Andrew nodded. "After they murdered my wife, I pretended to follow their plan, but I made one of my own. Some reporters were getting close to revealing our lie, so I decided to kill two birds with one scapegoat. A few days before the election, after appearing side-by-side with Cade Novikov's candidate, I fled the country, supposedly with all the money. That way, the government didn't get blamed for lying to the banks, and I tanked the communist pig's chance for election."

"You sacrificed your name for your homeland." Alice wiped at her tears.

"It cost me everything. My wife, my daughter, and my grandchildren. Everything." His brown eyes gazed into Alice's. "But into an old man's life falls the sunshine of my Kaya Kukla, and I can die in peace."

Alice hugged her grandfather, pressing her wet cheek against his broad shoulder. He rocked her back and forth, and they held onto each other, both crying unashamedly, the tears a mix of sadness and joy.

"Look at me bawling like a babe." Andrew leaned back and grinned. "Now tell me how you found me."

"I didn't. A friend did. She's waiting outside. Her name is Kiku."

Andrew sprang off the couch with the speed of a charging bear. He dashed toward the shotgun.

The front door swung open, and Kiku slipped inside, a pistol in her hand, and pointed at Andrew's chest.

"Stop." Kiku's voice was calm but firm.

Andrew halted mid-stride and stared at the shotgun.

"Kiku!" Alice stood up. "Stop pointing that gun at my grandfather!"

"Certainly, once he has taken a seat."

Andrew raised his hands and backed toward the couch.

"Stop moving, General." Kiku crossed to the open kitchen, keeping her gun leveled at Andrew's chest. She picked up a chair and set it at the edge of the living room. "If you do not mind, please sit here."

"Kiku, you're being ridiculous. You're afraid of him sitting on the couch?"

"Lift the cushion he sat on."

Alice lifted the cushion and was surprised to see a mini-Uzi underneath it.

Andrew sat down on the wooden chair. "Alice, you need to leave now."

"Kiku won't hurt you." Alice moved to stand at her grandfather's side. "She's my friend."

Her grandfather shook his head as he stared at Kiku. "I have heard your name before, Kiku. It was mentioned in whispers. You were known then as Bezdushnyy Rebenok. The soulless child. A killer for the Yakuza even as a little girl. You are not helping my granddaughter because you are her friend. You do nothing out of the goodness of your heart, because there is no goodness there."

"Grandfather!" Alice gasped.

"You don't know her, Alice! It was someone like her who murdered my wife. Someone like her who killed your mother! Your father! Your brothers!"

The words crashed into Alice. She wanted to defend her

friend, but there was so much about Kiku that she didn't know and, in some ways, what he said was true.

Kiku's eyes narrowed. "And I know of you, General, and the things you did. You believe that since you were wearing a uniform and standing on a battlefield, that makes us completely different. It does not. Avramij Gurin smuggled you to America. I want his location."

"No."

"I am afraid you are mistaken, General. I am not asking." Kiku's finger moved over the trigger.

Alice's heart pounded in her chest. "Kiku. This is my grandfather."

"I am aware. But as I told you, this information means everything to me, and I will do anything to get it."

Andrew gently pushed Alice away. "I told you, Alice. She is a killer." He glared at Kiku. "I will tell you nothing. Shoot me."

"No!" Alice cried. "Please, Grandpa. Why don't you tell her where Gurin is?"

"Because she will kill him."

"No, she won't," Alice said.

Kiku shook her head. "You are mistaken, Alice. I swear Gurin will die."

"See!" Andrew scowled. "She condemns herself with her own lips. She is a monster!"

"Avramij Gurin made me a monster!" Kiku shouted. "He is one of the men responsible for my sister's death."

"You lie."

"He is the man who arranged a meeting of truly soulless men to buy weapons. There my sister was murdered, and I swore I would carve out the hearts of everyone there, including your friend's. Once I am done, you will thank me."

"Thank you? You are as mad as you are wicked," Andrew said.

"Why did Gurin smuggle you and your family out of the Ukraine?"

"I told you, he was my friend."

"No." Kiku shook her head. "Gurin is like me, lost beyond redemption. His only friend is money. Didn't you ever question how they knew where your wife and daughter would be?"

Andrew's eyes widened. "You lie!" He jumped to his feet, raising his fist over his head.

Alice grabbed his arm.

"Gurin is the one who arranged the bomb beneath your wife's car. Gurin sold the location of your daughter to Cade Novikov to secure a trade route and a steady supply of weapons."

Andrew's arm went limp in Alice's grasp. "I am a fool." He slumped onto the chair and hung his head. "My brother. My friend. Is there no one in this world who will not betray you for money?"

"She is standing beside you," Kiku said. "Give me the location."

"In Belarus. Mazyr. His mother still lives there."

Kiku put her gun behind her back and hid it with her shirt. "It is time to go."

"I can't go with you right now. I just got here." Alice stammered, panic rising inside her. "Please give me a little more time?"

Kiku smiled. "You truly are a friend, but this I must do alone." She set the keys on the counter and said to Alice. "I hope you will give me the benefit of explaining later. I parked the car outside. Take it and go home when you are ready." Kiku slipped out the door.

Alice stepped forward.

Her grandfather grabbed her wrist with a firm grip. "No, Alice. You can't go with her. Where she goes, only death follows."

56

Jack rode with Bill Bliss, Sabrina's head of security, in the elevator up to her penthouse. "Once I'm finished speaking with Ms. Hall, I need to ask you some more information regarding last night."

"I've been notified that if I want to keep my job, I'll have to have one of the company lawyers present during my questioning."

Jack raised an eyebrow. "Are you asking for a lawyer, or will you follow their orders?"

Bill crookedly grinned. "I don't like civvies giving me orders. Especially ones in suits. I'll talk to you when you're done."

The floor number lit up and chimed, announcing their arrival as the door opened. Jack shook Bill's hand and stepped off the elevator, where another security guard stood watch in front of Sabrina's door. The man nodded curtly, then knocked on the door. "The detective is here to speak with you, ma'am."

Sabrina, dressed in a black blouse and slacks, opened the door. She wore her blonde hair pulled back and gazed at Jack with a poker face. "Detective." She glanced at the guard.

"He's been searched by Bliss, ma'am."

She nodded. "Please search him again. I hope you understand, Detective. In light of recent events, I recommended they implement the same security protocols here as we have at the office."

"I understand." Jack held his arms out as the guard patted him down. "My phone, gun, and body camera are locked downstairs already."

"He's clean," the guard announced.

Jack followed Sabrina into the apartment, and she locked the door behind them. "I suppose this is all an overreaction, considering Oscar is dead." She motioned Jack over to a chair facing the couch. "There was a news report on TV earlier."

"You can't be too careful. Oscar's killer is still out there, right?" Jack sat on the chair while Sabrina took a seat on the couch. He glanced out the window behind him at the sun sitting low on the horizon. He wanted to interview Sabrina sooner, but he'd spent all morning and afternoon getting everything and everyone in place.

"How can I be of help, Detective?"

"I had some follow-up questions regarding your whereabouts last night."

Sabrina smiled and crossed her legs. "Here. Sleeping. Verified by not only my security but also the Sheriff's Department."

"No one can actually verify that you were here."

"Don't be ridiculous. They all saw me enter the building, and I never left."

"Actually, you did. You were dressed as your assistant and took her car."

Sabrina gave a tight smile. "With statements like that, it may be wise for me to summon my lawyer."

"You should, but you won't. You like the power play too much." Jack pointed back and forth between them. "Me, the bright-eyed detective on his first case. You, the experienced negotiator with a thousand victories under her Hermès belt.

You enjoy this sparring. Why spoil it? And you said it yourself, if any of this goes to court, it's your word against mine, right? Besides, I saw your poker style once. You like knowing what cards I hold. Do you want to see my hand now?"

Sabrina crossed her legs. "You are good. I do like playing games, and yes, I am fascinated by this preposterous theory of yours. Go on."

"It's simple. You wanted Dr. Mobley's project more than anything. It's brilliant. That's what everyone says. Revolutionary. And don't give me the line about being unable to use it. Eagle's technicians will make some tweaks and modifications, then call it their own."

"I suppose that what you're saying would be my motive?"

"One of them. The other is you mistakenly believed that Oscar tried to kill you. Jilted love is as powerful a motive for murder as money."

Sabrina glared. "This fairy tale is making me thirsty. Would you care for a drink?" She started to rise, but Jack motioned for her to remain seated.

"Allow me." He walked over to the bar.

"I'll have a screwdriver. Orange juice is in the mini-fridge." She crossed her arms. "I'm surprised at your naïveté. I admitted I had sex with Oscar. Love is not a necessary ingredient for sex."

"Sex changes things. A friend of mine always said that, and it's true." Jack poured the drink and brought it to Sabrina.

She sipped the drink, and her eyes flashed with anger. "This is a virgin screwdriver!"

"Otherwise known as orange juice, yes. You can have a stiff drink when we're done." Jack knew that anything she said under the influence of alcohol would be inadmissible in court.

Sabrina huffed. "Why on earth would you, especially you, say that I am mistaken in thinking that Oscar tried to kill me? You were there!" Her voice rose, and her hand shook.

"You are mistaken, Ms. Hall. Oscar Chambers did not try to kill you."

Sabrina chuckled. "Oh, please. Don't be so ludicrous to suggest that I faked that attack on my own life. Is that where you are going with this fiction?"

"No. Someone most definitely wanted you dead, but it wasn't Oscar who tried to blast you to bits."

"So who did? I'm waiting with bated breath." She flashed a sultry smirk.

"First, tell me if I'm right. You dressed up as your assistant, Tahirah Nadeau. It's amazing how a brimmed hat covers a face from the cameras. It even fooled trained security and Sheriff's officers watching the building. They all saw the car and the outfit, but not the person in the outfit."

Sabrina smiled smugly. "I so wish I had some popcorn. Please, continue."

Jack smiled. As far as liars went, Sabrina Hall was in a league of her own. He took a deep breath and continued. "You borrowed Tahirah's car and drove out to meet Oscar."

"And how was I supposed to know where Oscar was?"

"He called you."

"I admitted that. But, if I thought Oscar tried to kill me, which I still believe to be true, why would I go meet him?"

"To get the project for yourself and"—Jack held up his hand when Sabrina protested" —to hide any link between you, Oscar, and the other murders."

"I had nothing to do with the other murders!"

"I believe that. Do you know who else had nothing to do with those murders? Your boy toy Oscar. That you didn't know. You thought he was the killer clearing out the competition, and you worried if they traced the murders back to him, you'd also be linked to them."

"That's ridiculous," she said. "I am mildly embarrassed for you, Detective. It is a good thing this pitch of yours has an audience of one. It pains me to point out your errors, but I simply must. Otherwise, you risk appearing the fool, and your first case as a detective will be your last. May I?"

"Please, show me the flaw in my theory."

"Obviously, Oscar killed the other members of the project. He was the last man standing."

"True, but the actual murderer would have killed Oscar, too, if given time. But you saved them the trouble."

Sabrina coughed and sputtered her drink.

Jack handed her a napkin.

"And who is this supposed real killer?" she asked, dabbing her chin.

"I'll get to that. First, I know you killed Oscar, but proving it in court will be next to impossible. I'll admit that. I'm a realist. So, I'll make a deal with you—off the record."

"All of this is off the record, Detective. What could you possibly offer me?" Sabrina shook her glass. The ice cubes rattled.

"I'll give you the name of the person who successfully killed Doctors Mobley, Patel, and Chen and who attempted to kill you. Keep in mind, they will undoubtedly try to kill you again."

Sabrina scoffed, her foot bouncing nervously. "You're lying."

"Are you sure of that, Ms. Hall? If I were you, I'd want to know who was after me. If not, I don't think I'd ever be able to sleep, let alone leave my apartment. But then again, you'll be a sitting duck if you stay inside. What kind of life would you have waiting to be killed besides stressful and very brief?"

Sabrina dabbed the sweat collecting on her forehead. "How could you know Oscar didn't kill them? Besides myself, and I know I didn't do it, no one else had a reason."

"Oh, someone else had a reason, alright. But you've got to show me your cards to get the name."

"You are vexing, Jack Stratton."

"I get that a lot." Jack grinned.

"If a person kills someone who tried to kill her, it would be self-defense or justifiable homicide, et cetera. We live in a dog-eat-dog world, Jack."

"We are not on a first-name basis, Ms. Hall," Jack said to offset her attempt to take a power position. "I know you shot Oscar. Oscar called you because he was concerned about your safety."

"That's a lie. He wanted to lure me out and finish the job. He wanted me dead."

"Now you are ruining my story, Ms. Hall. That's not what I think happened at all. But, if you don't want to tell me the truth, I can leave you here to take your chances."

"You can't do that! You're sworn to serve and to protect! If there is a crazed killer out there, then it is your job to stop him! Now stop fooling around and tell me who it is!"

"Now I've lost my place." Jack looked up at the ceiling and tapped his temple as if trying to pull back the memory that had escaped him back in. "Got it! So after Oscar called, you exchanged clothes with your assistant, borrowed her car, and drove out to meet him."

"You say all this without a shred of evidence."

A crooked grin grew on Jack's handsome face. "It's just a theory, but humor me. You must've told Oscar to wait out of sight, and he did. He stood hidden off the road, chain smoking while he waited for you to show up. And when you did, Oscar ran over to the car, and you shot him. Right?"

Sabrina Hall glared at Jack and blinked repeatedly.

"Oh, come on! You know I'm right! We had a deal that I would tell you my theory, and I'd tell you the name of the person intent on killing you. I didn't peg you as a sore loser."

Jack had hit a nerve.

The rage in Sabrina's eyes flashed and cooled to a low simmer. "As I said, none of this will be admissible. It will be my word against yours. But I want that name, Detective."

"Then tell me the truth."

Sabrina's foot stopped bouncing. "You're right, it happened exactly as you said, but I am NO LOSER. My plan was genius! I dressed up like Tahirah and killed that weasel, Oscar. It was kill or be killed, and I'd do it again! Now give me the name!" Sabrina stood up, her hands balled into fists at her sides.

Jack grinned. He turned around and stared at the windows of the building in the distance. A light flashed three times.

"What is that?"

"Some friends." Jack stood up and took out his handcuffs. "Right now, I'm arresting you for the murder of Oscar Chambers."

"You can't. Everything I said is off the record. You have no proof!"

"I have a mountain of proof. I brought Tahirah in for questioning this morning, and when the gunpowder residue test returned positive, she threw you under the bus."

"What gunpowder test? She didn't fire a gun."

"Tahirah's hands tested positive for gunshot residue, but thank you for confirming that she didn't fire a gun. Ballistics show you shot Oscar as he came towards the car. You wore gloves, but we found gunpowder residue in the ceiling fabric of Tahirah's car and on the steering wheel. After you fired the gun, the powder transferred from your gloves to the steering wheel, then the gunshot residue got on Tahirah's hands when she drove her car again."

"It's still my word against hers."

"Your word is what will help send you away. Thank you for confessing."

"I'll deny it. This was no confession! It was meaningless banter."

"Call it what you want, but it's on video." Jack pointed at the building across the street.

"So what? Someone may be able to capture a picture from over there, but there is no way they could get audio."

"They don't need it. See, I have this wonderful friend who's a videographer. She's also deaf and can read lips like nobody else."

Sabrina raised her hand to strike Jack.

He slapped a handcuff over her wrist, spun her around, and cuffed the other hand. "I know. Vexing, right?"

Sabrina fumed as Jack read her rights. "You better believe I want a lawyer. You're going to pay for this, Stratton. I swear you will pay! That entire business of there being another killer was one big lie."

"No. That was true. Oscar didn't kill anyone. So let's hurry this up so I can go get the other bad guy, shall we?"

57

The sun burst over the trees, sending golden rays dancing across the lake's calm waters. It was the perfect morning for fishing, but Jack wasn't here for the trout.

He strolled across the boat ramp and over to the long dock stretching into the lake. Sitting at the end of the pier, in a foldable director's chair, a man was focused on a sizeable remote-controlled float plane bobbing on the water.

The plane's propeller spun. Its engine whined, rippling the water behind it. Slowly it glided forward, steadily picking up speed until it rose majestically into the air.

Jack stopped beside the man, and both focused on the plane as it started to circle the lake lazily.

"It's beautiful, Dr. Mobley," Jack said.

"Thank you." Dr. Mobley pressed a button on the large controller in his hands, and the plane leveled out. "I had a bad feeling about you the day you showed up at my house. Something about your eyes, Detective. Who would have known my picking the Jack of Spades would prove so prophetic? It appears you are a herald of my downfall."

"Is that a compliment?"

"Of sorts. I know I've failed because I am sitting here very much alive in your presence. What gave me away? I wore rubber gloves while preparing the playing cards and certainly didn't lick the envelopes, so it couldn't be that."

"The trophy your mother gave you. You took it with you before the explosion."

Dr. Mobley sighed and adjusted the plane's flight path to circle back around. "I'm a sentimental old fool. But surely that couldn't be enough?"

"Carl Wilson. I read his notes in his Bible, and I think he really turned his life over to God. So when Carl's friend OD'd on prescription drugs, Carl felt led to stop the dealer. That's when Carl discovered that the good doctor who had helped the police in the Sweet Sally bust to get drugs off the street had gone dirty. He had gone from being part of the solution to being part of the problem selling prescription meds on the street. That's why Carl came to your house."

"How could you have possibly figured out it was Carl's body in the explosion?"

"Honestly, I had a harder time wrapping my head around the fact that a doctor sworn to do no harm, with such a stellar reputation of doing good and being kind, could become so evil and do such vile things. But once I figured out you were alive, the body recovered in your house after the blast had to be someone else. That got me thinking, especially after the M.E. confirmed it was your body by your medical records."

"I thought that part of the plan was perfect."

"Nothing about murder ever is. Carl's granddaughter filed a missing person report. You used your position at the hospital to switch your medical file with Carl's. You're both the same age, and Carl's injuries from the war were similar to yours."

"Because I switched the records, the corpse at my house was an exact match for my medical record. You couldn't possibly tell it wasn't mine."

"Right, but you don't know what you don't know. Had you ever been a soldier like Carl, you would've known that all soldiers get a cocktail of shots before deployment. I remember my vaccinations syringe looking as if it were filled with peanut butter. I felt as though I had the flu for several days. No soldier forgets that. Carl was a soldier, and you weren't. We ran an antibody titers test, which was positive for both the Japanese encephalitis and anthrax vaccines."

"That was an oversight on my part. I'm stunned that wet-behind-the-ears M.E. didn't slap a toe tag with my name on the body you recovered after the blast. I never expected that newbie to do such a comprehensive exam."

"That 'newbie' wept at the sight of your body and asked me as a personal favor to find whoever killed you because she believed you were such a kind, good man. Dr. Mei Lai may be new to her current position, but she has the fine character she misattributed to the likes of you."

Dr. Mobley's eyebrows pulled together. "Just because my medical record didn't show the corpse's antibodies wouldn't be positive proof of the records switch."

"You're right. That's why I asked the IT folks to pull the hospital's backup data tapes from last year. The new records didn't match the old, confirming that you switched them."

"Excellent work, Detective. But you can't take credit for finding me. I told you myself where I'd be, didn't I?"

"Your favorite place in the world—Lake Winnipesaukee. The only question I don't have an answer to is why? Was it the money?"

Dr. Mobley shrugged. "No. It was the same thing that broke my body before—hubris. I flew too high. I put everything I had into that project, and when I spent all my cash and mortgaged my house, I got desperate. And a desperate man is capable of despicable things. When I helped the police years ago, I saw how easy it was for crooked doctors to make money hand over fist selling drugs. After all that work, they stole my project! And my contributions were not only diminished but erased! Imagine removing my name as the inventor? It wasn't just theft; it was the kidnapping of my brainchild and murder of my soul! How could I just let that happen?" Dr. Mobley continued to gaze at his plane as he spoke.

"I would have fought back, too, but in court. Why did you choose Carl Wilson?"

"I didn't. He showed up on my doorstep with a Bible in his hand, telling me that Jesus loved me and I needed to turn myself in." Dr. Mobley brushed the tear running down his face away and removed his glasses. "He actually thanked me for sending him to prison. He said it changed his life."

Jack's jaw flexed. He knew Carl's fate, so any sympathy for Mobley wasn't forthcoming.

"He gave me a chance to do the right thing. He suggested I go to a lawyer and get a good deal from the police. I thanked him by bashing in his skull with a fireplace poker." Dr. Mobley hung his head. "After I killed him, I knew it was only a matter of time before getting caught. So I came up with my plan."

"You blew up your house and killed Dr. Chen and Dr. Patel."

"But I didn't kill Oscar." Dr. Mobley stared across the water. "Tell me Sabrina Hall won't get a deal. I want to know she'll rot in prison."

"She will, but you're just as responsible for Oscar's death as she was."

Dr. Mobley nodded. "Yes. Yes, I am."

"Samuel Mobley, I'm placing you—"

The sound of an engine whining grew louder.

"There's a pound of C4 inside that plane," Dr. Mobley calmly said. "I would run, Detective."

Jack glanced down the dock to the shore. It was over twenty-five yards away. He'd witnessed C4's explosive power firsthand. Even sprinting, he'd never make it.

Dr. Mobley looked at the approaching plane and smiled.

Jack grabbed Mobley, toppling him from his chair. Mobley flailed and tried to punch Jack as he dragged him off the dock and into the water.

Jack tightened his grip on the back of Mobley's shirt and swam downward. His legs burned as he kicked as hard as he could, holding onto Mobley with his left arm and pulling desperately with his right.

A deep thrum pulsed through the water. Overhead flashed a brilliant red, orange, and yellow glow.

Jack changed course and headed for the surface. He gulped in air and waved as the shouts of the waiting backup policemen came from all directions.

Mobley coughed and spat up water.

Holding tightly to Mobley's collar, Jack swam until his feet touched the lake's sandy bottom. Jack dragged Mobley onto shore and dumped him onto the bank.

Mobley glared at him, "You should have let me die, Detective. I swear to you, you'll live to regret it."

Jack laughed. "That curse didn't take long to come true. I already regret saving you. Samuel Mobley, you're under arrest."

58

Jack knocked on the hospital room door as he walked in.

Ed sat propped up on the bed, his leg in a cast and suspended by cables. He glanced toward the door, then turned his attention back to the TV.

"We got him, Ed." Jack shifted the large gift basket in his arms.

"You got him," Ed muttered, keeping his eyes on the TV. "I had nothing to do with it."

"Are you kidding me?" Jack crossed over to the table by the window and set it down. "It was a team effort."

Ed shook his head. "Don't give me that crock of crap. You did it. All I did was get hit by the stupid car."

"No offense, Ed. But what you're saying is garbage and disrespectful to every other member of law enforcement that helped bring Dr. Mobley down."

"Don't start with the there's no I in team speech." Ed clicked the TV off. "I—"

"Shut up and listen." For emphasis, Jack placed a hand on the cable supporting Ed's leg.

Ed's eyes widened, but he kept his mouth shut.

"What about Kendra, Goodman, and Hicks? They did nothing?"

"Yeah, but—"

"Or Sheriff Morrison? Or Dr. Lai? What about dispatch? They all contributed, but truth be told, you outdid everyone, including me. You put yourself in harm's way to stop a killer. We would never have gotten to Dr. Mobley if it weren't for your sacrifice."

Ed sat up a little straighter.

Jack was laying it on thick, but he believed everything he was saying. "It wouldn't surprise me if you got a medal out of this."

"Really?"

Jack nodded. "So don't you dare start thinking you had nothing to do with solving this case. We did it." Jack held out his fist.

Ed stared at him for a moment before returning the fist bump.

"One more thing," Jack continued. "A friend of mine has a garage and says he can work with any insurance. I sent him pics of your car, and he thought he could get it done by the time you get out of here. We passed the hat at the station, and it should cover any cost your insurance company can't. Are you interested?"

Ed's eyes rounded, and his lip trembled. He fumbled for a basket on the table next to the bed and threw Jack his car keys. "I'm not crying." He sniffed. "It's the medicine. And the pain," he quickly added.

Jack caught the keys, smiled, and headed out the door. He had another stop to make.

~

Jack set the boxes he carried next to the door and rang the bell. This was the part of the job he hated. He hadn't slept last night, and his stomach was twisted in knots.

Naomi opened the door. She looked at Jack's face, and tears filled her eyes. "No. Oh, no." She walked out the front door, pulling it shut behind her. She moved over to the front porch railing in a daze and gripped it in both hands.

"Was it drugs?" Her voice was soft and filled with sadness.

"Your grandfather was murdered."

Naomi's knees buckled.

Jack helped her sit on the front steps and then sat beside her. He told her everything, starting with the death of Carl's friend. He explained Dr. Mobley's involvement and his twisted plan.

Naomi stared down at her hands. She didn't cry or ask questions. She listened attentively and, when Jack finished, hung her head.

Reaching back, Jack got hold of the corner of the box and dragged it over. "I have some of your grandfather's things. I know he'd want you to have this." He reached inside and pulled out the dog-eared Bible. "Your grandfather wrote several notes inside about you and your dad. When you're ready, they may bring you some comfort."

"Thank you."

"You were right, Naomi. Your grandfather had turned his life around. He died trying to do the right thing."

"And it got him killed."

Jack nodded. "He knew it was dangerous, but he was a soldier like you're going to be." Jack pointed at the Bible in her hands. "I read through some of his notes. I had to for the investigation. Your grandfather was so proud of you. Not only with you joining the Army. He said you're going to be a teacher?"

Naomi nodded. "That's why I want to join the service to go to college."

"What do you want to teach?"

"Math."

"Cool. My father was a math teacher." Jack laughed. "Where did you go to high school?"

"Washington Heights. Like you."

"Did you check out any of the scholarships available?"

"What would be the point? My dream is to teach, but I'm not a straight-A student."

"I knew a guy like that. Chandler Williams. There's a scholarship in his name."

"Was that the soldier that got killed trying to save a little girl?"

Tears sprang up in Jack's eyes. He wiped them away but more came. "Yeah. Can I ask you a question? Do you dream of going into the Army the way you do teaching?"

Naomi shrugged. "Not really, but I want to be a teacher, and the Army is my ticket."

Jack took a deep breath and pressed the palms of his hands against his eyes. When he took them away, he stared at Naomi and smiled. "Then you should apply for that scholarship. Trust me. You've got a chance to get it."

Naomi leaned away and looked at him sideways. "And why would that be?"

"Because you're the type of person that scholarship was made for. Chandler was my best friend. And I happen to know somebody else affiliated with the scholarship. I'd be happy to put in a good word for you."

"Really?"

Jack nodded. "Big goofy guy. I was always keeping him out of trouble, although he'd say the same of me."

While the sun rose into the sky, Jack sat on the front porch talking to Naomi about Chandler. After a while, she opened up about her grandfather. She shared stories about when she was little, and Carl used to come over. They talked, laughed, and she cried, but when they were done, Naomi did something that took him by surprise.

Jack was getting ready to get into his car when Naomi raced down the sidewalk and hugged him. She pulled him close, whispered, "Thank you," and let go just as quickly.

Jack smiled. "Be sure to visit the guidance counselor at school and ask about financial aid. And let me know when you've applied for the scholarship, and I'll call my contact."

"Do you think I have a chance?"

"I guarantee you've got a shot, but I need to warn you about something. If you get it, you'll have to work hard and keep your grades up. Chandler's sister Alice checks on all recipients and arranges tutoring or attitude adjustments. She can get a little crazy."

"If I get the scholarship, I'll give it all I've got! I'll work harder than anyone and everyone. I swear."

Jack smiled. "I know you will."

59

Jack opened the apartment's front door and groaned when something slammed into his chest. Stumbling backward, Jack held onto Alice as she clung to him like a monkey on a tree, her legs coiled around his waist and her arms wrapped around his shoulders.

"I missed you, too, and so has Lady. She is still downstairs at Mrs. Stevens." He smiled.

She grabbed both sides of his face and showered him with kisses. Over and over, she alternated between saying, "I missed you both so much" and "I'm so sorry."

"It's okay." Jack carried her into the apartment and over to the island in the kitchen. He doubted he could extract himself from her grip, but at least he could take some weight off his still aching shoulders.

"Welcome home." Jack brushed an errant hair from her face.

"I'm so, so sorry." She dropped her chin to her chest.

Jack tipped his head forward, lifted her chin, and looked into Alice's emerald eyes. "Next time, tell me. Agreed?"

"There will never be a next time."

Jack shook his head. "Don't kid yourself. Now that you're a Stratton, lightning strikes twice, Big Foot shows up, and stuff happens. So promise me that you'll tell me, okay?"

Alice wiped away a tear. "I promise. Please forgive me, Jack."

"All's forgiven. How's your grandfather?"

Alice smiled awkwardly. "Actually, I need to ask you something."

The doorknob to the front door rattled and swung open. An older man with a barrel chest and thick gray hair walked in. He spotted Jack, threw his hands up, and shouted, "AH!" The man rushed forward and embraced Jack in a bear hug. "You are my angel's angel!" He lifted Jack off his feet and squeezed.

Jack's tender ribs groaned.

"Maybe not so hard, Grandfather." Alice nervously looked at Jack.

"Oh, do not worry. Your man is strong." Andrew set Jack down and clapped two massive hands on Jack's bruised shoulders. "That is good!"

"Thanks." Jack forced a smile.

"Alice told me all about you on the ride here. We drove straight back. She was so homesick we only stopped for gas. You were all she spoke of. You are her hero. I am so sorry I missed the wedding, but I will make it up to you both. I will make you a dish to put some meat on your bones tonight." He pinched Alice's cheek and patted Jack's stomach.

"You don't have to do that, sir. I can take us all out if you'd like?"

"Nonsense. I love to cook! It's what I do as they say. I watch all the cooking shows."

Alice took Jack's hand and pulled him toward the bedroom. "I need to talk to Jack for a second, Grandfather."

"GeeGee," her grandfather said. "The word for grandpa in Ukrainian sounds funny. Your momma was so formal, but I'm old now. Call me GeeGee. You too, Jackie."

Jackie?

Alice squeezed Jack's hand and tugged. "Can I talk to you, honey?"

"You two go and chat. I'll check and see what ingredients we have to work with." Andrew started singing in Ukrainian, then shouted, "What a wonderful day! I have a family again. Now I can die right here, a happy man. I will never leave!"

Jack's mouth fell open.

Alice yanked him into the bedroom and shut the door. "I swear I didn't know. He said he wanted to come with me. I thought it was a good idea for him to get out of Florida and figured he'd stay with us for a couple of days while he looked for a place. But he started talking like that when we got here, and I didn't know what to do."

Jack laughed.

"What? Don't you get it? My grandfather thinks he's staying here. With us! Like permanently."

"Yup. I heard. I was alluding to this kind of surprise in my welcome to the Stratton family speech. Stuff like this happens. We have to roll with the punches."

"I thought I'd be peeling you off the ceiling because of this news flash. You don't mind?"

"You spent your whole life thinking your family was gone. Now that you found him, what am I going to do? We'll adapt. You may have to be a little quieter during our lovemaking—"

Alice reached up, tried to cover his mouth with her hand, and blushed crimson.

Jack laughed harder and pulled her close. "I love you with all my heart, Alice. I'm so happy you are home."

"I'm so happy you are fine with all of this. I love you, too." Alice reached up and began stroking Jack's hair. "Maybe they're right. Distance does make the heart grow fonder. I may need to go away more often!" Alice giggled.

"If you even think about that, I'll place you under house arrest." Jack wiggled his eyebrows, and Alice kissed him again.

"I'm going to take the trash out, then check with my grandfather on how long it will be until supper."

"I got the trash." Jack headed back to the kitchen. "I forgot, and it's probably starting to stink as bad as me."

"I think you smell good." Alice winked.

Jack grabbed the trash bag and headed out of the apartment and down the stairs. All he wanted to do was take an epic shower and drain the hot water tank dry.

He jogged across the rear parking lot, holding the green trash bag as far away from himself as possible.

"I should have taken this out three days ago. It smells like something died."

The gravel crunched beneath Jack's shoes as he crossed to the green dumpster. He shoved the black plastic cover up and let it crash back down.

He stood there staring at the closed dumpster, blinking rapidly.

"No way." Jack let the trash bag fall out of his hands.

Jack reached for his gun, but the weapon was sitting on his nightstand. Weapon or not, he had a job to do. Taking a deep breath, he shoved the lid up and over. The plastic cover banged off the back of the dumpster. Partially hidden by trash bags, a body was stuffed inside. A box obscured the torso, but legs were sticking out on the right side.

The hot, familiar glow of adrenaline clicked on and flowed through his veins. You can take the soldier out of the war, but the war in the soldier remains. There was murder at his doorstep, and he had a family to protect.

He took out his phone and called dispatch.

"This is Detective Stratton. I need to report a Code 54."

JOIN THE FREE PREFERRED READER PROGRAM

Visit ChristopherGreyson.com to sign-up!

ALSO BY
CHRISTOPHER GREYSON

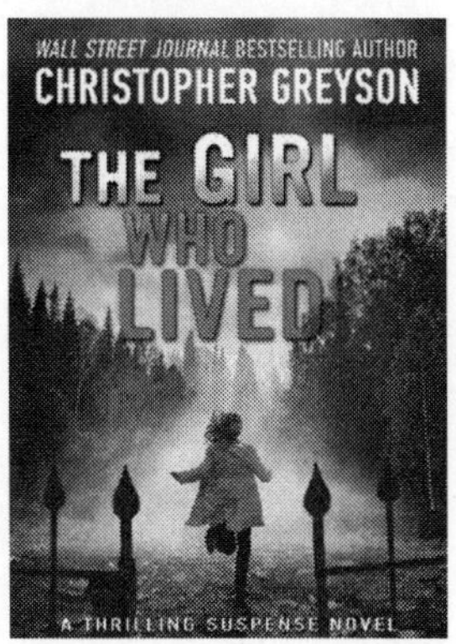

THE GIRL WHO LIVED

Ten years ago, four people were brutally murdered. One girl lived. As the anniversary of the murders approaches, Faith Winters is released from the psychiatric hospital and yanked back to the last spot on earth she wants to be—her hometown where the slayings took place. Wracked by the lingering echoes of survivor's guilt, Faith spirals into a black hole of alcoholism and wanton self-destruction. Finding no solace at the bottom of a bottle, Faith decides to track down her sister's killer—and then discovers that she's the one being hunted.

ONE LITTLE LIE

A LIE IS A WELCOME MAT FOR THE DEVIL...

Kate had high hopes when she moved to her husband's hometown, but her domestic bliss was short-lived. Blindsided by her spouse's public affair with his high school sweetheart, everything she worked for begins to unravel, along with her sanity. Confused, alone, and afraid, can Kate untangle the web of lies and unmask her stalker, or will she lose everything—including her life?

One Little Lie is a riveting suspense novel set in an idyllic town where money talks, gossip flows, and the court of public opinion rules. Jump on for a fun, fast-paced ride with a book you can't put down!

The Detective Jack Stratton Mystery-Thriller Series

The Detective Jack Stratton Mystery-Thriller Series, authored by *Wall Street Journal* bestselling writer Christopher Greyson, has 5,000+ five-star reviews and over a million readers and counting. If you'd love to read another page-turning thriller with mystery, humor, and a dash of romance, pick up the next book in the highly acclaimed series today:

And Then She Was GONE

A hometown hero with a heart of gold, Jack Stratton was raised in a whorehouse by his prostitute mother. When his foster mother asks him to look into a missing girl's disappearance, Jack quickly gets drawn into a baffling mystery. As Jack digs deeper, everyone becomes a suspect—including himself.

GIRL JACKED

They say a dangerous man is the one who had it all and lost it. But they're wrong, it's the one who lost everything but has a chance to get it back...

Guilt has driven a wedge between Jack and the family he loves. When Jack, now a police officer, hears the news that his foster sister Michelle is missing, it cuts straight to his core. The police think she just took off, but Jack knows Michelle would never leave her loved ones behind—like he did. Forced to confront the demons from his past, Jack must take action, find Michelle, and bring her home... or die trying.

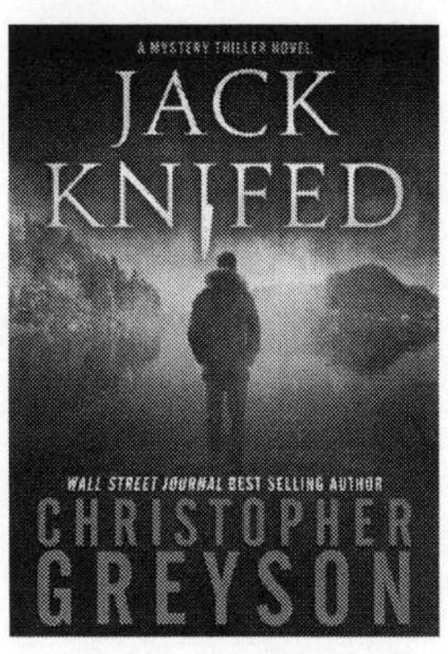

JACK KNIFED

How far would you go to uncover the truth of your past?

Constant nightmares have forced Jack to seek answers about his rough childhood and the dark secrets hidden there. The mystery surrounding Jack's birth father leads Jack to investigate the twenty-seven-year-old murder case in Hope Falls.

A heart-rending mystery-thriller about lost love, betrayal, and murder that will keep you on the edge of your seat.

JACKS ARE WILD

As the body count rises, the stakes are life and death—with no rules except one—Jacks are Wild.

When Jack's sexy old flame disappears, no one thinks it's suspicious except Jack and one unbalanced witness. Jack feels in his gut that something is wrong. He knows that Marisa has a past, and if it ever caught up with her—it would be deadly. The trail leads him into all sorts of trouble—landing him smack in the middle of an all-out mob war between the Italian Mafia and the Japanese Yakuza.

A strong hero, smart women sleuths, and more twists and turns than a piece of licorice.

JACK AND THE GIANT KILLER

A serial killer is stalking Jack's town--and no one's safe. But they don't know Jack.

Rogue hero Jack Stratton is back in another action-packed, thrilling adventure. While recovering from a gunshot wound, Jack gets a seemingly harmless private investigation job—locate the owner of a lost dog—Jack begrudgingly assists. Little does he know it will place him directly in the crosshairs of a merciless serial killer.

An action-packed thrill ride until the very end!

DATA JACK

Can Jack and Alice stop a pack of ruthless criminals before they can Data Jack?

Jack Stratton's back is up against the wall. He's broke, kicked off the force, and his new bounty hunting business has slowed to a trickle. He thinks things are turning around when Alice gets a lucrative job setting up a home data network.When the computer program the CEO invented becomes the key tool in an international data heist, things turn deadly. In this digital age of hackers, spyware, and cyber terrorism--data is more valuable than gold. The thieves plan to steal the keys to the digital kingdom and with this much money at stake, they'll kill for it. Can Jack and Alice stop the pack of ruthless criminals before they can *Data Jack*?

JACK OF HEARTS

Jack Stratton is heading south for some fun in the sun. Already nervous about introducing his girlfriend, Alice, to his parents, the last thing Jack needed was for the dog-sitter to cancel, forcing him to bring Lady, their 120-pound King Shepherd, on the plane with them. The dog holds Jack responsible and wants payback. On top of everything, Jack is still waiting for Alice's answer to his marriage proposal.

When his mother and the members of her neighborhood book club ask him to catch the "Orange Blossom Cove Bandit," a small-time thief who's stealing garden gnomes and peace of mind from their quiet retirement community, how can Jack refuse?

JACK FROST

What do you get when you mix the blockbuster television show Survivor with Agatha Christie's masterpiece And Then There Were None...

Jack has a new assignment: to investigate the suspicious death of a soundman on the hit TV show *Planet Survival*. Jack goes undercover as a security agent where the show is filming on nearby Mount Minuit. Soon trapped on the treacherous peak by a blizzard, a mysterious killer continues to stalk the cast and crew of *Planet Survival*. What started out as a game is now a deadly competition for survival. As the temperature drops and the body count rises, what will get them first? The mountain or the killer?

JACK OF DIAMONDS

All Jack Stratton wants to do is get married to the woman he loves—and make it through the wedding. It seems like he is finally getting his wish until he responds to a police distress call and discovers his old partner unconscious in an abandoned house. Investigators insist it was just an accident, but Jack fears there may be more to it. Sketches of women cover the walls, and among them is one sketch that makes Jack's blood run cold—a sketch of Alice, pinned up beside an invitation to a very special wedding—his own.

This time, "till death do us part"
might just be a bit too accurate!

CAPTAIN JACK

Looking forward to some fun in the surf and sand, newlyweds Jack and Alice Stratton are determined not to let something like a hurricane upset their honeymoon plans. But the storm's winds and churning tides unearthed a secret long hidden beneath the turquoise waters of the island paradise.

A local tour boat captain discovers a lost submarine and offers to sell the location to a man known only as the Dyab—the Devil. When the captain is murdered, the police suspect Jack and Alice and confiscate their passports. Trapped between the Devil and the deep blue sea, the handsome young detective and his blushing bride have nowhere to turn and everything to lose as they set out to prove their innocence and find the real killer.

JACK OF SPADES

The most dangerous killer is the one you don't see...

When a distraught man calls 911 to report a murder that hasn't even happened, police think it's a hoax or a crackpot until the caller turns out to be a highly respected Doctor. After his warning comes violently true, the killing thrusts Jack Stratton into his first official case as a new detective. Money, sex, and drugs are all motives. Still, these aren't your usual suspects: a tenured professor, a tech CEO, a mathematical genius, and a convicted felon have a million reasons to kill, but who did it? Can Jack follow the trail of victims and catch the mastermind, or will his first case be his last?

Hear your favorite characters
come to life in audio versions of
the Detective Jack Stratton
Mystery-Thriller Series!
Audio Books now available on Audible!
Listen Now

Novels featuring Jack Stratton in order:

AND THEN SHE WAS GONE
GIRL JACKED
JACK KNIFED
JACKS ARE WILD
JACK AND THE GIANT KILLER
DATA JACK
JACK OF HEARTS
JACK FROST
JACK OF DIAMONDS
CAPTAIN JACK

Fantasy Adventure

PURE OF HEART

Orphaned and alone, rogue-teen Dean Walker has learned how to take care of himself on the rough city streets. Unjustly wanted by the police, he takes refuge within the shadows of the city. When Dean stumbles upon an old man being mugged, he tries to help—only to discover that the victim is anything but helpless and far more than he appears. Together with three friends, he sets out on an epic quest where only the pure of heart will prevail.

Kiku - Rogue Assassin

Award-winning, *Wall Street Journal* bestselling author Christopher Greyson breaks the mold for action-thrillers. Join Kiku as she crisscrosses the globe from Chicago to Hong Kong, the streets of Japan, and the frozen tundra of Russia and takes on the mob, Yakuza, black market, and anyone else who stands in her way!

A BEAUTIFUL PLACE TO DIE

When you wound an angel, you unleash a demon.

It was supposed to be a simple assignment, get a DNA sample from a young boy, but it turns into a deadly trap. With a price on the boy's head and a target on her back, Kiku must not only shield him from the ruthless Russian mafia but also from a traitor within the Yakuza itself. Torn between love and honor, duty and scorn, Kiku must decide where her loyalties lie before it's too late.

KINDLE THE FIRES OF WAR

She's outnumbered 100 to 1.
They're going to need more men.

Kiku has gone rogue. Now hunted by the Russian mob and the Yakuza, Kiku heads to Hong Kong's underbelly to rescue her lover. Faced with impossible odds, Kiku must outwit, outfight, and outrun everyone trying to capture her and collect the two-million-dollar bounty. Rats fueled by greed or vengeance, driven by ruthless leaders, run rampant, all hoping to score. The mob, Yakuza, and Hong Kong's black market—they all wanted to fight. Kiku started a war.

DANCE OF DEATH

To save the one she loves,
she'll kill them all.

Kiku's quest to rescue her lover has gone disastrously wrong. With the odds stacked against her, her enemies think she'll run and hide to save herself. They're wrong—dead wrong. Kiku decides to take the fight to them instead. Now the hunter, Kiku, will stop at nothing to protect those she loves.

THE ADVENTURES OF FINN & ANNIE — MINIMYSTERY SERIES

In these heartwarming short stories, join Finn and Annie as they investigate their way through murder, arson, theft, embezzlement, and maybe even love, seeking to distinguish between truth and lies, scammers and victims. A MiniMystery series that will touch your heart and leave you craving more!

ACKNOWLEDGMENTS

I would like to thank all the wonderful readers out there. It is you who make the literary world what it is today—a place of dreams filled with tales of adventure! Word of mouth is crucial for any author to succeed. If you enjoyed the novel, please consider leaving a review at Amazon, even if it is only a line or two; it would make all the difference and I would appreciate it very much.

I would also like to thank my amazing wife for standing beside me every step of the way on this journey. My thanks also go out to Laura and Christopher, my two awesome kids, and my dear mother and the rest of my family. Finally, thank you to my wonderful team: Maia McViney, my fantastic editor—Anne Cherry, and the unbelievably helpful beta readers!

ABOUT THE AUTHOR

My name is Christopher Greyson, and I am a storyteller. Since I was a little boy, I have dreamt of what mystery was around the next corner, or what quest lay over the hill. If I couldn't find an adventure, one usually found me, and now I weave those tales into my stories.

My love for tales of mystery and adventure began with my grandfather, a decorated World War I hero. I will never forget being introduced to his friend, a WWI pilot who flew across the skies at the same time as the feared, legendary Red Baron. I love to hear from my readers. Please go to Christopher-Greyson.com and sign up for my mailing list to receive periodic updates on new book releases. Thank you for reading my novels. I hope my stories have brightened your day.

Sincerely,

JACK OF SPADES
Copyright: Christopher Greyson
Published: November 4th 2022

Find out more about the author and upcoming books online at
www.ChristopherGreyson.com.

V.I.II.I.22

Made in United States
Orlando, FL
12 December 2024

55490156R00209